A Tale of

Two

Courtships

by

Jann Rowland

One Good Sonnet Publishing

By Jann Rowland

PRIDE AND PREJUDICE ADAPTATIONS

Acting on Faith
A Life from the Ashes (Sequel to *Acting on Faith*)
Open Your Eyes
Implacable Resentment
An Unlikely Friendship
Bound by Love
Cassandra
Obsession
Shadows Over Longbourn
The Mistress of Longbourn
My Brother's Keeper
Coincidence
The Angel of Longbourn
Chaos Comes to Kent
In the Wilds of Derbyshire
The Companion
Out of Obscurity
What Comes Between Cousins
A Tale of Two Courtships

COURAGE ALWAYS RISES: THE BENNET SAGA

The Heir's Disgrace

Co-Authored with Lelia Eye

WAITING FOR AN ECHO

Waiting for an Echo Volume One: Words in the Darkness
Waiting for an Echo Volume Two: Echoes at Dawn
Waiting for an Echo Two Volume Set

A Summer in Brighton
A Bevy of Suitors
Love and Laughter: A Pride and Prejudice Short Stories Anthology

This is a work of fiction based on the works of Jane Austen. All the characters and events portrayed in this novel are products of Jane Austen's original novel or the authors' imaginations.

A TALE OF TWO COURTSHIPS

Cover Design by Marina Willis

Published by One Good Sonnet Publishing

ISBN: 1987929896
ISBN-13: 9781987929898

To my family who have, as always, shown
their unconditional love and encouragement.

CHAPTER I

Netherfield Park was an oddity among the estates near the town of Meryton in Hertfordshire. The neighborhood was dotted with small estates inhabited by country squires and their families, good people, though the more critical of visitors might have thought them provincial and not worth their time. Unlike to the other estates in its general vicinity, Netherfield Park was, in fact, a large estate, rumored to have generated an income in excess of six thousand pounds at the height of its prosperity. But whereas the other estates all had steady ownership, a guiding hand, and occupants aplenty, Netherfield had stood empty for many years.

Some of the older members of the population claimed they remembered a time when the estate had actually been inhabited. There had been a family there, they claimed, though none could recall the name of those who had owned it. Someone had obviously built the stately manor house which, while not counted among the great houses, was still large, boasting many bedrooms, several parlors, and even a ballroom of sufficient size to host everyone in the neighborhood. The current master, a Mr. Mason, had not visited the property in many years, and it was understood he possessed a great estate in East Sussex. As it was believed to be in the northern part of the county and not far distant from London, even the convenience of Netherfield's proximity to town was not enough to draw him thither.

That state of affairs was to change, however, for rumors began to circulate through the neighborhood that Mr. Mason had finally agreed to lease the property to a young man of good fortune. And soon those rumors blossomed, until the gentleman who was to live there was rumored to be single, wealthy, and to visit with a veritable army of young men of similar station and wealth. And as is the case when all such rumors are perpetuated, the excitement of the residents soon rose apace.

"His name is Mr. Bingley," exulted one Mrs. Margaret Bennet one morning after a visit with her sister. Mrs. Phillips was the wife of the town's solicitor, and one of the foremost gossips in the neighborhood. "I have just had it from my sister Phillips that Mr. Bingley inspected the place on Tuesday last and pronounced it charming and perfectly situated for a man in his position. The lease was signed, and he takes residence in the first week of September."

"Does he, indeed?" asked her husband. "Well, I suppose it will be good to have a neighbor who will actually look after the property. Assuming, of course, that this Mr. Bingley is a man of industry and not of sloth."

Elizabeth Bennet, the Bennets' second daughter, listened to her father with amusement, and no little exasperation. By the strictest sense of the word, she was aware her father was exactly that which he had just censured. He loved nothing more than the quiet of his bookroom and the benefit of the thick door, which separated himself from his wife's nerves. Mrs. Bennet, the mother of five daughters possessing little dowry, fancied herself nervous, which Elizabeth knew to be nothing more than an abject fear of her husband dying and leaving her destitute.

That was not to say that Mr. Bennet never took any thought for the estate. His children were never allowed to go wanting, and there was always food on the table to feed them. But as he had no heir and the estate was entailed on a distant cousin, Mr. Bennet had little reason or desire to work for its improvement. This lack of forethought Elizabeth generally declined to consider. Had he exerted himself, either in the improvement of the estate or in curbing her mother's spending habits, some small amount might have been put away for their eventual support. But Elizabeth had decided many years ago to exercise philosophy on the matter. She had always been her father's favorite and the recipient of his teaching and affection, and while she might have wished her situation was not so precarious, she decided it was best to be grateful for what she did possess.

"You will visit him when he comes?" demanded Mrs. Bennet of her husband.

Though it was clear Mr. Bennet was on the verge of some witticism at his wife's expense, he ultimately sighed. "You know I shall visit any gentlemen as is proper. Why would you think I would not in this instance?"

"I know no such thing, Mr. Bennet," said Mrs. Bennet. "There have been so few to come into our neighborhood that I am certain you have not been required to welcome a new gentleman for at least the past five years."

"I cannot dispute that, Mrs. Bennet," replied Mr. Bennet. "And for that paucity of new faces, I am profoundly grateful."

Mrs. Bennet did not seem to know what to make of her husband's words, but since he had agreed to visit Mr. Bingley, she decided it was best to simply allow the matter to rest. Soon Mr. Bennet had excused himself to his bookroom, as was his custom, leaving the ladies to speak on the matter. In reality, little was said which was of interest to Elizabeth. Mary, Elizabeth's younger sister by one, could be counted on to keep her own council—except for the odd homily she so loved to insert into any conversation—while Kitty and Lydia, the two youngest, more than made up for their elder sister's reticence, each declaring what a fine thing it would be if Mr. Bingley took a fancy to one of them. Jane, the eldest, was not present, as she was currently in London staying with the Gardiners, Mr. Gardiner being Mrs. Bennet's younger brother.

As this scene was little different from their usual behavior, Elizabeth ignored them. Kitty, though two years older, was the follower and Lydia the leader in their schemes. They had both come out earlier that summer when Kitty had turned seventeen years of age, a fact that offended Kitty—rightfully, in Elizabeth's opinion. But Lydia, being her mother's favorite, had managed to persuade her so, not that it had been difficult. Thus, instead of waiting until she was seventeen like her elder sisters had, she was out two years earlier. Given her general level of silliness, Elizabeth was not convinced she was in any way prepared.

In due time Mr. Bingley arrived to take possession of the estate, and Mr. Bennet visited him as he had promised. If his reports of Mr. Bingley were less than his family might have wished, it seemed to bother him little and amuse him a vast deal. No, he could not declare the color of Mr. Bingley's coat, for the hue of the garment had quite escaped his notice, and the only thing he could state about Mr. Bingley's person was that the gentleman was tall and slender and that his hair was blond. He was able to inform them that Mr. Bingley seemed a genial sort of man, but the rest was left to their imaginations. It became something of a game. His daughters would attempt to pull information from him, and he would reply with sly comments, designed to say nothing, and often contradicting what he had said previously. This would, of course, prompt cries of protest and ill-usage, which only served to amuse him more.

Fortunately for the sake of Mrs. Bennet's nerves, their curiosity was soon to be assuaged. The monthly assembly was scheduled for the week after Mr. Bingley's arrival, and as their good friend, Charlotte Lucas, had informed them, her father had invited Mr. Bingley to attend. He had accepted with enthusiasm appropriate for the occasion (or at least it seemed to be so, given the fact that they had nothing more than Sir William's word on which to base their suppositions.) The ladies prepared for the evening, in Elizabeth's case much as she had ever done. But nothing was good enough for Mrs. Bennet, who clearly had her heart set on one of them appearing irresistible to the still unknown gentleman.

"Come, girls," said Mrs. Bennet, chivvying them out of the house and to the waiting carriage. "We must arrive before Mr. Bingley comes."

"Do you have some secret intelligence which informs you that Mr. Bingley always arrives early?" asked Elizabeth, fighting to keep the smile from her face.

"Please keep a tight rein on the nonsense you usually speak, Lizzy," said Mrs. Bennet. "Of course, I do not. But if you are all before him and looking your prettiest, why he may have any one of you he chooses!"

It took a considerable amount of willpower to avoid informing her mother that she and her sisters were not prize horses at an auction. But Elizabeth, catching Mary's eye and sharing a commiserating glance, only stepped up into the carriage and took her seat. Soon they were off, accompanied by Mrs. Bennet's high-spirited statements and never-ending commentary about her expectations for the night. She instructed them on the best way to go about catching a wealthy gentleman—most of which was nonsensical, while the rest bordered on improper—and made minute adjustments to their appearances.

On more than one occasion, Elizabeth heard her mother muttering under her breath: "How I wish Jane were here. She would have no trouble catching the gentleman in a trice!"

Elizabeth loved her sister more than any other person in the world. But given how Jane had attained the age of two and twenty without experiencing hordes of gentlemen falling at her feet, Elizabeth was more than a little skeptical of her mother's conviction.

They entered the assembly room and her mother was quick to determine that Mr. Bingley had not yet arrived. Nor had most of their neighbors—they were at least fifteen minutes before their usual time, and the Bennets had never been known for anything other than punctuality. Thus made happy, Mrs. Bennet set about the task of lining her daughters up in a row within a clear view of the door, ensuring they were looking their best, both in appearance, posture, and whatever else she thought necessary. Elizabeth felt like she was in the army, being presented for the commanding officer's inspection.

It was fortunate, indeed, that Mr. Bingley arrived early himself, otherwise Elizabeth might have grown tired of standing in that attitude for so long. Her first glimpse of the man was favorable. He was a passably handsome man, though his hair was revealed to be more red than blond, contrary to her father's assertions. Sir William, who was always present near the door in his self-appointed role of host and usher combined, greeted him and the men spoke together for some moments. Since Charlotte and her sister and brother were standing nearby, they were immediately introduced to Mr. Bingley, who seemed eager to meet and speak.

"Come, Sir William," Elizabeth heard her exasperated mother mutter. "Do not keep Mr. Bingley to yourself. Your daughters are not nearly handsome enough to tempt him."

Though embarrassed by her mother's characterization of her closest friend, Elizabeth stood bravely while Mr. Bingley moved on with Sir William to some others to whom he had not been introduced. Mrs. Bennet ground her teeth together in frustration while Elizabeth did her best to ignore her. Then Mr. Bingley was before of them, requesting an introduction.

"Mrs. Bennet," said Sir William, his arms spread wide in expansive pleasure, "please allow me to introduce you to our new neighbor, Mr. Bingley. Mr. Bingley, this is Mrs. Bennet, and her daughters, Elizabeth, Mary, Kitty, and Lydia."

Mr. Bingley responded with enthusiasm, gratifying Mrs. Bennet exceedingly. She welcomed him, thanked him for his attention, and was unable to allow him to depart without saying something of the fifth Bennet girl. "My eldest, Jane, is not here tonight, for she is visiting relations in London. How I wish she was here! For you see, Mr. Bingley, she is widely accounted as the most beautiful and agreeable young lady in Meryton."

Not knowing quite what to say to such a speech, Mr. Bingley replied: "Then I shall be happy to make her acquaintance when she returns."

Then Mr. Bingley turned to Elizabeth and said: "Miss Bennet, if you are not already engaged, might I solicit your hand for the first set?"

"I am not engaged, sir," said Elizabeth, his infectious grin prompting her to give a similar response. "I would be happy to dance with you."

"Excellent!" exclaimed Mr. Bingley.

They spoke for some few more moments before Sir William pulled Mr. Bingley away from them to introduce him to some of their other neighbors. The moment he was out of range of her voice—though Elizabeth was skeptical such would be possible without actually leaving the assembly rooms—Mrs. Bennet began to exult in her daughter's success.

"It is only a dance, Mama," said Elizabeth after listening to her mother for a few moments.

"One dance may be the start of much more," said Mrs. Bennet with an airy wave. Then she turned a stern look on Elizabeth. "I shall ask you once again, Lizzy: please rein in your flippant tongue. You are well aware of our situation with respect to the entail. One of you must marry well, and Mr. Bingley presents the best chance we have seen in some time. Do not ruin it!"

And with that, Mrs. Bennet turned and walked away. Elizabeth watched her go with mixed feelings. Yes, she was very aware of her family's situation. But she would not put aside her principles and show more affection than she felt for the purpose of capturing a wealthy husband. She did not wish to marry without affection, and she knew feigned affection would be revealed soon after any marriage took place, forever ruining any chance of happiness.

It was soon evident to Elizabeth that Mr. Bingley would be an agreeable partner in a marriage, even, she suspected, should a woman worm her way into his affections under false pretenses. He was cheery and garrulous, amiable and handsome, and his conversation was interesting and plentiful.

But it was also soon obvious to her that they did not suit as partners. He was a good man and not lacking in intelligence, but it was clear they did not share the same interests, and some of the statements she made to attempt to gauge his interest in certain subjects resulted in nothing more than curious and uncomprehending replies. Thus, Elizabeth determined to simply enjoy his company without attempting to find a deeper subject on which to converse.

"Do you have any family?" asked Elizabeth when the subject arose.

"I do," replied he. "I have one older sister and one younger. Louisa, the eldest of us, is married to a man by the name of Hurst—Hurst is the master of an estate in Norfolk. Caroline, the younger, is staying with them in London at present, though a few weeks ago they were visiting friends in Bedfordshire."

"Then I hope we shall make their acquaintance," replied Elizabeth.

Mr. Bingley smiled and changed the subject. "I also have a very good friend—a Mr. Darcy, by name—who is to visit me at Netherfield and assist me with accustoming myself to the management of the estate."

"Mr. Darcy is familiar with these subjects?"

Elizabeth's question opened the floodgates, for there was much for Mr. Bingley to say of his close friend. "We met at Cambridge, you see. As I am three years younger than Darcy, he was entering his last year, when I was entering my first. I will be forever grateful he took me under his wing."

Laughing, Elizabeth said: "He sounds like a paragon of virtue, Mr. Bingley. But you did not answer my question."

"I suppose I did not," said Mr. Bingley. "Darcy has been master of his estate these past five years since his father's early death."

"I am sorry to hear of it, Mr. Bingley," said Elizabeth.

Mr. Bingley nodded. "It was a difficult time, for he was called home just before he was to depart on his grand tour to the continent. But as I have said, he is an excellent master of his estate and has much wisdom to impart. He has been delayed in the north due to some business. But I hope to persuade him to join me before long."

If Elizabeth thought that would be the end of Mr. Bingley's conversation concerning his friend, she was to be mistaken, for he had much more to say. This Mr. Darcy was given such a flaming character that Elizabeth began to feel impatient to make his acquaintance. But Mr. Darcy was not the only topic of conversation, for Mr. Bingley had many other things to say, and his words tumbled from one idea to the next without seeming forethought or hesitation. But he was pleasant and kind, and Elizabeth enjoyed speaking with him immensely.

Had Elizabeth any indication of Mr. Bingley's interest in her, she might have been flattered. As it was, however, she knew him to be a friend, and she was content with that.

As the month progressed, Mr. Bingley became a regular participant in the events of society, and where the Bennets and Mr. Bingley came together, Mr. Bingley's preference for her company was noticeable to all. There were, of course, rumors of an attachment between them on the lips of many in local society, and as far as Elizabeth could determine, her mother was the foremost promoter of such rumors. But Elizabeth never thought herself in danger of succumbing to Mr. Bingley's charms and, furthermore, the more time she spent in his company, the more she realized that it was nothing more than his unguarded temperament which led him to be so open with her.

Elizabeth, where possible, refuted any claim of anything other than friendship between herself and Mr. Bingley, and after a time with no more overt signs of admiration, she thought the talk died down to a certain extent. While most of those with whom she shared the truth of her friendship with Mr. Bingley seemed to understand and did not comment further, there was one who deemed it her duty to "talk some sense" into Elizabeth.

It happened during a morning visit. Such visits were common between the Lucas family and the Bennets, for not only had Elizabeth always been close to Charlotte, but Lady Lucas and Mrs. Bennet were friends — gossiping partners, the cynical might say — and Kitty and Lydia, thick as thieves with the younger Lucas daughter, Maria. On the morning in question, a lovely autumn morning in which the leaves rustled in the breeze, accompanying Elizabeth as she walked the paths close to her home, she discovered the Lucas ladies on the front drive of her home and accompanied them inside. It was not long before she and Charlotte were ensconced on a sofa in Longbourn's main sitting-room, speaking as animatedly as old friends often did.

"I see you were in Mr. Bingley's company most of yesterday evening again," said Charlotte after they had spoken together for some minutes. "Good for you. You have made an important conquest, and one which may, one day, save your family."

Elizabeth was perplexed. Surely Charlotte, as an intelligent woman, having known Elizabeth for many years, would understand that Elizabeth's interest in Mr. Bingley was entirely friendly. Furthermore, Elizabeth would have thought Charlotte would recognize Mr. Bingley's seeming interest as nothing more than a man enjoying lively company.

"You are quite mistaken, Charlotte," replied Elizabeth, eager to correct her friend's misapprehension. "I have no notion of any interest on Mr. Bingley's side, other than that of a friend, and I certainly do not wish for a closer connection to him."

Charlotte fixed Elizabeth with a pointed look. It was one akin to those often bestowed on Elizabeth by her mother when she found her daughter exasperating. It was also one her mother had not used on her since she was sixteen years of age.

"You do not see Mr. Bingley's interest in you?" asked Charlotte. "I have rarely seen such a promising beginning with a gentleman, certainly beyond anything Jane has ever had. Should you only exert yourself, I am certain you could induce him to believe himself in love with you, sufficient to prompt a proposal."

"I cannot understand why you wish me to behave in such a way, Charlotte. You know I am not interested in marrying a man unless he is in love with me, and I with him."

"Ah yes," said Charlotte, her tone slightly mocking. "I had forgotten your romantic streak. I would, however, entreat you to leave such thoughts to the girl you were at sixteen and focus on the practicalities. Neither you nor I nor any of your sisters possess much in the way of dowries, and our connections and breeding are uninspiring at best. You may never possess so good an opportunity as that which has been presented to you now. Do not allow it to slip away."

"You have said quite enough, Charlotte," replied Elizabeth, feeling offended that her close friend would be promoting such distasteful behavior. "I have no interest in Mr. Bingley, nor has he any in me. We are friends. I will not feign love where such feelings do not exist."

"If you will excuse my saying, Elizabeth, your stance is short-sighted."

"And what should happen when my duplicity is discovered after we are married? Surely you do not think I can maintain the pretense for the rest of my life."

"Who is to say that ardor does not cool after one becomes accustomed to marriage?" asked Charlotte. "And even if your true feelings are revealed, it is not as if you dislike him."

"No, but I am certain if I feigned love and it was discovered, he would not be happy. I will have stolen any chance of his obtaining a true meeting of minds with a woman."

"Are you certain that is what he wishes for? Perhaps he is a man who would be content with a marriage of respect."

"I must think you a simpleton if you believe that," replied

Elizabeth. "Mr. Bingley's true strength is the passion with which he undertakes life. I cannot imagine he would approach marriage in any other manner."

"Then fall in love with him, if that is what you wish."

"Charlotte!" exclaimed Elizabeth, drawing the attention of the rest of the room to them. A little embarrassed, Elizabeth leaned forward and hissed: "One does not simply fall in love on command. Now, cease these objectionable assertions, I beg you."

Charlotte regarded Elizabeth for several moments, her expression unreadable, before she nodded, albeit slowly. "I see I shall not persuade you, so I will attempt it no further. But you are making a mistake, Elizabeth. You may never have such an opportunity again."

The rest of Charlotte's visit was spent in uncomfortable and stilted conversation. It seemed like every subject was now tainted and every understanding she had previously possessed of her friend was now overthrown. Elizabeth knew Charlotte was not romantic and had never agreed with her opinion of what would constitute a good marriage. Then again, Charlotte was not a Bennet, was not resident of Longbourn, and though she knew of the discord which often existed between Elizabeth's parents, she had not experienced it daily in such close quarters as a family home. Elizabeth was almost happy when Charlotte left a few minutes later.

"Lizzy," a voice interrupted her when she had remained on the sofa for some time after her friend's departure. Having completely forgotten she was not alone, Elizabeth looked up to see Mary watching her, curiosity written on her brow.

"I apologize, Mary. It appears I was woolgathering."

"Did something happen between you and Charlotte?" asked Mary. "It seemed to me you were arguing."

Elizabeth was surprised Mary was asking her such things. They had never been close, and Elizabeth often found Mary's sermonizing to be tiresome, and her conversation uninteresting, even medieval at times. She almost wished for Jane—then reality asserted itself. Jane would try to find some way to claim that Charlotte's opinions were anything other than distasteful. Perhaps, in this instance, Mary might shed some insight on Elizabeth's thoughts. At the very least, perhaps she could verify that Elizabeth's opinion was justified.

"I learned something of my friend which has disconcerted me," said Elizabeth with a sigh. Mary tilted her head in a clear question, and Elizabeth essayed to explain what had passed between them. When she finished, she sat for a few minutes, waiting with an emotion akin to trepidation for Mary to answer.

"Charlotte has always struck me as practical," said Mary. "I suppose it is not too much of a leap to assume she has more pragmatic opinions concerning marriage than you."

"Yes, yes," replied Elizabeth, a hint of impatience stealing into her voice. "That is understandable. But to feign love for the sake of a comfortable position. Is that not underhanded?"

Mary frowned. "I suppose it is," said she after thinking for a few moments. "I am sure you would not be surprised if I informed you I am also rather pragmatic about marriage?"

Elizabeth shook her head.

"A good character and the ability to provide a good home would be much more important than love. But I understand you and Jane have different opinions." Mary paused. "But I could not imagine ever attempting to hoodwink a man into marriage by showing more affection than I feel. I find I must agree with you in this instance — what Charlotte is suggesting is not proper."

Then Mary stood and departed, leaving Elizabeth to her thoughts. She felt vindicated, though she had never thought herself in the wrong. That Mary — staid, moralistic, scrupulously proper Mary, whom Elizabeth had often thought rather silly — should agree with her was strangely liberating.

It would affect her future relationship with Charlotte, Elizabeth knew. Matters had changed between them, and Elizabeth knew they would never be the same again.

CHAPTER II

It was the next day when a situation occurred which resulted in substantial changes for the entire family. The presence of Mr. Bingley when the circumstance occurred was entirely coincidental, though Elizabeth learned to be happy that he was able to assist, though mortified he had been witness to her family's near disgrace.

The day began much as any other. There were no events of society that day, and the Bennet sisters found themselves left to their own devices, Mr. Bennet having returned to the library and Mrs. Bennet, to her room, complaining of an indisposition. Mr. Bingley, as was often his wont, visited them that morning, and it was not long before he was seated on the sofa at Elizabeth's side, engaged in another animated discussion.

Though Kitty and Lydia were no less than struck by ennui due to their elder sisters' refusal to allow them to walk into Meryton that morning, their salvation soon arrived in the persons of three officers of the regiment which had recently arrived at their winter quarters in the district. The officers were, in Elizabeth's opinion, generally good men, with nary an objectionable character among them. But she did not consider them to be particularly interesting either, for few seemed to be able to carry on an intelligent conversation. To Kitty and Lydia, however, they were practically gods walking in the guise of men on earth. Their conversation of late had been restricted to "Lieutenant Denny is so handsome" or "Captain Carter said" followed by a long and uninteresting account of whatever had been discussed. Thus, when they appeared, Elizabeth was happy to leave their entertainment to her younger sisters while she conversed with Mr. Bingley. That Lieutenant Denny and Captain Carter were among the visitors increased her younger sisters' enthusiasm for them.

"Your sisters appear to be quite . . . friendly with the men of the regiment," said Mr. Bingley when they had sat down again after the officers' arrival.

"That was quite diplomatic, indeed," said Elizabeth, grinning at her friend. "You could have stated that they are incorrigible flirts and been entirely correct."

Mr. Bingley laughed, though Elizabeth thought she detected a nervous quality in it. He said: "They are yet young. I believe maturity and experience will bring them a greater understanding of the limits of polite behavior."

"I hope you are correct, Mr. Bingley," said Elizabeth, her eyes seeking out her younger sisters almost of their own volition.

Mr. Bingley seemed to sense that Elizabeth did not wish to discuss the antics of the youngest Bennets, so he smoothly changed the subject. "I believe I have mentioned my close friend, Mr. Darcy, in the past?" Elizabeth allowed that he had—in fact, the subject of Mr. Darcy was one which was raised quite often. "I have just received confirmation from Darcy that he will join me at Netherfield, and he will be bringing his sister with him."

"That is surely good news from your perspective, Mr. Bingley," said Elizabeth. "I must own that I will be happy to make Mr. Darcy's acquaintance, for you have given him a virtuous character, indeed."

"Darcy is all that is good, to be certain. He is, perhaps, not adept at making new acquaintances, for he often struggles to know what to say when among those he has never before met. But he is the best of men. I am grateful I have gained his friendship."

"And do you know when your guests will arrive?"

"At present, I do not, unfortunately," was Mr. Bingley's reply. "I would guess Darcy will arrive by Michaelmas, though it is possible he may be delayed again."

"Then I shall pray for a swift and safe journey." Elizabeth paused, not at all certain she should be speaking of her next point, but her curiosity demanded it be assuaged. "I am curious about the members of your family, however. Do your sisters mean to travel to Hertfordshire to stay with you? I would think they would be eager to do so, as your taking control of an estate must be a momentous occasion."

It seemed to Elizabeth that Mr. Bingley appeared more than a little shamefaced. But he gamely gathered himself and attempted to make a response. "It *is* a momentous occasion. But as for my sisters' absence . . . Well, you see, it may be *possible* that I neglected to inform them."

Elizabeth gaped at her companion, and Mr. Bingley allowed himself a chuckle, though it was clear he did not at all feel like laughing. "Yes, I can imagine you are surprised at my words. I would not give you a poor opinion of my sisters before you have had the opportunity of taking their likeness yourself.

"You see, though I am prodigiously fond of both of my sisters, they have a tendency to part with their opinions rather freely. I am my own man, and I have decided that Netherfield fits my needs. I have grown fond of it. I am quite content in accustoming myself to Netherfield without well-meaning sisters whose opinions may be contrary to mine. As such, while I will be happy to host them later, I wished to take my own measure of my new home without listening to their thoughts."

"That is a wise decision, I would say," replied Elizabeth. "I commend you for it. Then am I to suppose that your sisters will likely not visit until after Mr. and Miss Darcy are already staying here."

"Perhaps later than that," confessed Mr. Bingley. "Darcy is . . . Well, he is good to tolerate my younger sister for the sake of our friendship, but in truth, he finds her civility trying. Caroline, you see, considers herself to be a close friend of Darcy's, though his friendship rightfully belongs to me. Darcy has no interest in her other than as my sister, and she has not yet accepted this fact."

It was clear to Elizabeth what Mr. Bingley was not saying, and though she supposed she should wait to make her own judgment, she thought she already knew much of at least one of Mr. Bingley's sisters. While she knew it was best to avoid basing her opinion of those she had never met on Mr. Bingley's careful words, it was difficult. In her mind, she thought of the scenes which might ensue when Mr. Darcy came to visit, and when Miss Bingley came herself. From her brother's words, she sounded like the worst of social climbers, a woman who had dedicated herself to ensuring *she* was the only choice as the next mistress of the man's estate. The lengths to which such a woman might go to realize her ambitions nearly prompted Elizabeth to smile.

After a few minutes of such thoughts, Elizabeth roused herself to push them to the back of her mind. Mr. Bingley had, as usual, changed the subject and was now happily informing her of the visit he had paid to Lucas Lodge only the day before. As he spoke, Elizabeth endeavored to give the man her full attention.

While she was speaking with Mr. Bingley, Elizabeth was, in fact, watching the state of affairs in the sitting-room. There were times, it was true, when Kitty and Lydia were speaking in voices too loud or laughter too raucous for young ladies of their station. But they had not descended *too far* from what was proper, and Elizabeth meant to maintain such a state of affairs. Mary was present, of course, and watching them carefully, but Kitty and Lydia did not respect Mary and would not listen to her, not to mention how Mary's manner of expressing herself did not inspire obedience. Thus, Elizabeth thought it prudent to remain vigilant.

"Lizzy!" exclaimed Lydia in her usually loud voice, startling Elizabeth at the suddenness of it. "We wish to show the officers the back lawn now."

"Very well, Lydia," said Elizabeth. "As long as you stay within sight of the house and your sisters at all times."

Lydia pouted a little at such a stricture, though in truth such a reminder should not have been required for a young lady of any sense. She soon brightened, however, at obtaining permission, and set about guiding the men out toward the back of the house.

"I should be happy to accompany you and your sisters, Miss Bennet," said Mr. Bingley when Elizabeth turned back to him.

The time for his visit had elapsed, and Elizabeth knew it would have been proper for him to excuse himself. But he clearly had seen something in her sisters' behavior which gave him pause, and perhaps even something in that of the officers. Elizabeth was grateful for his offer and accepted it with alacrity.

They soon made their way through the house and out toward the back lawn. As they went, they came across Kitty and Lydia arguing. Elizabeth sighed — this was also not unusual, for while they were close, they were almost always engaged in little spats between them, in which Lydia, especially, could be quite cruel.

"You know the officers only pay attention to you when I am engaged, Kitty," Lydia was saying. "They appreciate my liveliness and vivacity — Mama always says so."

"They do not!" was Kitty's predictable reply. "I am just as popular among the officers as you are, and more so. I have more than a bit of fluff in my head, unlike some that I could name."

One might have thought that such a stinging insult might have prompted Lydia's retaliation, but Lydia only sniffed and turned away. "You may think what you like, Kitty. But I will thank you to stay away while I am speaking with Denny, for he likes me much better than you."

Kitty stormed after her sister, leaving Elizabeth with Mr. Bingley's escort. She was surprised when she heard a chuckle issue forth from his mouth and turned toward him with a look askance.

"Your sister's argument has reminded me of some of those to which I have been witness between *my* sisters. Some of their disagreements have been quite the sight to behold!"

"But surely they have never argued about so silly a subject."

Mr. Bingley scratched his chin. "Perhaps not. Remember what I said about your sisters, Miss Bennet. Though you may despair of their behavior at present, remember they are full young. Surely maturity will improve their dispositions."

In the privacy of her own mind, Elizabeth thought Mr. Bingley's assessment was overly rosy. She doubted either girl would ever improve without intervention from their parents, and such instruction was unlikely in the extreme. Still, she appreciated his encouraging words and nodded in thanks, if not agreement.

The day was, as her sisters had averred, pleasant, if somewhat overcast. The wind—what there was of it—still carried the warmth of early autumn, and the leaves, while almost all yellow or brown, still rustled pleasantly. In the back of the house, there were several benches on which to sit and an old rope swing they had played on as girls. It was to this swing Lydia had gathered the three officers, who obliged by pushing her, while Kitty watched, sullen and offended. Mary, though she had brought a book with her, watched her younger sisters more closely than her book. Elizabeth, though worried her sisters would betray them all, thought they were well enough protected for the present. That state of affairs, unfortunately, was not to persist.

Deciding it was best to attend to the officers as well as Mr. Bingley, Elizabeth struck up a conversation with Lieutenant Denny, while Mr. Bingley approached Captain Carter. This was not at all to Lydia's liking, for it was clear she had determined to keep the officers' focus on herself. But when Elizabeth directed a pointed glare at her, she subsided with a huff, confining her devotion to Lieutenant Sanderson, who obliged her by continuing to push her on the swing. Elizabeth, mindful of her other sister's feelings, beckoned Kitty and was rewarded when Kitty gratefully joined them.

How it all happened, Elizabeth could not be certain, but soon after, she found herself speaking with Mr. Bingley and Captain Carter, while Kitty was left to Mr. Denny alone. How long this persisted, Elizabeth was not certain, but it was not long before Mary brought a problem to Elizabeth's attention.

"Lizzy!" hissed she, pulling Elizabeth to her. "Where is Kitty?"

Elizabeth looked about, seeing for the first time that Mary was correct—Kitty was nowhere to be seen. Furthermore, Mr. Denny was also missing from their party. It seemed Mr. Bingley had also noticed the same, but that good man distracted Captain Carter and directed him toward where Lydia was still speaking with Sanderson, ensuring he did not notice the change in the numbers of their party.

"Stay with Lydia," instructed Elizabeth, motioning toward their youngest sister. "Ensure she does not do anything she should not. I will find Kitty."

It appeared Mary would have liked nothing more than to find her sister herself, but she nodded and did as Elizabeth was bid. Elizabeth noticed Mr. Bingley watching her, and she grimaced at him before turning away to search for Kitty. As she moved toward the house, she thought she heard a giggle to her right, and she hurried toward the corner of the house, certain Kitty was around the other side. When she turned the corner, it was just in time to see Kitty throw her arms around Mr. Denny's neck.

Elizabeth let out a soft cry at the scene, which prompted Denny to abandon his obviously amorous intentions. He stepped back, disengaging himself from Kitty's arms, and Kitty, eyes wide at being discovered, turned to Elizabeth, a fearful expression suddenly appearing on her countenance.

"What is the meaning of this?" demanded Elizabeth.

The officer was shamefaced while Kitty looked at the ground and would not meet Elizabeth's gaze. They appeared like a pair of naughty schoolboys, caught in some mischief. Had the situation not been so dire, Elizabeth might have found it amusing.

"If you will excuse me," Mr. Denny finally roused himself to say.

"I think not," said a new voice, as Mr. Bingley stepped around the corner. "I believe Mr. Bennet will wish to have a word with you."

Again embarrassed that Mr. Bingley was witnessing such a scene, Elizabeth was still grateful for his insistence. It was clear Mr. Denny was reluctant in the extreme to speak with Mr. Bennet, but one look at Mr. Bingley's implacable countenance informed him the gentleman would not be gainsaid. As such, he allowed himself to be led away into the house toward the master's bookroom. Elizabeth prayed their absence was missed by those remaining.

At the sound of their knock, Mr. Bennet called out permission to enter, and Elizabeth led the assorted company into the room. The smile he summoned at the sight of Elizabeth turned to a frown when he noted her companions and became positively cold when he noticed the apprehension of Mr. Denny and Kitty's fear.

"I would welcome you all, but I suspect your errand is one which I will not find agreeable. Will you not explain why you are here, Lizzy?"

Though Kitty shot Elizabeth a pleading glance, it was much too late to reconsider, even if Elizabeth were inclined to grant clemency. "Your second youngest daughter was being a little too forward with the lieutenant. It is fortunate it was *I* who caught them in a compromising position."

Mr. Bennet's gaze found Kitty, and she seemed to feel the weight of it. "Is this true, Kitty?"

"It was nothing, Papa," said Kitty, finding a hint of her courage. "Lizzy is attempting to make more of it than she should."

"One thing I have learned about your sister," said Mr. Bennet, the rebuke clear in his words and tone, "is that she does not embellish concerning matters of a serious nature."

Then Mr. Bennet's gaze swung to the disgraced militia officer. "And you, sir. What have you to say for yourself?"

Mr. Denny's gaze darted around the room. It appeared he had finally realized the true measure of his error. Couples had been forced to marry for less egregious mistakes than that Elizabeth had just witnessed, and while she did not think her father would insist upon it, the lieutenant was likely wondering how he could possibly support a wife on the wages earned by a lieutenant in the militia. And well he might, Elizabeth thought with some disgust.

"I understand this appears damning," said Mr. Denny carefully. "But nothing happened between us."

"At present, I know nothing of what happened," was Mr. Bennet's short reply. "Perhaps you both would be so good as to elucidate?"

Neither Kitty nor Mr. Denny were eager to relate the particulars, but with some patience, much cajoling, and some insistence from the master of the estate, the story was soon told. It seemed the interlude they had witnessed had been at Kitty's instigation, and although they found it impossible to determine exactly what stratagem she had used to lure him away from the others, Kitty had planned it, though she had not counted on being discovered.

"Lydia thought she was much more popular with the officers," said Kitty after they had drawn much of the story from her lips. "She will be so jealous when she hears how attentive Denny was to me."

The lieutenant's pinched countenance upon discovering he had been the means by which Kitty had wished to gain the advantage of her sister might have been amusing to Elizabeth. But she allowed nary a smile to escape her lips. In fact, she was far too furious with her thoughtless sister for putting them all at such risk to show her even an ounce of anything other than her disgust.

"It seems, then, that the incident was not as bad as I might have feared. You have escaped the hangman's noose for today, lieutenant. You should be grateful you have made a narrow escape."

No one in the room missed the great sigh of relief released by the lieutenant, least of all a suddenly offended Kitty. But she remained silent when she noticed her father's glare, one of the few sensible acts Elizabeth could remember from her silly sister.

"Now, lieutenant, we should discuss your future conduct. Given the narrowness of your escape this time, I assume I need not worry that any rumors of my daughter will be spread throughout the neighborhood?"

"Of course not, sir," Denny was quick to reply. "The matter was a trifle and not worth repeating. You may be assured of my secrecy."

"Excellent!" replied Mr. Bennet. "Then you are free to go. However, I expect you will be more circumspect in the presence of *all* my daughters from this day forward. In fact, it may be best if you were to refrain from approaching them, except when necessary. I would not wish for such a . . . lapse to be repeated."

"You have my assurances, Mr. Bennet. I agree with your assessment without reservation."

"Thank you, lieutenant. I believe you will thank me someday. I would not be surprised if you were beset by gratitude even now."

Then Mr. Bennet waved his hand, a gesture of clear dismissal. Mr. Denny hesitated not an instant — he rose and quit the room with almost unseemly haste. Then Mr. Bennet turned his attention to Elizabeth and Mr. Bingley.

"I *am* curious at your involvement, Mr. Bingley."

"Denny would have fled had Mr. Bingley not insisted upon his attendance, Papa," said Elizabeth.

"Then I am indebted to you — we all are."

"It is nothing, Mr. Bennet." Mr. Bingley turned a slight smile on Kitty. "I believe that I would appreciate it if another man were to step in to assist *my* sister, should the situation warrant it. Your daughters are charming, sir, and not without their own share of good qualities. I hope Miss Kitty learns from this experience."

A witticism was on the tip of Mr. Bennet's tongue — Elizabeth knew it. But he refrained at the last moment, his eyes finding his daughter and softening ever so slightly. He then nodded once.

"I hope you are correct, Mr. Bingley. And to that end, I would request you and Lizzy leave me alone with Kitty, so we may discuss her behavior. Once again, I thank you, sir."

"It was my pleasure," replied Mr. Bingley.

As they quit the study, Elizabeth heard her father say in a voice brimming with resignation: "Come and sit, Kitty. There is no need to fear your old papa."

"I add my thanks to that of my father, Mr. Bingley," said Elizabeth. "I doubt Mr. Denny would have been so easily persuaded to see my father, had you not been present."

"Oh, he was on the verge of fleeing," replied Mr. Bingley, the light of amusement dancing in his eyes. "I doubt he would have said anything to any of his fellow officers for fear of provoking your father. But it is best to ensure he understands the gravity of the situation. I was happy to be of assistance."

By the time they reached the back lawn, the three officers' departing forms could be seen walking down the long lane away from the house toward the village. Mary was still keeping a close eye on their youngest sister, who was not shy about venting her annoyance at her fun suddenly being interrupted.

"I do not know where you all got to, Lizzy, but the officers departed with almost unseemly haste! And where the deuce is Kitty?"

"Please moderate your language, Lydia," admonished Elizabeth. "Do not concern yourself with Kitty. I am certain you will see her again later."

"It does not signify," replied Lydia, carelessly waving her hand. "Let us all walk into Meryton. Though Carter and Sanderson proved to be dull today, I am certain some of the others will be walking in Meryton at this hour."

"No, Lydia. We shall not walk to Meryton. I believe there has been enough amusement for one day."

And nothing Lydia said could change Elizabeth's mind. She was forced to be satisfied with the visit she had received, though she was not of a mind to be thankful. In fact, her bitter railing against the cruelness of her sisters sent both Elizabeth and Mary to their own rooms after Mr. Bingley departed, if only to escape from her constant complaints.

CHAPTER III

$\mathcal{M}$iss Catherine Bennet emerged from her father's bookroom, later that day, chastened. Elizabeth, who had retired to her room to escape Lydia's complaining, had left it as soon as she confirmed her sister had gone to her own room. Though she had completed some of her own tasks while waiting for Kitty's emergence, in reality, she was mostly involved with listening for any hint of what was happening in the room. There was little enough to be heard—Mr. Bennet was not a man given to raising his voice with much frequency, and whatever happened between father and daughter was quiet enough that Elizabeth could not hear it.

When the door finally opened and Kitty made her way toward the stairs, Elizabeth was the recipient of an angry glare. But Kitty did not say anything, instead climbing the stairs quickly. A moment later the sound of her door impacting the frame echoed through the house—while Kitty had not precisely slammed the door, she had not been gentle in closing it either.

Mr. Bennet, Elizabeth soon found, was in a pensive mood. As Kitty left the door to the study opened, her father noted her presence in the hall and called her into the room. It was with much curiosity that Elizabeth joined him, wondering what had happened between himself and her sister.

"Well, Lizzy?" said Mr. Bennet. "What do you think of this business with your sister?"

With a sigh, Elizabeth said: "I do not think the incident in itself was all that serious. Lydia, as usual, taunted Kitty, teasing with her so-called popularity with the officers. What happened with Mr. Denny was about Kitty proving her ability to best her sister, though Lydia as yet knows nothing of it."

A snort escaped Mr. Bennet's lips. "I am sure that shall not last long. Kitty will be eager to crow to her sister of her perceived victory."

"True," replied Elizabeth. "I am much more worried about the direction in which their behavior is trending. If there had been others nearby, or if the other officers had seen what happened, Kitty's reputation might have been ruined, and her sisters' along with it."

"Surely they would realize it was naught but a bit of mischief," said Mr. Bennet in an attempt to be lighthearted. "No one of sense would think it anything else."

"If you will pardon my saying, sir, there are many people in the world of little sense, including my youngest two sisters. Would *you* wish her married to an unserious man such as Denny, to live in squalor and hardship? You know he has not the means to support her. And heaven forbid he should sire any children with her."

"No, you are correct, Lizzy," replied Mr. Bennet with a sigh. "I would not wish it—for her, or for any of you. Even Lydia, who is as silly a flirt as ever lived."

While Elizabeth did not appreciate the manner in which her father spoke of his youngest, she knew his words contained more than a hint of truth. She had always been thankful for how he tolerated her open opinions with him, for she knew many fathers would not accept such censure from a daughter. Still, nothing changed with respect to her sisters, and she could not help but wish he would act.

"You have given me much on which to think, Lizzy," continued Mr. Bennet. "Let me consider the situation and decide what is best to be done."

"Very well. And thank you, Papa."

The matter came to a head later that evening—much sooner than Elizabeth had ever expected. Kitty had quite obviously been sent to her room, for she did not emerge until called for dinner. Her door was locked from the inside and though Lydia attempted to enter several times, there was no answer from within, no matter how many times she banged on the door.

"Leave your sister be, Lydia," said Mr. Bennet, drawn from his bookroom the third time Lydia's demands had echoed through the house. "Find something to occupy yourself in your own chambers."

The reality was that Lydia was more than a little intimidated by her father. Whereas she listened to little her sisters said, and her mother encouraged her poor behavior, a sharply spoken word from Mr. Bennet was almost always enough to quell her outbursts. This occasion was no different, as Lydia made no comment, returning to her room without pause.

At dinner, there was less chatter than might usually be expected at the Bennet supper table. Mr. Bennet was usually quiet, watching his family or speaking with his eldest daughters in soft tones, and Mary rarely said a word at the dinner table, unless it was to deliver some sermon she had practiced in the mirror, waiting for what she felt was an appropriate time to deliver it. The conversation was usually carried by the two youngest and their mother. But on this evening, Kitty was sullen and uncommunicative, Lydia annoyed with the tedious afternoon she had spent by herself, and their mother quite obviously confused at the seeming distance between her two youngest. As they ate, Elizabeth could see her youngest sister becoming more annoyed with every passing moment, and it was not long before she could no longer control her tongue.

"Kitty! You have become so dull! You need not be so jealous of me just because the officers prefer me."

"I am not jealous," said Kitty with a smirk. "In fact, I have proof that I am quite as popular as you."

Lydia replied with a snort. "I have no idea to where you disappeared this afternoon, but Sanderson and Carter both stayed with me, and both were quite attentive. For a time, I thought they might come to blows over who would show me the most favor."

The huff from Mary told Elizabeth that Lydia's words were nothing more than idle boasting. Not that she had expected anything else, of course. But Kitty was not about to be outdone by her sister, especially when she had paid a heavy price for her actions.

"You may think that if you like. You did not see—"

A loud clearing of Mr. Bennet's throat brought Kitty up short and her eyes dropped to the table as she fell silent. Mrs. Bennet, however, was clearly confused.

"What happened? Of what are you speaking, Kitty?"

"She speaks of nothing more than fantasy," interjected Lydia, with a pinched, mean sort of glare directed at Kitty. "She could no more attract an officer to pay attention to her than she could fly to the top of the tallest tree on the estate."

"Thank you, Lydia," said Mr. Bennet, causing the immediate cessation of Lydia's nasty words. "You have managed to convince me with your mean-spirited behavior, and Kitty's attempts to return the favor have firmed my resolve."

Surprised, both girls turned their gazes toward their father. "Of what are you speaking, Papa?"

All eyes were on the Bennet patriarch. He seemed to feel amusement at the scrutiny, for he did not speak for a moment, while the girls waited impatiently for him to inform them of his meaning.

"It seems I have your undivided attention," drawled Mr. Bennet, the hint of sardonic amusement in his tone escaping the notice of all save Elizabeth, and perhaps Mary. "The fact of the matter is, I have been reviewing the behavior of my youngest daughters and have come to the conclusion that it is wanting. Neither Kitty nor Lydia take any interest in matters of rational thought and spend their days on frivolous nothings. While it might be acceptable for a child to behave in such a manner, sooner or later we must all grow up and begin acting like adults. It is clear I have been remiss in attending to the education of my youngest daughters. That must change."

"Oh, you do not need to worry, Papa," said Lydia in her usually flippant manner. "I am quite mature now. All the officers say so."

Mr. Bennet's glare silenced Lydia, and it prevented her mother from speaking. "You are not mature, Lydia. You chase after officers, fight amongst yourselves, and if I should leave you to your own devices, you shall ruin your reputations and that of your sisters.

"No, it is now clear to me. You must be sent to school to learn how to behave yourselves, for it is clear we, your parents, have failed in that respect."

The uproar that Mr. Bennet's declaration provoked was the least surprising facet of the evening's events. The first to voice her objections was Mrs. Bennet, who was offended at the suggestion that she did not understand how to raise her daughters properly. And Lydia and Kitty were not shy about voicing their own objections, though they were more easily silenced than their mother. In the end, Mr. Bennet was forced to order the girls to their rooms before peace was restored. When Mrs. Bennet persisted, he took the simple expedient of returning to his room.

Soon after he had left, Mrs. Bennet threw down her napkin and stalked away toward the sitting-room, complaining all the way of her ill-usage. Elizabeth watched her go and determined to follow her. But before she could rise, Mary's voice prevented her from her objective.

"Would you ever have thought Papa would come to such a decision?"

"No, I would not," replied Elizabeth. "But I think we must take this opportunity to attempt to educate Mama. If we do not, she may never understand."

Mary nodded. "I hope you will forgive me if I leave that task in your hands. I doubt Mama would listen to me, even if I made the attempt."

Though a part of her branded Mary a coward, she knew her sister was correct. Soon Mary rose and quit the room, leaving Elizabeth to marshal her strength for the upcoming discussion with her mother. When she felt she was ready, she rose and followed her mother to the sitting-room.

When she entered the room, she was not at all surprised by her mother's accusatory statement. "I suppose you are happy now, Lizzy. You have been clamoring for your sisters' censure for some time now."

"I *am* happy, Mama," said Elizabeth. Her mother's countenance tightened in response, but Elizabeth ignored her. "In fact, I am happy for Kitty and Lydia. I am also more than a little envious of the opportunity they shall receive."

Elizabeth's words confused her mother. "Envious of them? Why would you be envious? You have no need to go to school—none of you have any need of it. You have learned everything you need to know right here."

"Yes, Mama," replied Elizabeth, once again ignoring her mother's words. "I would have jumped at the opportunity to attend school when I was a girl. I have educated myself as best I can, but to receive formal instruction would have been a privilege. Your daughters will emerge from the experience more confident and poised, I dare say."

"But they will be away for at least a year, maybe more!" wailed Mrs. Bennet. "You must all make good marriages! How are they to marry if they are locked in school, receiving lessons instead of partaking in society as they ought?"

"Oh, Mama!" exclaimed Elizabeth. She sat by her mother's side and caught one of her mother's hands in her own. "Have you not considered that rather than make it more difficult to marry, their experience in finishing school will make it more *likely*?"

"How can you say such a thing?"

Elizabeth sighed. "Because, Mama, their behavior is not what it ought to be. I know you fancy Lydia and Kitty are the favorites of the young men of the neighborhood, and of the officers in particular. But do you not also see the censorious looks they elicit? Do you not notice how the gentlemen are happy to dance with them but laugh at them when their backs are turned? Have you never seen how their behavior may one day disgrace us? If their reputations are ruined, none of us will ever make a good marriage."

Mrs. Bennet eyes widened in abject terror, and she shook her head with vigor, denying Elizabeth's assertions. But Elizabeth, though she knew she was distressing her mother, was not about to recant her words.

"It is true, Mama. Consider Jane's behavior. She is mild and kind, quiet, yet friendly, and she never makes a spectacle of herself. Our society prizes young women who are demure and proper. Liveliness is also prized, yes, but only when it is tempered by proper manners and restraint. Kitty and especially Lydia are not restrained in anything they do. In fact, they are rude, loud, and obnoxious, they flirt with anything wearing pants, and I dare say if they are left to their own devices, all your daughters will end as despised spinsters, shunned by all of any reputation whatsoever.

It was some time before Mrs. Bennet found the voice necessary to respond to Elizabeth's assertions. Elizabeth had chosen her words carefully, for nothing could obtain Mrs. Bennet's attention as quickly as the suggestion her daughters might not marry. Having pinned all her hopes on their success, the specter of being forced from her home with nowhere to go was always just under the surface in Mrs. Bennet's mind.

"But Jane is beautiful," said she. It was a pitiful last-ditch effort to protect the opinions she had cherished for many years.

"She is, Mama. But though her beauty will attract the notice of a man, it is her character which will hold them. Beauty fades with time. But character will always be a part of us. Papa is correct to fear for Kitty and Lydia, and I fully support his decision to see them educated. It will give them the best chance to reach their potential, and that, in turn, will give them the opportunity to make a rewarding marriage."

When Elizabeth fell silent, she could see the conflicting emotions warring across her mother's countenance. There was nothing more she could do, and so she rose and exited the room, leaving her mother to think on the matter. Elizabeth hoped she would come to the correct conclusion.

Above stairs, a more contentious conversation was taking place. Upon leaving the dining room, Mary had gone directly to her sisters' rooms, intent upon seeing them understand, and though she was not certain of her success, she knew she needed to make the effort. Mary hoped Elizabeth appreciated her efforts—she had not missed Elizabeth's expression when she had hurried from the room.

"Kitty!" snapped Mary as she opened the door.

Her sister, who had been moping on her bed, started to her feet, watching Mary as if she had never seen her before. Mary had counted on this—it was the reason she had chosen to come to Kitty's room first. Kitty was much more easily led than Lydia.

"Come with me now," commanded Mary. "I wish to speak to both you and Lydia."

"But Mary—"

Mary cut her sister off mid-whine. "This instant, Kitty! *Now!*"

The harshness of her tone and the scowl Mary displayed persuaded Kitty it would be best to do as her sister demanded immediately, and she rose and followed Mary from the room, though not without reluctance. Lydia's room was the next door toward the back of the house, and Mary proceeded there without delay, threw open the door, and ushered her sister inside.

"What are you doing?" screeched the indignant voice of the youngest sister. "Get out! I do not wish to speak to you!"

"I do not care *what* you wish, you spoiled child!" hissed Mary, provoking a visible start from Lydia. "Kitty, come in here and sit down next to your sister. You will both listen to what I have to say."

Kitty plodded into the room, reluctance in every step, while Lydia watched them both with her mouth wide open. For the briefest of moments, Mary was gratified that her youngest sisters, who had never listened to her and had tormented her as often as not, were actually doing as she bid them. Then Mary pushed that feeling aside. Her words were far too important for such petty considerations.

"I know you are both upset that our father has decreed you are to attend school," said Mary, delving into the heart of the matter without delay. "But it seems to me neither of you comprehends your good fortune."

"And what good fortune is that?" was Lydia's snide query. "You were never commanded to attend school, and neither were Jane or Lizzy."

"No, we were not. But any of us would have appreciated the

chance."

Both girls gaped at her. "You would wish to go to school?" demanded Kitty.

At the same time, Lydia snorted and said: "It is just like you, Mary, to wish for such dreariness as school lessons. I have no need of such things."

"You have more need of it than most, you silly child!" hissed Mary. "Do you not know how close to the brink of ruin you two have brought the entire family? Do you wish to live in degradation and want the rest of your lives?"

The girls gaped at her, but Mary would not allow them to respond. "Kitty, do you not know the probable result of your adventure today? Do you know what you might have cost the family?"

Apparently, Mr. Bennet had spoken to Kitty somewhat concerning the consequences of her actions for she hung her head. Lydia, however, turned to Kitty, her confusion clear.

"What did Kitty do today?"

Kitty's eyes immediately rose to Mary's, but the plea within was not gratified. "She threw herself into Lieutenant Denny's arms without thought to her own reputation."

"Why you little traitor!" cried Lydia. "You knew he preferred me!"

"Silence!" demanded Mary. Lydia, though she was still angry at her sister, obeyed. Kitty only glared at them both, mutiny in the depths of her eyes.

"I care nothing for your petty rivalry," said Mary. "I wish you to understand the consequences of your actions. Do you not know, Kitty, that had you been discovered by anyone other than our sister, you would have been forced to marry Mr. Denny?"

"All the better," replied Kitty, the flippancy in her tone positively infuriating. "I have proven that he likes me better anyway."

"Oh, so you wish for a life of poverty, do you?"

Kitty's eyes bulged out in her shock, but Mary continued mercilessly. "That is exactly what it would be, Kitty. A man in Mr. Denny's position struggles to pay for his own upkeep, let alone the necessary expense of a wife. If you were to fall with child, the situation would worsen."

"But he might be promoted," ventured Kitty.

"You cannot count on that," rejoined Mary. "And even if he was put forward for promotion, would he have the means to purchase the next commission?"

Mary paused, allowing her sisters to think on it for a moment.

"Now, it is possible Mr. Denny might have a family who supports him. But lest you think your thoughtless actions might have been mitigated," Kitty was doing exactly as Mary expected, her face lighting up in a smile, "I should remind you that you know *nothing* of the lieutenant's situation. Am I correct?"

Kitty scowled again and allowed Mary to be correct.

"Then why on earth would you wish to marry such a man? You are used to living on this estate which, while it does not make Father a wealthy man, it provides us with a comfortable home, food on the table, and fine fabrics from which to make our dresses. As the wife of Mr. Denny, you would be wearing the same dresses five years from now, patching them when they became worn, all because you cannot afford to buy new ones. How long do you think you would be happy in such a situation?"

"Do you wish us to be like you?" demanded Lydia, a sneer directed back at Mary. "Should we spend our lives moralizing and quoting scripture? Should we determine to end old maids?"

Though hurt by Lydia's words—and it was not the first time she had heard them—Mary pushed them away. It was nothing more than Lydia's typical thoughtless meanness, and further evidence she had no business being out and every reason to be in the strictest school her father could find.

"None of us wish to be old maids, Lydia," said Kitty, surprising Mary with her support.

"Thank you, Kitty," replied Mary. "Indeed, I do not wish to be an old maid. But I also wish to marry a man who can support me and any children we may have. I will readily confess I am not nearly so romantic as you or Lydia—or even Jane or Lizzy. But I *do* wish to marry eventually.

"But the longer you girls run amok with the officers, the less likely it becomes that *any* of us shall ever marry."

"How can it affect you?" demanded Lydia. "What can our behavior be to you?"

Mary threw her hands up in the air and began to pace the room. "Have you nothing but frivolities in your head? Do you know so little of society that you do not know the answer to your own question?"

When Lydia did nothing but stare at her in uncomprehending silence, Mary sighed. "Anything any one of us does is reflected on our sisters. We will be tainted by association. Society prizes virtue and good manners. If one sister is fallen, gentlemen will not only not wish to be connected to the one who is proven weak, but some will assume that as one sister behaves in such a manner, the others will as well."

Both girls gasped. "But that is the silliest thing I have ever heard!" exclaimed Lydia, Kitty nodding along with her. "Everyone knows that we are all very different. To expect you to behave the same as Lizzy is nonsensical."

"Perhaps it is," replied Mary. "But it is what it is. Kitty's adventure today could have brought blame down on us all. We would be made pariahs, never to be invited to any events of the neighborhood, shunned in Meryton, to hear whispers whenever we showed our faces in town. You would never attend another assembly."

The shock her sisters displayed told Mary that neither had ever heard of such things before—or if they had, they had not listened or understood. To think that they had embarrassed their elder sisters for years due to nothing more than a lack of understanding was almost beyond belief. Given their reactions, Mary finally felt the smallest hint of hope in her breast that their behavior could be amended. Her father's determination to send them to school would do them good.

"I implore you both," said Mary, approaching her sisters and resting a hand on the shoulders of each, "use this opportunity to become proper young ladies. None of us wish to be ruined by your thoughtless actions. But equally as important, we wish you to be happy in your lives. A marriage to an officer of the militia might sound like a grand adventure. But I assure you it would be nothing like you imagined. Do not subject yourselves to such a life, for you will regret it if you do."

With those final words, Mary let herself from the room.

"And there you have it. Kitty and Lydia shall be sent to school, and the sooner the better, according to my father."

"How do your sisters feel about it?" asked Mr. Bingley. "Given their love of society, I dare say they were not happy with your father's edict."

"They complained quite loudly after my father made the announcement." Elizabeth paused, thinking about Lydia and Kitty of the previous night. "But they were strangely subdued this morning. Mary told me she spoke to them, but I doubt they listened to her. They never listen to Mary."

"Then perhaps they have learned something from the incident."

"As strange as that may seem, you must be correct."

Mr. Bingley directed a pointed look at Elizabeth, and she felt the heat rise in her cheeks. "You must understand, Mr. Bingley, we have all despaired over my sisters' behavior for many months. Jane, Mary, and I have often attempted to take them to task, but it has done little good. I will rejoice if their transformation proves to be enduring. But I had never truly had much hope it would ever take place."

"You must have faith, Miss Bennet. I believe all shall turn out well."

"I hope it does," replied Elizabeth with feeling.

"Now," said Mr. Bingley, changing the subject, "I have often heard mention of this mysterious elder sister, but you have not told me much of her. Will you not do so?"

"With pleasure, sir," replied Elizabeth with a laugh. They spent an agreeable time speaking of Jane. The matter of Kitty and Lydia was pushed to the back of her mind. Perhaps she should not worry about them much since they were to go away. She felt lighter because of what had happened. For the first time in many months, she now had hope.

Chapter IV

*While Kitty and Lydia had been subdued the morning after their father had made his intentions known, that did not mean they were immediately resigned to their fates. They were, after all, still the same girls—no amount of firmness on their father's part nor admonitions from their sisters could affect a change with such haste. Lydia, in particular, was not known for acquiescing with such ease to others' decrees.

In fact, she seemed determined to test her father's resolve. Wherever Lydia went, Kitty was certain to follow, and while Kitty remained less vocal than her sister, she was no less determined to avoid her fate, if she could.

"It is not as if I have been *very* naughty," Lydia would say, oblivious to the way Mary and Elizabeth would shake their heads at each other. "I have learned my lesson. There is no need to send me to school."

This, of course, was not appreciated by Kitty. "You are the one who usually leads us into our adventures," would be her response, spoken in a sulky tone.

"Perhaps," replied Lydia in an offhand tone. "But I have never gone so far as you have. *I* have enough sense to know not to jump into the arms of an officer."

"Oh?" asked Kitty, her voice dripping with scorn and resentment. "What of the time where you were hanging all over Sanderson in town?"

And then they would descend to arguing, and their sisters would be obliged to separate them if they were to have any peace. And every time this would happen, their father would look on with sardonic amusement. And invariably he would say:

"You are proving yourselves to be quite mature, indeed."

When reminded in such a way, the girls would immediately fall silent, though the reproachful looks they directed at each other would not cease. It was odd, but Elizabeth noted that several times Mary would direct a pointed look at each, often when one or the other would bring up the officers. When that happened, they would almost immediately fall into a chastened silence. The most surprising thing of all was when Mrs. Bennet took a direct hand in silencing them after this had gone on for some days.

Their mother was not ignored in their attempts to avoid their fate. But in the immediate days after, they focused their efforts on their father as the author of their current difficulties. When it became clear he would not be moved, they turned to their mother in desperation. Not that it profited them anything since Mrs. Bennet would listen to them, look to her husband or Elizabeth herself, and declare they would obey their father. Until one day a noisy and boisterous week later.

On the day in question, Elizabeth had been finding it especially difficult to tolerate her sisters. She knew, from the pinched expression on Mrs. Bennet's face, that she was not the only one, to say nothing of Mary. Mr. Bennet had, only moments before, joined the family in the sitting-room long enough to inform them he had heard back from the headmistress of the school he had chosen for them, and that they were to depart the following week for Bedfordshire. Then with a wink and a soft word of congratulations to the two girls for their upcoming adventure—which they appreciated not at all—he left to return to the solitude of his bookroom. Knowing an explosion of temper was almost certainly in the offing, Elizabeth thought to return to her own room. But she did not move quickly enough.

"Mama!" cried Lydia, almost as soon as the door had closed behind her father. "You must tell Papa that we have no need to go to school!"

Elizabeth witnessed her mother's eyes darting in her direction when Mrs. Bennet sighed and repeated her well-worn refrain: "Your father has already made his wishes clear, Liddy. Nothing I say will change his mind."

With a growl of frustration, Lydia rose and began to pace the room. "This is all nonsense! What can they teach us at school that we cannot learn at home? No, I refuse to go to school! There will be no officers, and it shall be ever so dull! You must talk some sense into Papa."

The entire time of Lydia's diatribe, Elizabeth watched her mother, wondering how she would react to her youngest daughter's demands. She certainly had not expected what was to follow.

"Sit down, Lydia!"

Though Mrs. Bennet's voice was shrill and displeased, it by no means lessened the note of command inherent in it. Shocked by the sound of her mother's raised voice—something which happened with great frequency, but which was rarely directed at *her*—Lydia sank into the chair in which she had been sitting. She did not even possess the presence of mind, in her shock, to be offended at the obvious inference in Mrs. Bennet's actions which should have told her that her last desperate effort to avoid finishing school would be almost certainly denied.

"This is unseemly, Lydia," said Mrs. Bennet, her tone quieter, but still forceful. "Your father has made a decision and will not be gainsaid."

"But, *Mama!*" whined Lydia again. Kitty, at least, possessed the sense to remain silent. "I do not wish to go to school!"

"Which is why you must go, my dear. Just think of it," said Mrs. Bennet when Lydia would have spoken again, "you shall make friends and learn the best of good manners, and I do not doubt you will come home with the knowledge of how to capture a proper gentleman. You shall both marry very well, indeed—I am absolutely certain of it!"

"We can do that very well without going to school," said Lydia, her pout making her look quite ridiculous.

"You will come to see the wisdom of it in time, Lydia," was Mrs. Bennet's cold response. "Whether you do now is immaterial. Your father and I have decided that this is how it shall be, and that is the end of it. I do not wish to hear any more of your complaints."

Lydia opened her mouth to speak again, but the look from her mother silenced her. The day Mrs. Bennet finally declared herself on her husband's side of the dispute was the last time the matter was discussed openly. Kitty and Lydia—particularly the latter—still muttered and complained, but it seemed when they discovered their mother against their position, that the fight left them. They were resigned, if not eager.

The rest of that week was spent preparing them to depart. Their trunks were packed with clothing and all other manner of personal effects, and their mother gifted them each a small diary, which would fit in their reticules.

"I have never been to school, girls," said she, a wistful quality in her tone. "When you have time, write your experiences in your journals, for I would be pleased to read your thoughts when you come home."

Elizabeth was surprised at her mother's sentimentality and thoughtful mood. It would, indeed, have been better had Mrs. Bennet attended school as a young girl, for her behavior would, no doubt, be better than it was. Perhaps she was, herself, understanding this on some level.

On the appointed day, the carriage was brought around, the girls' trunks loaded onto it, and Mr. Bennet took his leave with his two youngest daughters from the rest of the family, promising to return on the morrow. Tears were shed between the two travelers and their mother, but in the end, they entered the carriage and embarked on their way to a new adventure. Elizabeth herself was feeling a little envious, for she had wished to be able to attend school herself when she was Lydia's age.

As it turned out, Longbourn was to receive new visitors later the morning of the youngest sisters' departure. Mr. Bingley was soon announced to visit them, and with him, he brought a young man, some few years older than he was himself, along with a young lady of about Lydia's age. The man was tall—taller even than Mr. Bingley. He carried himself erect, the bearing of a man of confidence and poise, and within his countenance, Elizabeth thought she detected a hint of an aristocratic quality. He was also one of the handsomest men Elizabeth had ever seen, his jaw strong, his eyes a deep blue, and his hair a dark brown, curling about his ears as if in need of a cut.

The familial resemblance between the man and the girl was evident, though in truth they looked little alike. Whereas the man was dark, the girl was fair, standing tall and slender like her brother, her eyes the same shade, but the angles of her face softer, more delicate. Her hair was long and flaxen, tied up in an elegant bun behind her head, and though she possessed some of his noble features, hers were tempered by the obvious shyness with which she regarded the company. At that moment, Elizabeth was grateful Kitty and Lydia had already left, for their unguarded ways would more than likely astonish this shy creature exceedingly!

"Mrs. Bennet," said Mr. Bingley, while smiling at Elizabeth and

Mary, greeting them as well. "If you will oblige me, I should like to introduce my friends to your acquaintance."

"Of course, Mr. Bingley. Any friend of yours is welcome at Longbourn, I am sure."

Mr. Bingley grinned at her before he gestured to the gentleman. "This is Mr. Fitzwilliam Darcy, my friend from university. With him is his sister, Miss Georgiana Darcy. Darcy, Miss Darcy, allow me to present Mrs. Bennet, Miss Elizabeth Bennet and Miss Mary Bennet, my closest neighbors." Mr. Bingley paused and looked about with interest. "Is Mr. Bennet also present?"

"I am sorry, Mr. Bingley," said Mrs. Bennet, a hint of nervousness appearing in the way she wrung her hands. "Mr. Bennet has departed with my youngest daughters this very morning, though we do expect him back tomorrow."

"Very well," replied Mr. Bingley with a knowing glance at Elizabeth. "Will the youngest Miss Bennets be returning with your husband?"

"They are for school, actually," interjected Elizabeth, much to her mother's relief. "My sisters will not return until Christmastide."

"I hope they enjoy themselves," replied Mr. Bingley. "I suppose Miss Darcy shall simply have to content herself with your friendship, and that of your sister."

"Of course," said Mrs. Bennet. She rose, captured Miss Darcy's arm, and led her to the sofa beside Elizabeth. "Come and sit with Lizzy, Miss Darcy. I dare say you are fatigued from your journey. I assume you only arrived yesterday?"

"Yes," said Miss Darcy, managing to answer before Mrs. Bennet spoke again.

"Traveling is such a bother—do you not agree? I have not left Longbourn in some few years, but even when I did, I found it a tedious business." Mrs. Bennet paused and directed a piercing glance at Miss Darcy. "I am sorry, Miss Darcy, but from where did you journey?"

"My brother's estate is in Derbyshire," replied Miss Darcy. Her voice was quiet, with a timidity Elizabeth would not have expected of a young woman who was a member of what she suspected was a prominent family.

"I understand Derbyshire is a lovely county," said Mrs. Bennet, when it became apparent that Miss Darcy would not say anything more. "My sister Gardiner was a resident of the county for some years in her youth. She has much to say about her time there. One might think it was a little bit of paradise on earth."

The way Mrs. Bennet eyed Miss Darcy, Elizabeth was certain she was bursting to ask her more of the Darcy estate, most likely including the income it generated, the Darcys' exact position in society, and the positions in society of all their nearest relations. But Elizabeth directed a steady look at Mrs. Bennet, and her mother caught it and seemed to divine its meaning. She sighed and sat down in her chair nearby, watching the proceedings with keen interest.

Miss Darcy, though clearly wishing to stay silent, hazarded a glance at her brother, who was watching her, seeming to provide encouragement with nothing more than the slight smile with which he favored her. This seemed to give her courage, for she turned to Elizabeth and in a small voice asked:

"Do you know where your aunt lived?"

"How could I forget?" said Elizabeth with a laugh. "She is continually regaling us with tales of the beauty of the place. It is a little town called Lambton, as I recall."

Miss Darcy's eyes widened. "Why, Lambton is only five miles from Pemberley, my brother's estate!"

"Ah, yes," said Elizabeth. "I believe I have heard my aunt mention the name of that estate too. I believe she toured it once as a girl and called it very lovely."

"I cannot argue with your aunt's opinion, for it quite mirrors my own." Miss Darcy fell silent for some moments, in which she seemed to be struggling to find something to say. After a moment, she settled on a quietly spoken: "Have you traveled to Derbyshire, Miss Elizabeth?"

"I have not," replied Elizabeth. "In fact, we have rarely gone anywhere other than to visit my aunt and uncle in London. My father, you see, detests travel and prefers to stay close to Longbourn."

"That I can well understand," replied Miss Darcy. "It can be quite fatiguing, indeed."

Those few words seemed to pierce Miss Darcy's reticence, and the conversation began to flow a little more easily as a result. It still took some coaxing on Elizabeth's part to elicit many words from the girl's mouth, but soon the subject changed to music—Miss Darcy was quite the musician, it seemed—and other subjects of mutual interest. And as the visit progressed, they found enough common ground to move their discussion forward with greater ease. Perhaps surprisingly, Mary also joined in speaking with them, and as she was as interested in music and the pianoforte as was Miss Darcy, soon they were also speaking in an animated fashion.

It was not to be supposed that Mrs. Bennet remained entirely silent, as she did interject a few comments here and there. For the most part, she spoke to Mr. Bingley, who seemed agreeably engaged in speaking with her. But the whole time she was speaking with Mr. Bingley, Mrs. Bennet's eyes often strayed to Mr. Darcy, seemingly attempting to understand the man, and particularly his position in society. Thankfully, Mrs. Bennet made no impertinent or vulgar inquiries.

As for Mr. Darcy, for the first few moments of their visit, Mr. Darcy stayed silent and aloof, watching them all with an unreadable gravity. He did not appear to be displeased, as far as Elizabeth could determine. The cut of his clothes and his bearing suggested he was used to much finer surroundings than Longbourn could offer.

At one point, about halfway through the visit, Miss Darcy noted Elizabeth's frequent glances at Mr. Darcy, and she chuckled a little, leaning toward Elizabeth to say in a soft voice: "Has my brother fascinated you, Miss Bennet?"

Embarrassed at being caught out, Elizabeth felt the heat rise in her cheeks. "I am simply curious that he has said little thus far. I hope he is not displeased to be here."

Miss Darcy only shook her head. "He is almost always a little reticent when in the company of those to whom he is newly introduced. Once he comes to know you, however, you could find no firmer friend than he."

"Perhaps you and he are not so different, then," said Elizabeth, her tone teasing.

A blush stained Miss Darcy's cheeks. "Perhaps not. But . . . I have found it easy to speak to you and your sister."

"I am happy to hear it, Miss Darcy. We would wish you to feel welcome at Longbourn."

A smile of gratitude brightened the girl's countenance. Soon, by her request, they were referring to each other by their Christian names, and the conversation continued apace. Elizabeth was so engrossed in it, she did not notice the fact that she was, in fact, the recipient of some interested glances from their new visitor. As it happened, when Georgiana had turned to Mary to speak of some piece they had both learned on the pianoforte, Mr. Darcy approached Elizabeth and began to speak to her.

"Miss Bennet," said he. "I must inform you that I am quite astonished."

Several thoughts ran through Elizabeth's mind at that moment, some of them not precisely complimentary, no doubt incited by his relative aloofness with them that morning. But she quashed them all—there was no reason to suppose he was disapproving of them, after all—and opted to simply ask his meaning.

"It is my sister," said Mr. Darcy in response to her query. "She rarely makes friends easily and has been quite reticent of late in particular. And yet it appears that you and your sister have quite drawn her out and made her feel comfortable."

"I am glad you think so, Mr. Darcy," said Elizabeth, thankful she had suppressed her baser instincts. "She is a wonderful girl, sir. I understand you are her primary guardian. I must commend you, for you have done well in raising her."

"I *am* joined by my cousin in her guardianship," said Mr. Darcy. "But as he is in the army and is rarely at home, you are correct in supposing she has been primarily my responsibility. I must ask, however, what formula you have used with her. If I had it, I could prompt her more active participation in other situations as well."

"Brother!" protested Georgiana, having overheard Mr. Darcy's final words to Elizabeth. "You will have Elizabeth thinking I am some sort of recluse with such an account of me."

"No, dearest," said Darcy, while Elizabeth laughed at Georgiana's protest. "But I *know* you, and I am happy that you have taken to these ladies with such rapidity."

"I am happy to have made their acquaintance," was Georgiana's shy reply. "I have so often been witness to much pretension that I am happy to meet ladies who display none of it."

Then before Elizabeth could reply, Georgiana turned back to her conversation with Mary. All the while, Mrs. Bennet was speaking with Mr. Bingley, but she appeared smug in the knowledge that two of her daughters, at least, had managed to impress her new visitors, who must be, in her opinion, of at least a wealthy situation in life.

"You see, Miss Bennet?" Mr. Darcy's voice brought her attention back to him. "My sister is never this open. She has friends she made at school, but even with them, there is an underlying sense of reserve in her manners. I have rarely seen her so open with *anyone* who is not a member of the family."

"I think, Mr. Darcy, that she is not so different from her brother."

Mr. Darcy's countenance changed not a whit, but she thought she saw amusement shining in his eyes. "You have managed to understand us both with exactness, Miss Bennet. I am not, as you have understood, the most comfortable in situations where I am with others I do not know well. That trait sometimes leads to giving offense, though I have no intention of it. I hope that is not the case in this instance."

"Is it offensive to speak little when one is not comfortable?" asked Elizabeth rhetorically. "You have no need to fear being judged in such a manner as that here, Mr. Darcy. As a family, we are a disparate group of characters. I hope you do not think us so closed-minded as to look down on someone because they are different."

"Yes, I heard your mother mention something of younger sisters who are off to school. Have you any brothers?"

"No—we are five sisters, my eldest having been in London these past months with an aunt and uncle. I have always wished for a brother, though. I imagine it would be a fine thing to have a brother as attentive to me as you are to your sister."

Ever after, Elizabeth could not say why she had been so open with Mr. Darcy. She thought a man would consider her overly flattering because of her words, but Mr. Darcy merely thanked her and the conversation moved on apace. That morning there was no time for deep philosophical discussions, though Elizabeth knew instinctively that Mr. Darcy was entirely capable of having them, should he so choose. But the subjects of which they did speak were rendered all the more interesting because of the intelligent manner in which he spoke, and the way he listened to her opinions and did not contradict her when she disagreed with his own.

Mr. Darcy, Elizabeth decided, was like an onion. In the few moments they had spoken that morning, she had managed to peel back the outer layer, brown and leathery, which protected the goodness which lay inside. But there were many more layers to discover, she was certain, and she found herself eager to embark on such a worthwhile journey.

So interested in their conversation were they that the elapsing of the thirty-minute time for a morning visit passed with little notice. In fact, it was some minutes past the time they should leave when Mr. Bingley rose reluctantly and announced they had best depart. The surprise shown by Mr. Darcy was such that Elizabeth knew he had been as lost in their conversation as she had.

"Thank you for bringing your charming friends to visit, Mr. Bingley," said Elizabeth's mother when they rose to depart. "Please know you are welcome to return to Longbourn at any time.

"In fact," continued Mrs. Bennet, her finger tapping a lip in thought, "I think it has been some time since we had you to dinner. Would you be available the day after tomorrow, when Mr. Bennet will have returned?"

Mr. Bingley glanced at his friends, and when neither voiced any objection to the invitation, he was happy to respond in the affirmative. "We would be delighted. I thank you, Mrs. Bennet, for your hospitality."

The Bennets saw their guests to the door to bid them farewell. But as they walked, Elizabeth noted that Georgiana had slowed her pace, allowing the others to move a little ahead of them. When they had gained a hint of privacy, she turned amused eyes on Elizabeth.

"It seems my brother was quite happy to speak with you, Elizabeth. When we first arrived, he could hardly remove his eyes from you. When he finally made his way to your side, he would not be moved from it."

Astonished at Georgiana's suggestion, Elizabeth could only gape at her. This, of course, prompted Georgiana's giggles.

"I am interested to see where this leads, Elizabeth. Even though we have just met, I feel confident in stating you would be an excellent sister, should my brother be so fortunate as to secure you."

Then she hurried ahead, the sound of her laughter floating back to Elizabeth. Elizabeth soon followed and made her farewells as was proper. As she did, however, she noticed that Mr. Darcy *did* watch her in particular, and she found herself returning his interest. Could a connection be made with such alacrity? Elizabeth did not know. But she knew she would be happy to make the discovery.

CHAPTER V

Not much was said on the return to Netherfield. Darcy, as a man of few words himself, did not notice, even though Bingley, who most certainly *was* a man of many words, was silent himself. Even the knowing grin with which Bingley regarded him was beyond Darcy's notice. He was far too engaged in contemplating the face of a pretty woman, in which was set a pair of the finest dark eyes he had ever seen. Darcy was glad that Longbourn had been their last call that day, for he was not certain he could have mustered the necessary focus to do another visit any justice.

The journey passed swiftly, and soon the carriage was pulling up in front of the estate. When the footman opened the door, Bingley nudged Darcy, saying: "We are here. Do you wish to disembark, or should we, perhaps, spend the afternoon in the carriage?"

Georgiana giggled at Bingley's tease, but Darcy only shrugged and stepped from the carriage, putting a hand out to help his sister down. They went inside and separated to their rooms, Georgiana informing him she would rest for a time. Darcy, assisted by his valet, repaired his appearance after the short time in the carriage, and then made his way to Bingley's study, where he expected his friend would eventually join him. He was not incorrect.

Bingley was in a good mood that day if his grin was any indication. He said nothing when he entered the room, instead going to the sideboard and pouring himself a small measure of port. He gestured to the bottle, a silent inquiry in Darcy's direction, but Darcy only shook his head. It was much too early in the day for Darcy to imbibe.

"It seems to me you enjoyed our visit to Longbourn," said Bingley as he raised his glass to his mouth. Bingley turned and sat in one of the chairs in front of the fireplace, lifting an eyebrow in Darcy's direction. "I have rarely seen you so voluble when first meeting a new acquaintance. Is there anything you wish to tell me?"

Darcy's defensiveness reared its head at the tone of Bingley's voice. "Of course not."

The look Bingley directed at him was brimming with disbelief, but he took a different tack from what Darcy had expected. "You know," said he after taking another sip of his drink, "I had thought Miss Bennet might be the kind of woman who would interest you."

"I have no notion of what you speak."

"She is intelligent," said Bingley, ignoring Darcy's protests. "So intelligent that sometimes I find myself out to sea when speaking with her. She can hold her own in any conversation, and if you disagree with her, you had best be able to back your words up with rational thought, or she will cheerfully tear your arguments to shreds. And yet, she does it in such a disarming fashion that it is impossible to take offense."

"She does, does she?" asked Darcy, unable to help himself. "We did not have much opportunity to speak, of course, but I caught more than a hint of her intelligence."

"Try her," said Bingley, grinning once again. "I do not think you will be disappointed."

Darcy paused, thinking about what Bingley had said. "I *do* find her intriguing. Though I will assert that any of the fanciful notions you have in your head are premature. But this is a fine to do—*you* are the one who falls in love with every pretty girl you meet."

"I am glad you are owning it, Darcy," replied Bingley.

"And why are you not already pursuing her? She is far and away the handsomest girl we have yet met in the neighborhood."

"Oh, the handsomest by far," was Bingley's offhand reply. "But though she is pretty, I knew at once she was not for me. I think I should like a girl who was much calmer, more restrained, for I am loquacious enough for us both."

"That is the truth," replied Darcy with a chuckle. "Whereas I require the opposite, lest nothing be said between us all day long." Darcy paused. "What of her family?"

Bingley chuckled. "All different, to be sure. Miss Mary is tolerable, though she can almost be a little puritanical. The mother, you have met, and she is not the cleverest of women, nor the most proper. Her younger sisters are off to school, and a good thing it is too, for they are very nearly wild. Her father is quite intelligent, though I dare say a little odd. The fifth daughter I have not met, though Miss Bennet's reports of her are intriguing. I hope we shall be introduced too."

Darcy nodded slowly. "Not all objectionable, then, though perhaps lacking in connections. Any lack of fortune bothers me not at all."

"Then there is no impediment. You can use this time to come to know her, and if you find she is not to your taste, then you have lost nothing. But if she *is* . . ."

"Then your finding this estate for lease has been entirely providential," replied Darcy, nodding.

"The only problem I can see might be Caroline."

The quick glance from his friend did not go unnoticed, and Bingley sighed, putting his glass down on a nearby table. "Caroline is not happy that I leased an estate without her 'permission,' though the word she prefers to use is without 'consulting' her. It is the reason why she is not here yet. But in recent letters, she has begun to imply that she might join me soon to inspect the 'hovel' I have leased, so she may turn up at any time."

"You need not worry about me, Bingley. I am capable of fending off your sister."

"I am aware of it, my friend," replied Bingley. "But you know how she can be. I suggest you use whatever days of grace we have been granted wisely, for Caroline shall surely interfere when she comes. Then it will be doubly difficult to woo Miss Bennet."

"I intend to," replied Darcy, seeing no reason to deny it yet again. Perhaps nothing would come of it, but there was something about Miss Bennet which had caught his eye. And he meant to discover what it was.

The days after Mr. Darcy's arrival were similar to those when Mr. Bingley had first come to Netherfield. This time, however, Elizabeth was forced to own that there was something to the rumors which had begun to be whispered about the neighborhood. Mr. Bingley was a friend, a man with whom Elizabeth had connected on a friendly level. She knew that she had never had any interest in him on a basis which was anything other than friendly, regardless of what others said.

Mr. Darcy, however, was an entirely different matter. For one, he was far more physically attractive than Mr. Bingley, though she would readily confess that Mr. Bingley was also handsome, and another might have a completely different opinion. For another, Mr. Darcy was much more appealing to her in his intelligence and ability to debate certain subjects of mutual interest. Mr. Bingley was a much more playful conversationalist who, though not lacking in intelligence, was not as serious-minded as Mr. Darcy. Elizabeth found that to be greatly in Mr. Darcy's favor.

The first time Elizabeth met again with Mr. Darcy after their initial meeting, was when the gentleman in question came to Longbourn with his friend and sister for dinner. Mr. Bennet was interested to meet the gentleman and had been treated to a long discourse on the apparent benefits of the man's station, including — or perhaps almost solely — what she suspected about his situation in life. It seemed to Elizabeth that her father and Mr. Darcy shared much in common, for they spoke together for some time until called in to dinner.

In the dining room, Mr. Darcy escorted Mrs. Bennet and sat to her right as the highest ranking of their guests, and while he did not seem eager to speak with her, he acquitted himself well. For his part, Mr. Bennet escorted Georgiana, and while she would not speak more than two words together to Mr. Bennet, he did his best to make her feel at ease. Mr. Bingley escorted both Elizabeth and Mary into the room, with his usual jovial manners. The conversation in the room was at times stilted, as most of the diners were not natural matches in interests or disposition for those nearby.

When they retired to the sitting-room after the meal, Elizabeth was witness to the first amusement of the evening. Though she was forced to acknowledge her mother was behaving well, she still possessed the soul of a matchmaker and the burden of two unmarried daughters present occasioned her with a dilemma. Mr. Bingley was obviously meant for Elizabeth in her mind. That only left her one other daughter with which to tempt Mr. Darcy.

"Come, Mary," said she, after watching Mary for several moments, her eyes darting to Mr. Darcy. "You may sit beside Mr. Darcy and entertain him."

Mary was, fortunately, not of a mind to refuse her mother, little though Elizabeth thought she was interested in a man such as Mr. Darcy. She did her duty, however, and sat by the gentleman, speaking politely about banal subjects, if Elizabeth was any judge. Mr. Bingley was, of course, situated beside Elizabeth. When the tea and after dinner cakes were served, they all partook, with little conversation passing between them. But as is often the case, the conversations were fluid and there was some changing of positions. And soon Elizabeth found herself near Mr. Darcy and, soon after, engrossed in what he was saying.

"I have told you of my family, but I have not heard much of yours," said Elizabeth after speaking with him for a time. "Do you have any brothers or sisters other than Georgiana?"

"I do not," replied Mr. Darcy. "She is all I have left in the world, for my mother passed when I was twelve, and my father five years ago."

"I am sorry to hear it. It is odd, however, that there is such a large age gap between you. You must be at least ten years apart?"

"Twelve, actually," replied Mr. Darcy. Elizabeth did not miss the inference that his mother had likely passed at his sisters' birth. "I understand that my mother suffered several miscarriages between my birth and my sister's."

"I apologize for bringing up such painful memories."

Mr. Darcy favored her with a slight smile. "It is no trouble, Miss Bennet. Your curiosity is natural. These events are far enough in the past that they do not trouble me as they once would have—they are akin to a momentary sadness, rather than an all-encompassing grief."

From there, the discussion turned to extended families. Elizabeth told him of her mother's brother and sister, including their professions, and while she mentioned them in an offhand fashion, a part of her wondered if a prominent man such as he would find her connections offensive. She was thus surprised at his response, which was a little chiding.

"Your uncle—is he a good man?"

"The best of men," said Elizabeth, raising her jaw a little in defiance.

"Then that is what is important. Come now—you did not expect me to shun you because you have an uncle in trade, did you? You must know that Bingley's fortune was made in trade."

"I did," said Elizabeth, feeling properly chastened. "But he is now set on becoming a gentleman, while my uncle is quite content to be a tradesman."

"Ah, but Bingley is not a gentleman yet. And yet he is a good man. Though I will own that I possess a haughty streak at times, I try not to judge a man by his profession. If the opportunity presents itself, I would appreciate an introduction to your uncle."

Elizabeth, of course, promised she would do so. As they spoke, however, she noted that Mr. Darcy was eager to hear of her connections, but less so to speak of his own.

"What of your extended family, Mr. Darcy?" asked she after a moment. "Are their situations as objectionable as that of my own?"

It seemed he caught the teasing tone of her voice, for he smiled at her. "Not at all." He leaned in close as if imparting a secret. "They are, in fact, infinitely worse."

Elizabeth could not help but laugh at his jest, which drew the attention of the room. Her father smiled indulgently and returned to his conversation with Mr. Bingley. Mary and Georgiana only shook their heads. But Elizabeth noted her mother with her eyes fixed on them, a grave expression on her countenance. Elizabeth was grateful her mother stayed watchful and did not speak up.

"Do not concern yourself, Mr. Darcy," said Elizabeth. "I will not judge you, as you did not judge me."

Mr. Darcy shook his head and chuckled before his manner became serious again. "On the Darcy side, I actually have no close relations. There are various cousins several generations removed, some who bear the same name and some who do not. But we are not at all close to them."

"And your mother's side?"

Again Mr. Darcy hesitated. Then he glanced at her and seemed to make up his mind. "My mother's brother and sister are both alive — my uncle has two daughters and two sons, while my aunt has a single daughter. My grandfather — my mother's father — was actually the Earl of Matlock, while my uncle now holds that position."

"Oh," said Elizabeth, instantly understanding why Mr. Darcy was hesitant to inform her of his connections. "Those are high connections, indeed. Are you close to them?"

"My uncle and his family, yes," replied Mr. Darcy, seeming a little relieved. "My aunt I visit every Easter, but in truth, she is a domineering woman who is not beloved of anyone in the family. I honor her as my mother's elder sister, but I attempt to keep my distance from her as often as possible."

With a laugh, Elizabeth then turned a stern glare on him. "I hope I have passed your test, Mr. Darcy. I will not turn into a fortune seeking miss simply because you possess connections to an earl."

"I suppose, then, we are equal," replied Mr. Darcy with a wry grin. "I do not look down on your relations, and you do not flatter me to gain access to mine."

Elizabeth laughed at the way he phrased it. "I suppose that is true,

Mr. Darcy. Let us leave this testing of the other behind."

"Agreed." He paused. "But I do hope you will keep mention of my connections in confidence. Though *you* have passed the test, I am sure there are others in the neighborhood who would not."

"My lips are sealed, Mr. Darcy."

Soon their discussions turned to subjects of much more substance. They met almost daily, with the Longbourn ladies visiting Georgiana at Netherfield—which they had not been able to do before when Mr. Bingley was alone—or Mr. Bingley and his party visiting Longbourn. Interspersed with this were several events of the neighborhood, including card parties, teas, or dinners at one or another of their friends' residences. It was an eventful time for Elizabeth, and she often found herself in company with Mr. Darcy. Although there were machinations aplenty, young ladies attempting to garner the attention of the two new and single gentlemen, they almost always found themselves together by choice and circumstance.

At a card party held at the Goulding residence, Elizabeth was subject to the first overt censure of a jealous lady. Miss Geraldine Goulding was a young woman of about Charlotte's age, and one of less physical beauty than Elizabeth's friend, not that Elizabeth had ever considered Charlotte deficient. The evening had been spent playing whist or fish, with the younger members of the assembled largely engaged in the latter. And after a while of this, Elizabeth stood with Mr. Darcy as was their wont, speaking of various matters of interest to them both.

"I find that I am parched, Miss Bennet," said he when they had been standing together for some time. "Can I bring you a cup of punch?"

"Thank you, Mr. Darcy," replied Elizabeth. "I would like that very much."

He had not been gone for more than a moment when Miss Goulding approached, and from the disdain she showed Elizabeth, it was certain her claws were about to be unsheathed.

"It seems to me that Miss Lizzy is attempting to keep the attention of *all* new gentlemen in the neighborhood to herself," said she to another woman, a Miss Tanner, who was five and thirty if she was a day, and firmly on the shelf. "First it was Mr. Bingley, and now Mr. Darcy. Do you think she fears becoming an old maid?"

"She should," replied Miss Tanner, who looked down her nose on Elizabeth. "I understand the Bennet girls will have nothing to live on when their father passes on."

"I wonder at the two of you speaking of such matters," replied

Elizabeth, not caring what they thought of her. "Had either Mr. Darcy or Mr. Bingley shown any interest in you, I would have gladly ceded their attention."

They were known to be catty and unkind to all and sundry, and Elizabeth had never had much interest in speaking with either. Miss Tanner's father's position as the least consequential gentleman in the neighborhood made her assertions especially laughable, though it was true she had a brother who could provide for her.

Penelope Long, who was one of Mrs. Long's nieces, happened to be nearby. Knowing the two ladies, and being on friendly terms with Elizabeth, approached and made her sentiments known. "That is rather amusing coming from you, Miss Tanner. I rather think that you wishing for Mr. Bingley's attention is akin to cradle robbing. Would you not agree, Miss Goulding?"

It was difficult, but somehow Elizabeth managed to avoid snickering at her friend's slight. The two tabbies were offended, not that either of the younger ladies minded in the slightest.

"I suggest you pay heed to your own cares, Miss Long," hissed Miss Goulding. "We have no need of your witticisms."

"And I suggest you take your innuendos elsewhere," said Elizabeth. "Approach Mr. Darcy if you wish, for I do not constrain his conversation partners."

Elizabeth could see that Miss Goulding meant to do exactly that. She raked them with a disdainful glare and turned away in a huff, Miss Tanner following closely behind.

"I thought she would order you from the house," said Miss Long.

"She cannot," replied Elizabeth. "Mr. Goulding is a close friend of my father's, and he is well aware of his daughter's character."

"It is no wonder she has not yet married." Then Penelope turned to Elizabeth. "It looks, however, like you will never suffer the shame of being an old maid, unlike those two viragos."

Elizabeth blushed, but Penelope only laughed and gave her a brief embrace. "It seems obvious to me, Lizzy. Though many thought you and Mr. Bingley were making a connection, it is quite obvious you are much closer with Mr. Darcy, though his residence here has been much shorter in duration."

"I do find him a fascinating man," confessed Elizabeth.

"Then I hope you will invite me to your wedding."

Then with a wink and a smile, Penelope stepped away. A few moments later, Elizabeth saw that Mr. Darcy was moving toward her, two cups of punch in his hands, when he was waylaid by a predatory

Miss Goulding. Mr. Darcy spoke with her in what appeared to be a congenial manner for a few moments, but then excused himself and made his way to her side. Elizabeth had all the satisfaction of seeing Miss Goulding glaring after him. She managed to avoid directing a smirk at the objectionable woman, but it was a near thing.

On another occasion, the Bennets, Darcys, and Mr. Bingley had been invited to Lucas Lodge for dinner. There, they were treated to the civility of Sir William, the friendship of Lady Lucas, and Elizabeth found herself once again in the presence of her closest friend. But before long, Elizabeth was wondering if Charlotte could actually claim that privilege any longer, given the vast difference in opinion which had recently become evident.

Elizabeth did her best to avoid speaking with Charlotte alone that evening, though at times she wondered if she was not being silly. Charlotte was still the same person she had always known, after all — it was simply that Elizabeth had not known her as well as she had always thought. But she could not avoid her the entire evening, though after the fact she might have wished she had.

"The neighborhood is speaking of you and Mr. Darcy now, Lizzy," said Charlotte when she had managed to get Elizabeth alone.

"It is unsurprising they would do so," said Elizabeth. "After all, they were ready to betroth me to Mr. Bingley when all I wished from him was friendship."

Charlotte directed a long look at her. "I can see you are trying to deflect me. I do not wish to overstep my boundaries, but I wished to give you a piece of advice."

"Oh?" asked Elizabeth, wishing her friend would simply cease speaking.

"Yes. You see, I am worried that you will allow your romantic nature to overcome your good sense. It was, perhaps, shrewd of you to have put off the lesser gentleman in favor of the greater, but I would suggest you leave Mr. Darcy in no doubt of your feelings, whatever they may be. He is much less likely than Mr. Bingley to believe himself in love. Thus, you must leave *him* in no doubt."

Elizabeth returned Charlotte's look, feeling cross with her friend, but clamping down on her pique with ruthless determination. "You think I waited for Mr. Darcy when I might have had Mr. Bingley? That is nonsensical, Charlotte — how could I have known anything of Mr. Darcy before he came?"

"Perhaps not consciously. But Mr. Bingley spoke of his friend constantly — there is no telling what he said which might have informed you it would be better to wait for his friend to arrive."

"Oh, Charlotte," said Elizabeth. "I have not 'waited' for Mr. Darcy, as you suggested. I never had any interest in Mr. Bingley in that fashion. I believe I already informed you of that fact."

"That is why I decided to speak to you. Do not allow Mr. Darcy to escape, Lizzy. You will regret it when you are my age and staring at impending spinsterhood."

With those final words, Charlotte turned and walked away, leaving Elizabeth to watch her friend's back sadly. She understood the reason for Charlotte's advice, but she had never suspected her friend of such bitterness. Regardless, she would never betray her principles for such things, though she knew many would look on her with scorn for it.

"Are you well, Miss Bennet?"

Startled, Elizabeth's eyes darted to the side where she found Mr. Darcy watching her. She attempted a smile, realizing it was a sickly attempt at best.

"Have you ever realized, Mr. Darcy, that someone you thought was a friend was an entirely different person than you thought."

Mr. Darcy did not reply for a long moment, and he was as grave as Elizabeth had ever seen him. When he did respond, it seemed to her a great emotion had welled up within him, rendering her petty disappointment with Charlotte insignificant in comparison.

"I have experienced it, Miss Bennet. It is difficult, indeed. Might I assume your disappointment is with Miss Lucas?"

There was no sense in denying it, and Elizabeth did not even try. Mr. Darcy coaxed her to share her new insight concerning her friend, and Elizabeth did so, though not without trepidation. She was disappointed in her friend, it was true, but she did not wish Mr. Darcy to think poorly of her. She was entirely surprised when Mr. Darcy commiserated with her instead of censuring Charlotte.

"It is commendable that you think the way you do, Miss Bennet. But Miss Lucas's feelings are far from singular. It is, you realize, more common in the ranks of the gentry to marry for such reasons as your friend espoused than it is to marry for true emotion. For a woman in distressed circumstances, it is not surprising her aim is marriage above all other considerations."

Elizabeth sighed. "Well I know it, Mr. Darcy. I simply never suspected it of her." Elizabeth paused and grinned. "Of course, her circumstances are not quite so distressed. She has a brother who will inherit the estate, and she will always have a home. And though it might be common for people to marry for reasons of prudence, to feign more than one feels strikes me as underhanded."

With a nod, Mr. Darcy dropped the subject. It was only a few moments before Mr. Bingley approached them, and given the grin with which he regarded them, Elizabeth expected a witticism. She was not disappointed.

"I see you are speaking with this reprobate again, Miss Bennet," said Mr. Bingley, gesturing toward Mr. Darcy. "Should I be unhappy to be supplanted in your esteem with so little provocation?"

Mr. Darcy stifled a laugh and sipped on his drink. For Elizabeth's part, she arched an eyebrow at Mr. Bingley and said: "I do not know, Mr. Bingley. Should you be offended?"

"Touché, Miss Bennet," said Mr. Bingley.

"I am sorry, sir, but I had not expected such an answer from you. It would be infinitely more exciting should you be inclined to fight for my hand. Shall it be pistols at dawn?"

Both gentlemen laughed. "No, I think I will withdraw from the field, Miss Bennet. In fact, I am happy that you have both seen much to like in the person of the other. Should you marry, I believe I shall take full credit for having introduced you."

Elizabeth blushed, but before she could say anything, Mr. Bingley winked and walked away. When she turned back to Mr. Darcy, she noted that he was looking at her, intensity written upon his brow.

"It would not do to disappoint my friend, would it?"

Hardly able to believe what she was hearing, Elizabeth gasped and blurted: "Are you proposing, sir?"

"I could hardly do so in such an impersonal location as this. I believe I shall wait until we have a much more private venue."

He was serious—Elizabeth was absolutely certain. And she realized at that moment that she was grateful he was. She could hardly wait.

As it was, Mr. Darcy proposed only a week after he had all but promised to do so. Permission from her father was sought and given, and the family celebrated Elizabeth's good fortune. Ever after, Elizabeth could never remember exactly what he said and how he asked her. But she remembered the feeling his proposal elicited—a feeling of utter contentment, happiness, and above all, a feeling of rightness. This was the man for her, and she knew they would live happily and start a family.

Little did Elizabeth know that though she had gained her happiness, troubles were just around the corner.

CHAPTER VI

There were no two closer sisters than Jane and Elizabeth Bennet. At the same time, however, no two sisters were so dissimilar. Jane was quiet, reticent, and prone to attributing the best possible motives to all with whom she met, while Elizabeth, by contrast, was open, at times a little opinionated, and more than a little cynical. Even in looks, they were not alike as Jane was accounted to be the beauty of the district, standing tall and willowy, with a wealth of blonde hair. Elizabeth was more diminutive, slightly darker of coloring, and possessed of rich dark tresses. But while she was not as classically beautiful as her sister, Elizabeth was accounted very pretty by those who knew her.

But despite these obvious differences, the sisters were entirely devoted to each other. Elizabeth, as the more demonstrative, was quick to defend her sister against any perceived slight, but even Jane had been known to take up Elizabeth's cause on more than one occasion. They were a perfect blend—Elizabeth's cynicism balanced and softened by Jane's artlessness, while Jane obtained a clearer notion of the motives of others with Elizabeth's insight.

An invitation to stay in London with their Aunt and Uncle Gardiner had been tendered at the end of summer, resulting in Jane's departure for the city only a week or so before Mr. Bingley's arrival at Netherfield. But the sisters had been in constant contact, with letters flying back and forth between the estate and the London townhouse with great frequency. Jane, as was her wont, was supportive of her sister, words of encouragement gracing every line of her letters. Elizabeth, for her part, drank in her sister's words, buoyed by her sister's love, sharing all her hopes and fears in return. It was to Jane she had shared the secret of her first feelings of love for her suitor when she had not shared it with anyone else.

When the engagement was formalized, it was of no surprise to any of the Bennets or their London relations that Jane was wild to be home. When the letter requesting her return reached Mr. Bennet, he was quick to inform Elizabeth of it.

"It seems, Lizzy, that you have filled your sister's head with thoughts of handsome gentlemen and love," said Mr. Bennet in his usual teasing way. "Had your sister been present, I might have feared for my safety, given the way she accosted me by post."

"She is to return?" asked Elizabeth, attempting—and failing, she thought—to keep the eagerness from overflowing in her voice.

"Yes, she is." Though Mr. Bennet's tone was slightly satirical, his amusement shone through. "I have sent the carriage this very morning to retrieve her. Assuming there is no trouble with the roads, I expect she will arrive in time for dinner."

Mr. Bennet's prediction proved well founded, for as the daylight was waning in the western sky, the sound of a coach could be heard approaching the estate. Eager to greet the sister from whom she had been parted for several months, Elizabeth flew from the room, out through the vestibule and out onto the front step, where the carriage was just pulling to a stop. A moment later, Jane was in her arms, laughing and crying along with Elizabeth.

"Well, is this not a pretty sight?" Mr. Bennet's voice interrupted their reunion. "It seems the rest of us are not nearly enough of an inducement for our eldest daughter, for she only has eyes for her sister."

As one, and still holding each other closely, Jane and Elizabeth turned to their father. Mr. Bennet was a man known for quick and sometimes acerbic commentary, but while his comments might be construed as censorious, Elizabeth could see a hint of mist in his eyes, not to mention amusement. Jane, of course, greeted her family with affection, and they soon went inside, Jane's trunks being carried to her room by the servants. Elizabeth reserved the privilege of assisting her sister refresh from her travels for herself.

"You must tell me everything, Lizzy," said Jane as Elizabeth assisted her to remove her dress. When she was standing in her shift, Jane turned again to Elizabeth. "From your early letters, I expected a different announcement."

"Oh, Jane!" said Elizabeth. "I was sincere in telling you I had no interest in Mr. Bingley as a potential husband."

Jane shook her head. "I know you, Lizzy. You would claim that a man *could not* have any interest in you and that he would be a much better match for *me*."

Elizabeth blushed at this evidence of her sister's knowledge of her character. In fact, she had often thought that Jane would do well with Mr. Bingley and that he would be smitten with her. But she could not tell that to Jane—Elizabeth did not wish to risk her sister's discounting the man without even meeting him.

"I would not have done such a thing," said Elizabeth, prevaricating only a little. "I certainly did not do it with Mr. Darcy."

"According to Mama, he could not take his eyes from you from the very beginning."

"You know what Mama is like, Jane. In her eyes, every man must be in love with us at first sight."

"Mary said the same as Mama."

Elizabeth could not help the blush which stole over her countenance. "It *was* an instant connection."

With a smile, Jane turned away and began to busy herself washing the dust of the road off her face and hands. Elizabeth watched her sister, keeping a close vigil on her, for as Jane had turned away, Elizabeth thought she had seen an instant of utter sadness from her sister. Jane said nothing for several moments while she concentrated on her task. When she turned, she favored Elizabeth with a wan smile before moving to inspect her closet. She chose a light blue dress she had left behind when traveling to London, one which, incidentally, Lydia had attempted to appropriate for herself. Had the dress belonged to anyone other than Jane, Lydia might have been successful in persuading their mother. As Jane laid the dress out on the bed, Elizabeth rose to assist her.

"What is it, Jane?"

"There is nothing the matter, Lizzy. I am quite content."

"Jane," said Elizabeth, her tone chiding. "Just as you are familiar with my character, I am well enough acquainted with yours to know when you are prevaricating. Will you not tell me what is weighing down on you?"

Though Jane sighed, she said nothing while Elizabeth was buttoning her dress. When it was complete, she sighed again and sat on the edge of her bed, prompting Elizabeth to sit with her.

"I *am* happy for you, Lizzy. You must know this."

"I do," replied Elizabeth, her alarm rising at what might be happening in Jane's mind. "But what has that to do with this melancholy which seems to have beset you?"

For a moment Jane struggled to speak. "You know that Aunt Gardiner introduced me to many men of their general acquaintance while in London, do you not?"

"You found several quite agreeable," replied Elizabeth. Had one of them taken a liking to Jane? Was she acting this way because she thought Elizabeth might be angry if the attention of the neighborhood was diverted from her due to Jane's engagement?

"Are you engaged, Jane?" blurted Elizabeth.

Jane shook her head, a rueful sort of motion, and said: "Quite the opposite, in fact. I have been thinking of my situation—of our situation. Some of the men seemed interested in me, but when they learned of my circumstances they either fled or confined their overtures to simple friendship. I have begun to wonder if I shall ever marry, Lizzy."

"Surely my engagement is proof that the possibility also exists for you." Elizabeth was not surprised at Jane's fear, for they had spoken of it often. She *was* surprised that Jane seemed so despondent at present.

"I suppose you must be correct," replied Jane. "But I am two years older than you. A man does not wish to tie himself to a woman who has lost the bloom of youth."

"I hardly think you are a spinster yet, Jane," said Elizabeth. She grasped her sister's hand and leaned her head against Jane's shoulder, prompting her sister to mirror her. "Your future husband might be closer than you think," added she, thinking of her suspicions regarding Mr. Bingley. "But if nothing else, Mr. Darcy and I shall be certain to introduce you to all his wealthy friends. I am certain you will attract one of them.

Jane laughed. "I may hold you to that, Lizzy."

"There will be no need to, Sister dearest. I am sure we will be happy to have you with us. Have faith. There must be a man in this world who would see you for the gem you are, regardless of your situation."

"I shall try, Lizzy."

In an odd sort of way, Elizabeth felt like her family was restored to her, despite the continued absence of the youngest Bennets. Jane was everything to her, the bond they shared was only rivaled by that Elizabeth shared with her father. They stayed awake late that night speaking, as they had done many times since they were girls. On this occasion, Jane did much more listening than was usual, as Elizabeth shared a more complete account of the past few months than was possible in letters. Jane did speak of her time in London, her doings with their aunt and uncle and the society in which she had been immersed. But more often she appeared content to simply listen to Elizabeth speak.

Mindful of the feelings Jane had shared with her earlier that day, Elizabeth watched her sister, attempting to determine how deep Jane's melancholy ran. But her sister, always difficult to read, even for Elizabeth, to whom she was the closest person in the world, hid her feelings as well as she ever had. Elizabeth could detect no hint of sadness in her manner.

With her recent engagement, Elizabeth was, as was to be expected, eager to introduce her sister to her newly betrothed. The opportunity presented itself the very next day. During his visit the day before, Elizabeth had informed Mr. Darcy—or William, as he now preferred she call him—of Jane's impending return. Having heard much of the Bennet sister to whom he had not been introduced, she thought William was eager to make her acquaintance. When the residents of Netherfield entered Longbourn's sitting-room, Elizabeth was quick to make the introductions.

"Miss Bennet," said William, "I am pleased to meet you. Your sister has told my sister and me much of you."

At his side, Georgiana curtseyed along with his bow, her face alight with curiosity. For her part, Jane greeted brother and sister with the same poise and self-possession as she ever had. She watched both parties for any sign of discomfort or admiration—Jane was very beautiful, after all, and William very handsome. But she could not see anything in their manners. It was a measure of her insecurity, Elizabeth thought with a self-deprecating wryness. Jane had always turned heads wherever she went, and Elizabeth had wondered if Mr. Darcy would react as so many other men had. That he had betrayed no sign of it induced a warmth in Elizabeth's breast which could not be dispelled.

"Her letters have been filled with much of *you* this past month, Mr.

Darcy," replied Jane. "I feel as if I already know you and your sister, and I look forward to making your acquaintance in a more intimate manner."

Elizabeth looked at her sister with gratitude. Jane was a young woman of relatively few words—for her to speak to the Darcys in such open terms showed her commitment to coming to know these people who had become so important in her sister's life.

And then Mr. Bingley saw Jane. The man had stopped to speak with Mrs. Bennet and Mary as his party had entered the room and had missed the introduction. His comments were completed about the time that Jane was speaking of wishing to know the Darcys better, and as he approached from behind Mr. Darcy, Elizabeth was witness to the exact moment when he caught sight of Jane. His eyes widened, and his mouth fell open, and a look of utter stupefaction came over him. This lasted only a moment when the surprise turned to fascination and then adoration all at once, and he stepped even with Mr. Darcy.

"Miss Elizabeth," said he, "I remember you mentioning your elder sister who has been from home these past months, and from the marked resemblance between you, I must infer this is she. Might I beg an introduction?"

Elizabeth could not help the giggle which escaped at that moment. She had seen this exact sequence of events so many times that it seemed destined to happen whenever a man caught sight of Jane for the first time. Having had at least part of her theory confirmed—and not daring to look to Jane to discover the second half—Elizabeth readily agreed.

"Jane, this is our new neighbor, Mr. Bingley, who has lately taken the lease on Netherfield Park. Mr. Bingley, please allow me to introduce my elder sister, Jane. Jane is, and I believe I would not have much disagreement from my other sisters, the best of us all."

Upon making this declaration, Elizabeth finally hazarded a glance at Jane, noting the rosy blush which now spread over her cheeks. A glance back at Mr. Bingley suggested his prior adoration had increased to prodigious levels, and she smiled in a rather smug manner when she turned back to her sister.

"My sister only loves to tease me," said Jane, finally finding her voice. "In fact, I believe Elizabeth is as exceptional as anyone I know"

"Miss Bennet," said William, smiling at her before turning a more intense look on Elizabeth, "it seems to me you are one of the most perspicacious young ladies of my acquaintance. I cannot agree with you more about your sister."

"Here, here!" cried Mr. Bingley, though his eyes never left Jane.

"What an . . . interesting greeting," the amused voice of Mr. Bennet interrupted them. "Far be it for me to disagree with you good gentlemen, especially when you have spoken such exquisite words about my eldest progeny. Suffice to say that I believe it is, perhaps, best to dispense with this mutual admiration society for the present and sit down so that we may take tea together."

"Of course, Mr. Bennet," said Mr. Bingley with his usual joviality. It missed no one's attention that when they moved to the sofas, he maneuvered it so that he was able to claim a position next to Jane. Elizabeth watched it with contentment, certain she had been correct about their compatibility.

They sat down to tea as Mr. Bennet had suggested, and the conversation flowed effortlessly between the various members of the party. The initial discussion centered on Jane and her recent return to Hertfordshire, how the roads had been, and whether she had found her journey fatiguing. Jane answered the questions with her usual quiet poise, and Elizabeth thought Georgiana, in particular, was beginning to look on Jane with something akin to worship. Georgiana's character resembled Jane's more than Elizabeth's, and as such, she would see in Jane someone she could emulate. Far from being offended by such an insight, Elizabeth thought to encourage her future sister to look up to the sister with whom Elizabeth had been raised.

As they sat for a time, Elizabeth noted that Mr. Bingley's attention became much more fixed on Jane to the exclusion of everyone else in the room. And far from being made uncomfortable or being annoyed by him, Jane appeared to be quite content to respond to his overtures.

When she could hold her amusement no longer, Elizabeth cleared her throat a little to gain Mr. Bingley's attention. She was surprised when he actually looked at her, for she had thought him too engrossed in what her sister was saying to respond.

"It seems, Mr. Bingley, that what is good for the goose is also good for the gander. I seem to remember you speaking of how my attention had completely departed from you in favor of William. Now it appears you have no more attention for me in the face of my sister's presence."

There was a smattering of laughter at her sally, primarily from Mr. Bennet. Mr. Bingley only grinned. "Perhaps you are correct, Miss Elizabeth. But as I have not been able to draw your attention away from my friend in some weeks, I cannot imagine you would miss mine now."

"Oh, I do not censure you, sir. In fact, I can think of few worthier of receiving your notice than my beloved sister."

"I could not say it better myself."

Though Jane directed a hard look at Elizabeth amid her embarrassment, she was soon absorbed in Mr. Bingley's conversation again. Once more Elizabeth felt vindicated at being proven so spectacularly correct regarding her suspicions, and after watching them for a short time, she turned to William to speak to him, thinking to obtain his thoughts on the matter.

What she saw there surprised her. Before she could say a word to her betrothed, Elizabeth caught the grave expression with which he was regarding the newly introduced couple. It seemed as if he disapproved of what was happening before his eyes!

A burst of anger entered Elizabeth's breast and she opened her mouth to deliver what would likely have been a cutting comment. But before she made it, she paused and considered the situation. William's scrutiny was not so much disapproving as it was pensive. And furthermore, William was now engaged to Elizabeth herself—could he possibly be so hypocritical as to disapprove of his close friend marrying a Bennet? Surely not! Elizabeth knew William better than that, knew that while he often appeared grave, he was a caring and amiable man. He would not disapprove of a marriage of affection on *either* side. There must be some other explanation. Elizabeth was determined to discover what it was.

"William," called she, drawing his attention back to herself. As soon as his eyes found hers, his countenance softened, and the light which had been extinguished in his eyes was once again kindled. This was the man she had come to know so intimately in such a short period of time.

"How do you like my sister?" queried Elizabeth before he could speak. "Is she everything you had expected?"

William gave her a teasing smile. "Indeed, she is not. Given your description of your sister, I expected her to glow with a bright light and float above the ground. By your account, she is too good to sully her holy feet with the soil on which we walk."

Elizabeth gaped at her betrothed's teasing and then swatted at him playfully. "You are not allowed to tease me, William. I believe that is within my purview."

A chuckle was his response, followed by an amused: "I dare say that if you are able to use your wit on *me*, then I must be permitted to respond. Else it is hardly fair."

Though she grinned at him, Elizabeth did not reply, instead waiting for him to answer her question. He did so with alacrity.

"In fact, you drew an accurate picture of your sister, indeed. Miss Bennet is perhaps one of the sweetest women to whom I have ever been introduced. In fact," a smirk crossed his face, "I may wish to consider which Bennet sister I mean to marry. Miss Bennet does not possess the sharp tongue of her younger sister."

"You may be surprised at that, sir," replied Elizabeth with a saucy wink. Then she sobered and remembered her observation instead of the bantering. "Then what was the meaning of your frown when you looked on Jane and Bingley together? I cannot think you disapprove, considering your understanding with me."

Mr. Darcy appeared surprised for a moment that Elizabeth had understood his expression. With a shaken head he said: "You are entirely too quick, Elizabeth. I shall never be successful in hiding anything from you if you can read me with such little effort."

"You mean to hide things from me?" demanded Elizabeth, arching an eyebrow at his confession.

"Nothing of any substance, unless I should wish to hide the purchase of a gift, for example, until it has been given to you.

"Regardless, you are correct—I have no quarrel with your sister and believe she would make him an excellent wife. Her calmness and intelligence would no doubt curb his impetuosity, making him more thoughtful in turn. Yes, I think she would do very well for him."

"Then is your pensive expression reserved for Mr. Bingley?" asked Elizabeth, unable to fathom such a thing. In this instance, however, it appeared the unfathomable was the truth.

"I am . . . concerned, it is true," confessed he. "They have only known each other for a few moments, but Bingley shows all the signs of infatuation which I have seen many times over."

At Elizabeth's concerned frown, William was quick to clarify: "He is no rake, Elizabeth. He will not trifle with your sister, nor will he attempt any improper behavior. Bingley is as scrupulously upright a man as I have ever known, and that includes my cousin, with whom I am exceptionally close.

"But Bingley's fancy is often captured by a pretty woman, and he falls in and out of love with frequency." William paused and then chuckled. "Of course, that is an exaggeration. He fancies himself in love often. It is not long, however, before he loses interest. This usually happens when he realizes the woman is not who he thought she was, or when he learns that she allows his presence because of his fortune."

"Jane will not act in such a manner. Other than concerning herself for the ability of a man being able to provide for her — which *all* women must consider — she cares nothing for a man's wealth."

"I never suspected she would," said William. "It is obvious within moments of meeting her that your sister is a woman of substance."

"We have always determined between us that we would marry for nothing but the deepest love," said Elizabeth, feeling the heat rising in her cheeks at her declaration. But she was determined that he understood her without the possibility of error.

"Well do I know it," replied William, one hand reaching up almost of its own accord, a soft finger caressing the skin of her cheek. It was as much as he had ever touched her, other than a hand on her arm or a kiss on the back of her hand. He always behaved with scrupulous propriety. "I thank you for bestowing your love on me, Elizabeth. I do not know if I deserve it."

"Shall we simply say that we, neither of us, deserve it, and resolve to be happy, regardless?"

William chuckled and grasped her hand, squeezing it to show his affection. "That sounds like a marvelous plan, my love."

Though she basked in the warmth of his love, Elizabeth's worry for her sister was too strong to ignore. Jane and Mr. Bingley were involved in an animated conversation at present. Beyond them, Elizabeth could see her mother watching them carefully. Though much had changed with Elizabeth's betrothal to Mr. Darcy, Elizabeth doubted that her mother would do anything other than promote the potential match with all the enthusiasm she could muster. That would complicate matters, especially should Mr. Bingley choose to be fickle.

"What can we do, William?" asked Elizabeth.

"There is nothing we can do except watch them," replied William. "I am . . . reluctant to speak to Bingley directly, for he is his own man, and our relationship of late has been changing to reflect that. I can do so should it become necessary, but only as a last resort."

"I suppose I should tell Jane to guard her heart," said Elizabeth. "If she waits until it is obvious that he wishes to strengthen their ties together, she should avoid most of the hurt if he should lose interest."

"Elizabeth." Turning, Elizabeth noted his fixed look on her and she flushed a little. "Perhaps it is best to simply watch and wait. Your sister is an intelligent woman. Surely she will know to guard her own heart and gage his interest from her own observations."

Though she was not certain of that at all, especially given what Jane had confessed only the day before, Elizabeth was forced to acknowledge that William's plan was best. But she would not shirk in protecting her sister should it become required. Mr. Bingley would not hurt Jane callously. If he wished to make her an offer and Jane wished to accept, they were both mature enough to decide on their own.

Thus decided, Elizabeth turned back to William and focused her attention on him. But that did not mean a small portion of her consciousness never left her sister.

CHAPTER VII

*I*t is the fate of all men to wish to protect the woman they love against heartache and trial, and Fitzwilliam Darcy was no different in this respect. It was irrational, Darcy knew, for there was little any man could do to create a cocoon which would insulate his love from the world and all the trials and hardships she would ultimately face. But Darcy loved Elizabeth Bennet, and he wished to protect her to the best of his ability.

The cynical of society would point out that he had only known his betrothed for a little more than a month. How could a man truly love another in such a short period?

But Darcy knew they were wrong. His heart had been long prepared for Miss Elizabeth Bennet to come into his life. The example of his mother and father, the love they had shared, the example of his aunt and uncle, had mingled with the desire to have his own love with a good woman. In a strange way, his years in society, being sought after by the simpering debutantes, none of them holding a candle to the brightness which was his Elizabeth, had prepared him for this time. He had something with which to compare her, and as such, he had known almost immediately that she was different, that he could forge a lasting relationship with her if he could only induce her to feel the same way.

In Elizabeth's case, he knew that any sorrow suffered by her closest sister would be felt keenly in her own breast. And even after only one meeting, Darcy felt highly of Miss Jane Bennet. She was a bright and beautiful soul. While Darcy did not think that she would have suited *him* nearly so well as did Elizabeth, as the sister of his future wife, he had an interest in her happiness as well.

"Well, the initial fascination certainly has not dimmed," said Elizabeth to Darcy the day after Bingley and Jane had been introduced.

"No, it has not," replied Darcy. "The only subject about which Bingley wished to converse last night was your sister. Had I not been in the room, I think he might have been content in speaking to the wall."

Georgiana, who was nearby, snorted in laughter, but it was largely missed by the couple walking in front of them, who were absorbed in their own conversation. "I would not have thought they would come together so quickly," said Georgiana. "And I witnessed the courtship of my brother and his affianced. They are liable to come to an agreement even more quickly than you!"

While Georgiana chuckled at her own joke, Elizabeth and Darcy only looked at each other, their countenances mirroring their concern. But there was little to be done at present. Then, on another occasion, they met at a dinner given by another family in the neighborhood.

"Jane told me last night that she has never seen such happy manners, nor met such a pleasant man in all her life." Elizabeth paused. "I have never seen her so affected by a man."

"Bingley is the same," replied Darcy. "It is almost as if . . ."

After Darcy fell silent for a moment, Elizabeth prompted him to speak. "Well? What did you mean to say?"

Darcy grinned at her—her query had been no less than a demand. "Bingley seems a little different from the way I have seen him before. He puts his whole heart into it, and this time is no different. But his interest seems . . . more mature than it was in the past, though I am not certain I am saying it properly."

"Then I hope it is sincere," replied Elizabeth. The way she looked back at Bingley told Darcy that she was more hopeful than she had been but still uncertain.

More than the desire to protect the ones he loves, however, Darcy knew that as Miss Bennet's future brother, it was his *duty* to protect her as best he was able. He had not wished to speak to Bingley on the matter. They were long-time friends, and as he had informed

Elizabeth, Bingley was coming into his own as a man and master of his own life. It was officious to attempt to direct his friend.

But in this instance, Darcy thought a little subtle probing of his friend's feelings was warranted. It only required the opportunity to do it in as indiscernible a manner as he could manage. That opportunity arrived the very next day, and in a manner which heartened Darcy. He knew it would please Elizabeth as well.

Having declared herself fatigued, Georgiana excused herself for her chambers, leaving Darcy in Bingley's company. The friends stayed in the sitting-room, Bingley not even thinking to suggest they retire to the study. The conversation consisted of the usual subjects, the estate, about which Darcy had been sharing what he knew, the neighborhood, and other banal subjects. On this evening, Bingley seemed to be avoiding the subject of his angel.

After a time, they both fell silent, and Darcy began to contemplate retiring to his room for the evening. It was only a moment longer before Bingley spoke.

"Darcy, I had wondered . . ." The man paused and fell silent, and for the first time in their friendship, Darcy was treated to the sight of Charles Bingley lost for words. It did not last long.

"Oh, hang it all!" exclaimed Bingley. He shot to his feet and began to pace the room. "I do not know that I have ever been so tongue-tied!"

"I would tend to agree with that assessment, my friend," replied Darcy. By now he was amused, certain he knew what was causing Bingley's disconcertion.

Bingley paced for a few moments before he whirled and faced Darcy. "What do you think of Jane Bennet?" blurted he.

"I think much of her, indeed," replied Darcy. "She is my future wife's sister, and beyond that, I think her an entirely estimable woman in her own right."

"That was not what I was asking."

"Then perhaps you should be more explicit."

Bingley threw his hands up in the air. "I was asking you for your opinion of what she thinks of me."

That surprised Darcy. "I beg your pardon?"

As abruptly as he had started pacing, Bingley threw himself once again into his chair. "It is just . . ." Bingley laughed, a nervous sound. "She is the most deucedly difficult woman to understand. Almost every other woman with whom I have been acquainted was obvious in their affections. But Miss Bennet does not give a hint of them."

"And what did that gain you with these other women of whom you speak?"

Bingley frowned. "I am not sure to what you refer."

With a prayer for strength when dealing with blind friends, Darcy shook his head. It seemed Bingley was not as ready to be as independent as Darcy had thought.

"Did your interest remain with any of those ladies?" demanded Darcy. "Furthermore, were they being sincere in showing their feelings, or did they have ulterior motives?"

"I suppose you must be correct," said Bingley, looking a little shamefaced. Then he frowned. "Are you suggesting that Miss Bennet is different?"

"I only suggest that she is not prone to feigning feelings she does not possess. If you examine her behavior, she is entirely proper. She is demure and accepts the attentions of anyone with pleasure, but she does not attempt to solicit interest. She is perhaps the best-behaved lady I have ever had the pleasure of meeting."

"Then how am I to ever know what she truly thinks of me?"

Darcy chuckled. "That, my dear Bingley, you must determine for yourself. Does the woman seem to welcome your advances? Does she react with pleasure when you speak with her? It is not proper for a woman to seek a man out, though there are many who do not obey this simple rule. It is for the man to decide on her level of interest and act accordingly."

"Please, Darcy," said Bingley, regarding him with beseeching eyes. "If you have some knowledge of Miss Bennet's feelings, please tell me." Then Bingley's eyes widened. "Has Miss Elizabeth told you something of her?"

"No," denied Darcy. "Miss Elizabeth has made no claims concerning her sister's feelings. And Bingley, you have only known her for a matter of days."

"Did you not offer for Miss Elizabeth less than a month after making her acquaintance?"

"I did," replied Darcy, unruffled by his friend's implicit accusation. "But I was not agonizing over her feelings only days after meeting her." Darcy sighed. "You know, my friend, that your history with respect to the fairer sex does not inspire confidence. The last half of the season was Miss Cartwright, was it not? Then before that is was Miss Farnsworth. And before that, it was—"

"You have made your point, my friend," said Bingley with a nervous chuckle. "And I can see where you have some interest in the matter at hand, considering your betrothal with Miss Elizabeth.

"Perhaps I have told you this previously with other young ladies, but I truly feel that Miss Bennet is different from any other lady I have ever met. I am well aware of my propensity to fall in love easily. But I cannot imagine ever losing interest in Miss Bennet, now that I have met her."

"I am glad to hear it, Bingley. I will not attempt to direct you or influence you. But I will give you this advice if you will hear it."

Bingley gestured for Darcy to continue.

"If you have interest in Miss Bennet, then, by all means, see where it will lead you. Should it take you three weeks to become convinced of your feelings, then that is what it shall be. But if you are not certain—or if you are not certain of Miss Bennet's feelings—do yourself and Miss Bennet a favor and proceed slowly. You are still a young man, so there is no rush. Be certain before you make such a life-altering step as to ask her to marry you."

"That is sage advice, indeed, my friend. I will do as you ask. As you say, there is no reason to rush."

They fell silent for several moments, each lost in their own thoughts. Something from their conversation pricked Darcy's memory, and he turned to his friend again, his curiosity demanding to be assuaged.

"What of Miss Cartwright, Bingley? As I recall, she is one of your sister's friends, is pretty and accomplished and has a large dowry, and was not pretentious in the slightest."

"By pretentious, I am certain you mean that she did not immediately throw me over for you when she discovered your prominence."

Bingley's tone was ironic, and Darcy laughed with him over it. There was no sense in denying it—Bingley had learned the true measure of more than one of the women for whom he had become infatuated by that exact means.

"She is a good woman, indeed," said Bingley. "But I found that I had little in common with her, and she did not excite in me that passion I have always thought I should have for my future wife.

"Furthermore, she was not as acceptable for me as you might have thought. Her dowry *is* large—she is her father's sole heir, and his property is not small. But the Cartwrights are not of the upper echelons of society, and Caroline has always wished that I make a match with a woman who would ensure her inclusion in the first circles."

Darcy snorted. "If you will forgive me saying so, finding such a woman would be very difficult, as you are just now establishing yourself in society."

"I never said Caroline's dreams were rational," replied Bingley. "You must own this, however: she does not do things by half measures."

"No, I suppose she does not."

The conversation had been illuminating for Darcy. It seemed to Darcy that Bingley's account of his loss of interest in Miss Cartwright was eminently sensible, unlike some of the other accounts Darcy had heard from his friend in the past. Perhaps Bingley was closer to maturity and responsibility that the early part of their conversation had indicated.

When Darcy related his conversation with Bingley to Elizabeth, he could see the relief which flowed out from her, though he knew she was still not completely at ease. "I am happy to hear it, William. I suppose there is nothing left for us now but to trust them to act in a way which will assure their happiness, whether it is together or apart."

"I believe so. In the end, we have no ability or right to live their lives for them. They are both mature enough to make their own decisions, even if one or another of them is hurt in the process."

"I will give Jane whatever support she requires. But I will not interfere."

Darcy grasped her hands, squeezing them and allowing his affection for her to shine through. "That is all you can do, dearest. They will be well. We simply need to trust them."

The very day after Darcy's conversation with Bingley, a group of unwelcome visitors arrived at Netherfield. Though Darcy supposed they were not precisely visitors and Bingley might be justifiably offended were Darcy to refer to them in such terms, it did not change his feelings a whit. The tepid interest with which Georgiana greeted the newcomers informed Darcy that his sister was in agreement with him.

"Charles, what a miserable hovel this is," the strident tones of Miss Caroline Bingley rang out as she entered the sitting-room where the three had gathered before setting out to Longbourn. "I can hardly believe even *you* would consider such a place sufficient for our needs. Why—"

Miss Bingley trailed off as she caught sight of both Darcy and Georgiana, her jaw falling in her shock. Her sister, who had been walking behind her, almost impacted with Miss Bingley's still form, and Hurst, who was bringing up the rear, was heard to say: "I say,

Caroline. What the deuce are you doing?"

"Hello, Caroline," said Bingley, rising to his feet. "I am surprised to see you all here, for I have had no notice of your coming."

"Mr. Darcy!" exclaimed Miss Bingley. But Darcy did not miss the angry glare she shot at her brother. "I had no notion you were in Hertfordshire. And dear Georgiana too! Had I known, I assure you I would have hastened here without delay, for I dare not think that you have been comfortable here without a mistress in residence to see to your stay."

"We have been quite well here, Miss Bingley," said Darcy. "I trust your journey to Netherfield was tolerable?"

Miss Bingley shot another harsh glare at her brother. "It was adequate, though I cannot think why brother has made a year's commitment to such an estate as this. I am sure our father had a much grander property in mind for my brother's purchase."

It was clear Miss Bingley was thinking of Pemberley when she said those words. In the past, Darcy might have found himself annoyed at the woman, or frustrated by her never-ending designs with respect to his person and property. It was amazing what the love of a good woman and a betrothal—to someone who was *not* Miss Bingley— could do for Darcy's mood! His engagement to Elizabeth must end all such notions on Miss Bingley's part. Darcy need not concern himself for her actions again.

"I *am* surprised to see you here, Darcy," said Hurst. The Hursts had stepped into the room when Miss Bingley had darted forward, and while Mrs. Hurst was standing in an attitude which clearly showed her support for her sister as she always did, Hurst's feelings were much more ambiguous. "Is the sport on the estate adequate? If it is, I would be happy to sample it in your company when we are settled."

"I am afraid we have not had much time for sport, Hurst," replied Darcy. Hurst was a simple soul in essence, and while he was not an objectionable companion, he was not precisely scintillating company either.

"Not much time for sport? If that is so, I wonder what in the blazes you have been up to since coming."

"I am certain Mr. Darcy has been providing his excellent advice on the proper management of an estate," interjected Caroline smoothly. "What else could they have been doing here? I am certain the local society must be nothing but a punishment, and there is little other reason to be here." A cunning look came over her. "In fact, perhaps we should all return together to London for the little season. There is no need to be in residence here at present, for it is not as if there is much work to do on an estate at this time of year."

Darcy did not bother to correct the woman's misperception. He left the response to Bingley, who was already showing signs of exasperation with his sister. "We are quite comfortably settled at Netherfield, Caroline. I have no intention of going anywhere at present, and I am confident Darcy agrees with me."

"Well then, perhaps it is better to stay here for the present. I will take up the reins of the house, of course. Perhaps I can do something with the servants and arrange a more comfortable stay for our guests. In the meantime, however, I believe I would like to refresh myself. I will speak with the housekeeper before dinner." She smiled at Darcy. "I appreciate your enduring the conditions you have until now, Mr. Darcy, but I will not allow them to continue."

And with that, the woman turned and walked from the room. Out in the hall, Darcy could hear her imperious demand for the housekeeper to attend her, and he pitied the woman. She was certainly capable of performing the duties of a mistress, but she would not be easy to please, especially when she considered him a captive audience. Perhaps it was not gentlemanly to think in such a way, but Darcy almost found himself anticipating the communication of his betrothal which must be made soon.

Of a necessity, their visit to Longbourn must be canceled—which was a particular annoyance for Darcy. As Sir William was to host a gathering at his house the following evening, Darcy knew he would not see Elizabeth until then. As he was betrothed to Elizabeth, Darcy decided it was his responsibility to make the communication. As such, he dashed off a quick note to Longbourn, explaining the circumstances, knowing that Elizabeth would almost certainly find the situation amusing. At least she would until Miss Bingley discovered the betrothal and released her jealousy and spite.

For the rest of the day, they were treated to the presence of Miss Bingley and her airs. If she was not boasting of her prowess as a hostess, she was paying every deference to Darcy. When she was not focused on Darcy himself, she was ingratiating herself with Georgiana. And through it all, she lamented her brother's unfortunate choice of an estate and spoke of her determination to raise the standards, little though she expected success.

"I am sure you must understand, Mr. Darcy," said she, completely confident of his concurrence, "it is sometimes difficult to acquire good help in such places as this. Hertfordshire is not Derbyshire, after all, and an estate such as this cannot be expected to be the equal of Pemberley."

"There is no need to concern yourself, Miss Bingley," replied Darcy. "We have been quite comfortable here, and I have not had any complaints about either the house or the staff."

"That is to your credit, I am sure, and due to your friendship with my brother. But I will not stand for anything but the best which can be offered. I will not rest until I have obtained it."

By the end of the day, Darcy was fatigued by the woman's constant presence and was amazed that she had been able to prompt that reaction from him in the space of a single day. In this, Georgiana was of a like mind.

"She is determined, is she not?"

Darcy laughed. "She is, indeed, Georgiana. You, at least, are insulated by your need to see to your studies and Mrs. Annesley's presence. I, unfortunately, must be a good guest and be attentive to my hostess."

"I am grateful for it," replied Georgiana.

She leaned back in her chair with a sigh. After attending their hosts in the music room that evening, the Darcy siblings had retired to the sitting-room attached to Georgiana's bedchamber. He had been grateful to escape—Miss Bingley had attempted to entice Darcy by showing him her skill on the pianoforte. It had been a failure, as Darcy much preferred the performances of Elizabeth and his sister, even though Miss Bingley was the technically superior performer.

"I assume you have not informed Miss Bingley of the death of her hopes?" asked she.

"I have not yet," replied Darcy. "But I suppose it must be done soon."

"Despite how much she might deserve it."

The Darcy siblings shared a rueful smile.

"I do not trust Miss Bingley, Brother," said his sister after a moment, once again completely serious.

"In what way?" asked Darcy. His question was an idle one, for his mind had turned to a much more agreeable subject—that of his betrothed. Foremost in his thoughts was the lament that he had not seen her that day

"Do you think a matter so trifling as an engagement will defeat her?" Georgiana's snort informed him of her opinion on the matter. "She will not give up until you have shared your vows with Elizabeth, and even then, she might still hold out hope of you 'coming to your senses' and divorcing her."

Darcy scratched his chin. "I suppose you might be correct. But while she will be unpleasant and supercilious toward Elizabeth and her family, I doubt she will stoop to anything underhanded. She does have a reputation to uphold, you know. She will not understand Elizabeth's allure and will assume she can turn me away from her at any time she pleases."

"You may be right," replied Georgiana. "She *is* that blind."

"She is, indeed."

"Then when will you inform her?"

A sigh escaped Darcy. He knew it must be done, but he did not anticipate her reaction at all. "I suppose it must be done before we attend the Lucases tomorrow. We would not wish—for Bingley's sake—for her to humiliate herself in front of the entire neighborhood when she learns the truth."

Georgiana was silent for a moment, and when she spoke, Darcy could feel nothing but amusement, though he supposed he should censure her. "Would you think less of me if the thought of Miss Bingley embarrassing herself fills me with satisfaction?"

"If I did, then I would share in the censure, dearest. She is quite deserving."

CHAPTER VIII

*D*arcy discovered the next morning that while making the determination to inform Miss Bingley of his engagement was all well and good, actually doing it was problematic. Miss Bingley was a determined woman, and among her curious quirks of character was an ability to see and hear only that which she wanted. She was also determined, especially when in his company, to carry the conversation, rarely allowing others to state their own opinions. It was these qualities which made informing her virtually impossible.

What she was not was an early riser—none of the Bingley family was, in fact. As Darcy was himself, he knew that his only moments of peace while in residence with the woman would be in the mornings before she rose. On the morning in question, however, Darcy found himself surprised when Bingley appeared at the breakfast table earlier than was his usual wont. When Darcy looked up with curiosity at his friend, Bingley only took his place at the table, with a smile and a nod for Georgiana, and set about eating his breakfast.

"With the arrival of my family, I must inform Sir William and ask his permission to include them in our party this evening."

It was a point that Darcy, as a guest, had not considered, though he knew Miss Bingley and the Hursts could not go to Lucas Lodge without an invitation. "I doubt Sir William will refuse. He seems quite fond of society."

Bingley agreed and further stated: "I only hope that Caroline can suppress her disdain for my neighbors. She has not been exactly circumspect about what she thinks of Netherfield. I can hardly expect she will have a different opinion of my new friends."

Darcy and Georgiana shared a glance, and he knew they were both thinking the same: how could she judge them without having made their acquaintance? Bingley, unfortunately, noticed their glance and grimaced.

"You know she does not require a reason." He forced his voice higher, a credible imitation of his sister's strident tones. "What a dull community you have chosen to force upon us. I am sure the locals are positively without redeeming qualities. Oh, how I wish we were at Pemberley, for there is no society so agreeable or sophisticated as that surrounding Mr. Darcy's home!"

While Darcy was surprised his friend had mocked *his* sister in front of *Darcy's*, the sound of Georgiana's laughter, coupled with his recollection of Miss Bingley saying almost those exact words, brought out Darcy's mirth as well. Bingley watched them with a grin, though Darcy noted the rueful quality it contained.

"I apologize for behaving in such an ungentlemanly manner," said Bingley, looking at Georgiana, "but the unfortunate fact is that it is true."

"You have my apologies too for laughing, Bingley," replied Darcy. "But I remember her saying almost those exact words to me."

"I know," replied Bingley, his smirk drawing further laughter from the siblings. "I was reciting from memory, I assure you."

Before they could say anything more or allow their mirth further reign, the subject of their laughter glided into the room, dressed more like she was attending an event of the season, rather than a morning at home in the country. The bronze dress and feathered headdress were elaborate and obviously made of costly material, but though she favored dresses of a similar shade, Darcy had always thought it made her complexion look sallow. A memory of his childhood flashed in Darcy's mind, of his father informing his mother how very beautiful she looked. Though Darcy could not remember what she had been wearing that morning, he was certain, given what he remembered of her, that it had been a simple day dress. Had Miss Bingley known what the daughter of an earl married to a wealthy and prominent landowner had worn most days she would have been scandalized.

"Good morning," said she, her voice containing a hint of enthusiastic excitement. "How wonderful it is that we are all here together. I hope breakfast is to your liking. I had a firm word with the housekeeper and cook last night and will be very displeased if it does not meet my high standards."

"Everything is excellent, Miss Bingley," said Darcy. "It has been since our arrival."

The woman preened as if it was all her doing. "Thank you, Mr. Darcy. I am eager to ensure your stay is as comfortable as I can make it. Should you — or your lovely sister — require anything at all, I will be happy to provide it."

Darcy assured her he was quite content and turned back to his plate. The next ten or fifteen minutes passed in exactly the same fashion as Darcy would have expected. Miss Bingley spoke incessantly about matters which were of no interest to Darcy, and yet she spoke as if he was hanging off her every word. She spoke of her recent time in London, the events she had attended, her expectations of their residence together in Hertfordshire, all woven about with innuendo concerning their *friendship* and how she expected it to deepen over time. There was little to be guessed at concerning her words, for she was as blatant as she obviously thought herself sly.

Eventually, Bingley excused himself. "I have a letter I must write at once. Darcy, if you will, perhaps we could ride later this morning."

Darcy assented, and Bingley departed. It was only a moment after his departure that Miss Bingley's claws were unsheathed. "Charles mentioned some sort of little function this evening. I assume the letter of which he spoke concerned that."

"I expect it was, Miss Bingley," replied Darcy.

"There is little to be done, I suppose. Since we are here, society cannot be avoided." Miss Bingley paused, and a truly ugly smirk settled over her countenance. "Dare I ask after the state of society in this insignificant speck?" Then she paused and laughed. "Of course, there is no reason to ask! I cannot expect them to be anything less than savage, as I am certain you already know. Perhaps it would be best to leave poor Georgiana here with me tonight, for you cannot wish her to be subjected to the crassness of the masses."

"On the contrary, Miss Bingley," replied Georgiana, her manner unconcerned, "I have found the local society to be pleasing. They are simple people, but they are little different from those in Derbyshire."

"I am certain it must seem that way to you, Georgiana," replied Miss Bingley. Though the woman herself saw nothing, Darcy could see his sister's frown at her patronizing tone. "But please allow those of us who possess more experience in society the greater understanding of the denizens of insignificant neighborhoods such as this. I know your brother has kept his true stature from these people, but he is unable to hide his true nobility of character from them. Why, it is in his very bearing and manners, though they have not the wit to see its true measure.

"Furthermore," continued she, oblivious to their mounting anger, "I am certain there are some poor country squires in this neighborhood who have come to see your dowry as their own. You must take care, lest the fortune hunters of society prey upon you."

"Miss Bingley—" began Darcy, but the woman continued, likely not even hearing he had spoken.

"You must know your brother has existed in society all these years, successfully fending off those who would attach themselves to him for his position and wealth. You must learn the same, Georgiana."

I have successfully kept them all at bay, *thought Darcy to himself. There is* one *who still clings to hope, but I cannot divest myself of her unless I forgo friendship with her brother.*

"I assure you, Miss Bingley, that there is no danger of succumbing to any such predator, either for Georgiana or myself."

"Of course! I never doubted you for a moment! Naturally, you would have taken the necessary steps."

"Indeed, I have," replied Darcy.

"Then let us speak of it no more!" exclaimed Miss Bingley, once again interrupting him when he sought to explain the situation to her. For the rest of the meal, she continued to speak without cessation, and neither sibling was able to fit a word in, to say nothing of informing her of his engagement. By the time they had sat there for another five minutes, Darcy was wild to be out of her company, finishing his breakfast hastily and excusing himself.

When he left the room, Georgiana followed him, along with her companion—who had sat down the table, watching Miss Bingley while remaining unobtrusive. The coming weeks promised to be difficult, for Darcy doubted that Miss Bingley would be silenced. She would only become worse when she learned of his engagement.

"You did not inform her, Brother," said Georgiana.

"When did I have the opportunity?" asked Darcy.

Georgiana giggled at the rhetorical question. Even Mrs. Annesley, who was strict in demanding proper behavior from her charge, smiled at Darcy's words.

"What will you do then?"

"She will discover it at the gathering tonight," said Darcy with a shrug. "She is too conscious of her image to make a scene. Or at least I hope she is."

"Let us all hope so."

Not long after, Bingley found Darcy and informed him that Sir William had responded to his query with an affirmative. Thus, the players were set for the evening. But while Darcy wished to spare his friend the embarrassment of a humiliated sister, a part of him could not help but anticipate the evening. It would not be dull, whatever else happened.

Despite their relationship having suffered in recent weeks, Charlotte was the first person Elizabeth sought out when her family arrived at Lucas Lodge that evening. And as they began speaking, Elizabeth could almost imagine that all between them was much as it ever was.

"I suppose you are eager for the Netherfield party's arrival this evening for two reasons," said Charlotte once their greetings had been exchanged.

"Oh?" replied Elizabeth, though knowing to what her friend referred.

"Mr. Darcy's coming, of course, must be one reason. The other, I would think, is the opportunity to finally make the acquaintance of Mr. Bingley's infamous sisters. Father received a letter this morning, requesting permission to include his newly arrived family. It was granted with much enthusiasm, as you may well expect."

"We received a similar communication yesterday morning," replied Elizabeth. "I will own to a certain level of curiosity, though I suppose it does not affect me much."

"Ah, but it may affect Jane if what I hear about Mr. Bingley's attentions to your sister is correct."

As it happened, Elizabeth was still a little concerned about what she had heard about Mr. Bingley. Thus, she ignored the comment. "By everything Mr. Bingley has said, I expect his sisters to be high-quality ladies, at least in the confines of their own minds."

Charlotte laughed. "So you have informed me. If they are so, do you suppose they will be fashionably late tonight?"

"I rather expect them to do everything in their power to avoid attending at all," replied Elizabeth. "I do not think anyone in this neighborhood will meet their standards."

"Ah, that is unfortunate," was Charlotte's mock-sorrowful reply. "I hope there is some benefit to come of their visit then. Perhaps they will simply enjoy being away from the city."

"I hardly think that is likely, but I find myself unconcerned about their predicament. If they behave in such a manner, they will bring whatever consequences arise of their own free will."

Before long, the Lucas home had filled with many of their neighbors and friends. Though Lucas Lodge was not at all a large manor house, Sir William was so fond of company that rarely did his gatherings exclude any of their neighbors. As such, the rooms were filled with people, all talking and laughing and enjoying the refreshments set out by their hosts. That evening it was truly a press because the officers of the militia had also been invited, and red-coated uniforms dotted the gathering.

At one point, Elizabeth saw Lieutenant Denny in the group speaking with Penelope Long. He noticed her looking at him, and she saw a hint of a blush climbing his cheeks. He did a credible job of feigning unawareness of her presence, however, and Elizabeth decided against tormenting the man. He had learned his lesson, presumably, and would not take the chance of approaching any of the other Bennet girls. The remaining Bennet sisters' lack of interest in the officers did not go unnoticed.

"Miss Elizabeth," said Sir William, as he approached her not long after, "I am surprised at you and your sisters. I have not seen one of you exchange more than a word with one of these fine, upstanding defenders of our realm. What can be the meaning of it?"

Elizabeth returned the man's grin fondly. Since the family had moved to Lucas Lodge a decade or so before, Elizabeth had a soft spot for Sir William. It was true that he was not the cleverest of men, nor was he blessed with the most sense, but he had a good heart and a jovial spirit, and Elizabeth liked him prodigiously.

"I am afraid that Jane, Mary, and I do not care much for the officers. It is Kitty and Lydia who find them so agreeable."

Sir William frowned. "Surely you do not suspect them of nefarious purposes."

"No, indeed!" exclaimed Elizabeth with a laugh. "I know no harm of them. I speak with them when the opportunity presents itself, but I find myself drawn to other elements of our society which I find much more interesting."

A sly grin came over Sir William's face, and he laughed, his belly shaking in time with his mirth. "Nay, you need not say anything more, for I fully understand your meaning." He leaned forward and said,

"Let me say how happy I am for you. Mr. Darcy is a fine man—the finest we have ever seen in this neighborhood. I hope, my dear, that I will see you at St. James's court in the coming months. I shall look forward to it, I assure you!"

Then he excused himself, still chuckling softly. Elizabeth watched him go, reflecting at that moment how she would miss this neighborhood when she moved to her new home. Society in Meryton had grown stagnant after the novelty of her coming out had passed, but it was at times like these that she remembered how fond she was of some of the characters of her home.

As it happened, the Netherfield party's arrival came a few moments later, about fifteen minutes after the hour indicated in their invitation. When they appeared in the doorway to Lucas Lodge's primary sitting-room, Elizabeth could only exchange an amused glance with Charlotte. The behavior of the sisters had been proven with an exactness of which Elizabeth might have felt proud, had it not been so obvious.

The Bingley sisters were generally pleasantly featured women, though the younger was more so than the elder. They were both taller than Elizabeth, though not so tall as Jane, Mrs. Hurst's hair a light brown, while Miss Bingley's was a redder shade, approaching the hue of her brother's locks. Their family resemblance was pronounced, both possessing long, angular faces, handsome, rather than pretty, with long noses and delicate jaws. They were also dressed in fine clothing, the fabrics costlier than anything which could be found in Meryton, which made them stand out among the more modest costumes of the rest of the company. Elizabeth suspected that distinction was by choice, rather than by accident.

When they entered together, the two sisters—plus a man whose arm the elder sister was holding—stopped by the door. While the man looked out over the assembled, apparently bored—until he saw the refreshment table and his eyes lit up—the women spoke together in soft tones.

"I see what you mean," said Charlotte in Elizabeth's ear.

Elizabeth, who had not known her friend was close by, turned and arched an eyebrow at her. "I assure you I know nothing of them."

"But Mr. Bingley has spoken of them, and you are intelligent enough to read between the lines."

"Do you suppose someone has added vinegar to the punch?" asked Elizabeth, feigning innocence. "They appear as if they are smelling something foul."

Charlotte only snorted. "I shall have to ask Father. I hope he has not been adding brandy."

The friends laughed together, and Charlotte turned away. While they were speaking, Sir William had approached the newcomers and welcomed them, eager to be introduced to them. The sisters responded with cold civility—Elizabeth could almost feel the arctic wind which accompanied them all the way from the door by which they stood. William, however, chose to ignore them and guided Georgiana to where Elizabeth was standing, bowing and kissing her hand, while Georgiana greeted her with a more enthusiastic embrace.

"I cannot tell you how happy I am to see you, Lizzy," exclaimed Georgiana. "I have been anticipating this all day."

"Why, have you not had interesting company today at Netherfield?" asked Elizabeth. "I would think the arrival of Mr. Bingley's family would be an occasion for happiness. You must be a merry party!"

The curt shake of Georgiana's head provoked Elizabeth's laughter. William only watched them with indulgent amusement. Elizabeth turned to him and gave him a pointed look.

"Can I suppose that *all* your party knows the full measure of our circumstances?"

William appeared more than a little ashamed, which surprised Elizabeth. She had thought he would waste no time in informing the woman, if only to halt her pursuit of him before it even started.

"She did not give William an opportunity to inform her," interjected Georgiana. "Her conversation consists of her doings in London, her expectations for our *felicity*, and her certainty that she will leave Hertfordshire an engaged woman."

"Though she certainly does not speak of such matters in anything other than innuendo," added William.

"She wishes to be engaged, does she?" asked Elizabeth. "Perhaps Samuel Lucas would do. He is Charlotte's brother, as you know, and is in search of a woman of substantial dowry." Elizabeth paused and let loose a mournful sigh. "But I could not do such a thing to my friend's brother. I am sure she would drive him to distraction before their wedding trip ended."

The siblings laughed, though it consisted of rueful mirth. "I cannot say you are incorrect, Elizabeth," replied Mr. Darcy. "And it is likely for the best."

Elizabeth nodded, but her attention was caught by Mr. Bingley leading his sisters in their direction. Jane was standing nearby, speaking with one of the other ladies of the neighborhood, and as Elizabeth knew it was his primary objective to introduce the woman he had begun to fancy, she beckoned her sister. Jane greeted the Darcys, and they stood together, waiting as the Bingley's made their way to them. As they were interrupted at least twice, it was a few moments before they arrived.

"They are very elegant, are they not?" asked Jane of Elizabeth while they waited.

Though Elizabeth could see William shaking his head, knowing what he thought of their manner of dress, Elizabeth decided against saying such things to Jane. "It is clear they are not afraid to show their sense of fashion."

"I hope we shall be the best of friends."

That was entirely unlikely, but Elizabeth would not inform her sister of her suspicions. There was little else said between their little party, and a few moments later the Bingleys were before them. Mr. Bingley lost no time introducing them, and Elizabeth was heartened when Jane was presented with particular pride. It was clear, however, that even Jane was received with tepid interest, and Elizabeth with none at all.

"Miss Bennet," replied Miss Bingley, her voice devoid of any warmth. "I am pleased to make your acquaintance. Charles has not spoken much of the people here, but then again his mind is often occupied with other matters, so that is not unusual."

It was easy to see Jane's crestfallen mien at these words, and Miss Bingley's satisfied sneer at the sight told Elizabeth the woman had intended it to be so. Mr. Bingley, however, seemed determined to make his sentiments known, for he smiled at Jane and bowed over her hand.

"On the contrary, you have been so intent upon telling us of your doings in London, that I have not had an opportunity to speak of our neighbors." Miss Bingley frowned at her brother, but he only continued, saying: "In fact, I have rarely found a society more pleasing than I have in Hertfordshire. I find the Bennets especially agreeable, and as they are my closest neighbors, I am quite happy with the welcome I have received.

"In fact, Miss Bennet has recently returned from London herself. Perhaps you have a common topic of conversation?"

The critical look with which Miss Bingley regarded Jane was soon replaced by one calculating. She smiled at Jane, who was beaming at Mr. Bingley's words, and said: "Perhaps we do, Miss Bennet. I am interested to know if we have any common acquaintances."

It seemed from the woman's tone that she expected the opposite, but at that moment Georgiana began speaking to Elizabeth, and she lost track of anything Miss Bingley said. That did not mean she was not watchful. Miss Bingley's performance was not anything Elizabeth had not suspected. She would bear careful scrutiny, indeed.

There was nothing Miss Bingley could hide from Darcy, in her expression or bearing, for he had seen it all. The woman herself had been an acquaintance for more than four years. Furthermore, he had encountered many women of her ilk in society. Her feigned interest in Miss Bennet—and that of Mrs. Hurst, though she was less overt—had an ulterior motive. She had seen Miss Bennet as a possible impediment to her grand plan of marrying Bingley to an heiress to improve her position in society. And now, she was using a potential acquaintance with Miss Bennet as a means to discover something which would make her objectionable, something she could use to persuade her brother against her.

There were plenty of things, Darcy thought to himself, for her, if not for Bingley. The Bennet daughters had little enough of dowry, it was true, and they had little to no connections of society, though Darcy was intrigued by Elizabeth's account of the Gardiners. Had Darcy thought Bingley cared at all of such matters, he would have warned his friend away earlier. But Bingley was his own man, able to make his own decisions, regardless of Darcy's concern for his friend's constancy. Darcy knew he valued a connection with a potential wife more than anything else.

"I see my wife and her sister are at it again," said a voice by his side.

Darcy turned to the side to see Hurst standing there, a cup of punch held negligently in one hand. The man was watching the two women speaking to Miss Bennet, and Darcy could see the sardonic amusement he held for them.

"You would never know they are daughters of a tradesman, the way they act. Caroline leads, and Louisa follows—it has always been thus."

"If you are so contemptuous of them, I wonder why you married Mrs. Hurst."

Hurst responded with a self-deprecating chuckle. "I needed the infusion of Louisa's dowry to help return my estate to prosperity. My father drained us quite significantly. Otherwise, I might have just found some young thing like Miss Bennet. Now there is a handsome woman. I am not surprised Bingley has become enamored of her."

When Darcy gave him a skeptical look, Hurst only shook his head. "I know what you are thinking, Darcy. You are correct: I am not the most diligent manager of my estate. But neither am I a spendthrift, as my father was. We will do well enough now that we are back on firm footing. *If* Louisa will ever give me a son, I will be proud to pass it down to him."

Hurst drained his cup and went searching for another. It was then that Darcy noticed that Miss Bingley had detached herself from Miss Bennet and her sister and was approaching him. Inwardly sighing, for he recognized that determined and disgusted expression with which her gaze roved the room, Darcy braced himself for the cutting poison of her wit.

"I do say, Mr. Darcy," said she when she was close enough to speak quietly, "that I am rather surprised at you."

"In what way, Miss Bingley?"

She gestured to where Georgiana was speaking with animation to Elizabeth. The sight warmed his heart, for the weeks before they had come to Hertfordshire had been trying to say the least. Elizabeth was good for his only sister, Darcy decided — she had a way of bringing the best out in her.

"Why, that you are allowing her to speak with such people as we find here. I should have thought you wished her to be protected against those who would seek to use her to raise themselves in society."

Such as you? thought Darcy. Out loud, he said: "The Bennets are respectable members of society, Miss Bingley. In fact —"

Once again it appeared she was not listening, for she said: "There is no one to overhear our conversation, Mr. Darcy, so you need not be circumspect. Miss Elizabeth is not Georgiana's level of society. Perhaps it would be best if you redirected her toward me, for you would not wish her to associate with disreputable individuals."

"Miss Bingley," said Darcy, his patience exhausted, "I am afraid that associating with Miss Elizabeth is inevitable. You see, I have made her an offer. She is Georgiana's future sister."

CHAPTER IX

Contrary to Elizabeth's determination to watch Miss Bingley carefully, she became immersed in her conversation with Georgiana. She was a delightful girl, intelligent and kind. It required a little patience to unearth her ability to converse under her shyness, but the effort was well worth it in the end. Elizabeth did not think the likes of Miss Bingley had ever taken the time to come to know the true Georgiana. More was the pity for her.

When they had been speaking for some time, however, Elizabeth happened to glance to the side where Miss Bingley was standing not far distant from them. What she saw surprised her, for Elizabeth could almost fancy she could see daggers emerging from the woman's eyes, impaling Elizabeth where she stood. It seemed the communication had been made.

Miss Bingley, for her part, realized Elizabeth had noticed her scowl, for she approached them, an entirely feigned expression of friendship for Georgiana. Elizabeth, she ignored.

"My dear Georgiana!" exclaimed she. "We have not spoken of your recent lessons with your pianoforte master since our arrival in Hertfordshire. Shall we not do so now? I have a great interest in your exploits for as exquisite as your playing was the last time we met, I can only assume it is so much more beautiful now."

Georgiana glanced at her, and Elizabeth thought she was trying desperately to avoid rolling her eyes. Miss Bingley might have been successful in diverting the young girl's attention. But the woman grasped Georgiana's arm and attempted to pull her away. Instant annoyance swept over the girl's countenance, and she pulled her arm away from the harpy's grasp. Miss Bingley's shock suggested she had expected Georgiana to meekly follow her.

"I would be happy to speak with you, Miss Bingley," said Georgiana in a firm voice. "At present, however, I am speaking with my brother's *betrothed,* and I prefer to continue our conversation."

Elizabeth knew that Miss Bingley had been informed of the betrothal, but she was not certain Georgiana had. Fortunately, the woman did not make a scene. Instead, she focused her considerable displeasure upon Elizabeth.

"Yes, I had heard of that development. I commend you, Miss Elizabeth, for succeeding where many others have failed. You must share your secret with me, for I am afire with curiosity."

It did not escape Elizabeth's attention that the woman inferred something deceitful. Georgiana stiffened in affront, and Elizabeth was certain she was about to say something impolitic. Thus, she hurried to respond.

"There is no secret, Miss Bingley. In fact, my engagement with Mr. Darcy was driven by nothing more than unalloyed inclination. I, you see, vowed to never marry, if I could not find such a situation. I am fortunate, indeed, that I have found a man who fit my requirements."

An elegant eyebrow rose at Elizabeth's statement. "What . . . quaint notions you possess, Miss Bennet."

"It is fortunate for me that Mr. Darcy possesses the same quaint notions, is it not?"

It appeared she struck a nerve for Miss Bingley was silent for a moment, eventually responding with a curt "Quite." But she soon excused herself, much to Elizabeth's relief. In the next moment, however, she found that she was annoyed with Miss Bingley all over again.

"Come, Charles," the woman said, heading directly to where her brother was speaking with Jane. "I require you to attend me."

Mr. Bingley's initial surprise was unmistakable. But he realized her game quite quickly, to his credit. His response further endeared him to Elizabeth and gave her greater hope of his constancy.

"I am sorry, Caroline, but is this an emergency?" Miss Bingley gaped at him. "From your response, I shall assume it is not. As you can see, I am speaking with Miss Bennet at present. I shall attend you when we have completed our discussion."

Then he, quite deliberately, turned away from his sister, leaving her gaping at his back. She huffed and seemed ready to make a scene, but in the end, her sense of discretion returned, and she stalked away. Soon, she was ensconced with her sister on a sofa in the sitting-room, speaking in low tones. Their countenances gave them away as unhappy with what they surveyed, and their looks at both Jane and Elizabeth were filled with all sorts of dark undertones.

Elizabeth sighed. "It seems I have made an enemy tonight, Georgiana."

"Did you expect anything else?" asked Georgiana.

A laugh escaped Elizabeth's lips. "No, I suppose you are correct. It was inevitable, was it not?"

"I dare say it was. But I can forgive her anger, as I am quite happy that she did not manage to capture my brother."

"I can certainly agree with you," said William as he walked up to them. "It seems I have missed some excitement?"

"You have, indeed, William," said Elizabeth, welcoming her betrothed with a smile while he grasped her hand. She was pleased when he did not relinquish it as might have been proper, holding it in a manner which would not be seen by those in attendance. "In fact, Miss Bingley is quite put out with the eldest Bennet sisters. While I care not on my own account, I wonder how much influence she has over her brother."

William's snort answered Elizabeth's question, but then he spoke up to clarify. "Not as much as she supposes. Bingley will listen to her and will not disagree openly, as he abhors confrontation of any sort. But I have never known him to be persuaded from his course by the efforts of his sisters."

"Then let us forget about them for the present. I would not belabor such an objectionable subject when there are much more pleasant matters of which to speak."

Mr. Darcy smiled. "I cannot agree more.

A little later, as was common at these gatherings, the pianoforte was opened, and Mary, who loved nothing more than to display her talents, sat down to play. This lasted for some time until some of the younger members of the party begged her to play so they could dance. Mary agreed, though not without reluctance, and soon a small line had formed to one side of the room.

"Miss Elizabeth," said William, who was standing by her side. "It has occurred to me that though we are now engaged, I have never had the pleasure of dancing with you. Will you accept my hand for this dance?"

Elizabeth turned a look on him which prompted a grin when he recognized it as mischievous. "Are you certain that an impromptu dance, which is likely to be little more than prancing about, will not affect your dignity?"

"My dignity is quite intact, my dearest Elizabeth," replied William. "I have danced in situations of far less formality than this."

"In that case, I would be happy to dance with you."

When William grasped her hand and led her to the other dancers, Elizabeth was thrilled at the way he possessed it, as if he never meant to let go. The heady feelings of newfound love and devotion swept through her and she squeezed his hand, about the only show of affection she could indulge in while in company. A fleeting smile curved the corners of William's lips as he returned the gesture.

When they took their places, they found they were flanked at the end of the line by Mr. Bingley and Jane. Though Jane was as demure as ever—Elizabeth, of course, could see through her sister and recognize her pleasure and excitement—Mr. Bingley was grinning openly. His sister's ill humor had not affected him in any way, it seemed.

The dance proceeded much as such activities usually did in such a location, and there was much laughter among the company and more than a little silliness from some of the younger dancers. Elizabeth and William were amused at their antics, but their attention was largely fixed on each other. As first dances go, it was more lighthearted than the quadrille, but that did not make it any less precious as memories for Elizabeth.

"It seems there is *someone* who does not believe my dignity has survived this evening," said William in a low voice to Elizabeth not long after they began.

Though she already knew who it was, Elizabeth managed to catch sight of Miss Bingley during the next pass, and she noted the utter shock with which the woman was watching them. Then she noticed Elizabeth's gaze and scowled pure poison. Then she was gone, no doubt to sit with her sister and increase each other's disgust by complaining about their present circumstances.

"I suppose she has never seen you in this attitude, William," said Elizabeth when she came close to her fiancé again.

"She has never seen me in many attitudes," replied William. "I rarely let my guard down to this extent in her presence. Besides, given my position in society, she likely has certain expectations, the majority of which are incorrect."

"But she has been taught at an expensive seminary, has she not?" asked Elizabeth.

"And she is very proud of it too."

Elizabeth laughed at his tone and then shook her head. "I do not wish to speak of Miss Bingley, William. Let us enjoy this evening without the specter of the woman hanging over us."

"I could not agree more."

For the rest of the evening, they ignored the presence of the woman, if she was close, and avoided all mention of her. After the first dance, they exchanged partners, Elizabeth dancing with Mr. Bingley while Jane paired with William. After these two dances, they stood nearby for the most part, watching as the younger members of the party amused themselves. Mary played for some time, and when she grew tired, Elizabeth took her place at the pianoforte. Before she left him, however, she directed a pointed look at William, saying:

"Can I persuade you to dance with Mary? She rarely is solicited as a dance partner."

"Of course, I will," replied William. "Though I will say it might help if she showed a more willing countenance to the company."

Elizabeth laughed, glancing at Mary, noting her typical disapproval plain for them all to see. "I dare say she might."

Soon Elizabeth had all the pleasure of seeing Mary start with surprise at the application. But while she looked at Elizabeth, her suspicion evident, she did not protest, and soon she was dancing with Elizabeth's tall fiancé.

The dancing continued for some time after, Elizabeth dutifully playing for the company. While Miss Bingley kept her distance, Elizabeth did see her watching at times, the disgust she felt for the company and the disbelief at Mr. Darcy's behavior an almost physical entity. When she glanced at Elizabeth herself, it was clear she did not think much of Elizabeth's talents, a matter for which Elizabeth was not concerned in the slightest. She imagined there would be some unpleasantness when William returned to Netherfield, but she possessed supreme confidence in his ability to manage Miss Bingley's tantrums.

The only part of the evening which surprised Darcy was the fact that

Miss Bingley was able to hold her temper until after their arrival at Netherfield. Though Bingley chatted on about the pleasure he had found in the company—while he did not mention Miss Bennet by name, it was clear his thoughts were primarily of her—Miss Bingley said little, though what she did say was delivered with caustic connotations. Darcy contented himself with watching her, knowing she would have her say at some time or another. Had Elizabeth been present to witness the scene, she would have been proud of her ability to predict Miss Bingley's actions with amazing accuracy.

"I shall have a tea service delivered to the sitting-room," said she when they had entered the vestibule. "Perhaps a little conversation before we retire will be welcome."

While Darcy and Georgiana shared a look, knowing what the other was thinking, Darcy decided it would be churlish to refuse, though he wished for nothing more than to seek his bed. It was likely best to face the ordeal at once so that the woman would cease importuning him.

"You know this is not likely to deter her," said Georgiana in a soft voice as they made their way toward the sitting-room.

"No," replied Darcy. "But she will at least understand my feelings on the matter. If she wishes to waste her time continuing to importune me, then I can do nothing to prevent her. As long as she does not attempt to denigrate Elizabeth, I will be content."

Unfortunately, maligning Elizabeth was exactly what the woman had in mind, and she began to speak almost as soon as they had entered the room. It did not take long for Darcy's anger to build.

"Well, I suppose this evening was . . . interesting."

Miss Bingley had taken a high-backed chair which was flanked by two sofas, which Bingley, the Hursts, and the Darcys settled themselves on. Darcy was certain this was by design—it was so like Aunt Catherine, he might have laughed had he not already been preparing himself for the worst.

"Unfortunately," continued she, "my expectations of the company were met in every particular. There is not a hint of fashionable manners among them, and their noise and uncouthness is beyond appalling. Imagine! An impromptu dance where the locals cavort in unseemly cacophony. How is it to be borne?"

There was little to be said, and Darcy determined not to say it. Bingley, though his harsh glare at his sister showed his anger, also kept his peace. Instead, Bingley walked to a sideboard and poured three measures of brandy, returning with one each for Hurst and Darcy. Hurst accepted his, the sardonic grin with which he favored his sister-in-law not hidden in the slightest. Darcy sipped his, knowing he would require the fortification. Miss Bingley only watched her brother's actions with disdain before she began to speak again.

"I would simply ignore them. But it seems you have been infected with their lack of modesty. It must be the fact that you have been among them these last months. To stand up in such an occasion, and with those awful Bennet sisters! I can barely comprehend how such a thing can be imagined!"

"This is not the first time we have been to a function in which there has been impromptu dancing," replied Bingley, finally, it seemed, unable to hold his temper.

As was her wont, Miss Bingley ignored him. "I suppose their improper manners, however, have had the unintended blessing of opening our eyes to their faults. I am sure you, at least, Mr. Darcy, must be regretting the alliance you have entered. Or perhaps you have been tricked into it."

Miss Bingley's eyes widened as if the thought had just come to her. Unwilling to allow her to even suggest anything further, Darcy was quick to respond.

"My reasons for proposing to Miss Elizabeth are my own. Furthermore, I saw nothing more than your brother did this evening. A few of the younger members of the party became a little too excited, perhaps, but they were quickly settled by their elders."

"Then I think you must have been bewitched by *Miss Eliza*," spat Miss Bingley. Then she looked at him, suspicion evident in her manner. "Come, sir, you have stated that you have your own reasons, but I have never been so shocked as when you told me of it. How did this engagement all come about? My understanding is that you were only here a few weeks before we came, surely not enough time for an engagement to be formalized."

"William's engagement with Elizabeth came about in the usual manner," interrupted Georgiana. "I was witness to it all, Miss Bingley. I anticipate having Elizabeth as a sister, for I do not think I could have a better one."

Though quite obviously angry, Miss Bingley mastered it and threw Georgiana a patronizing look. "I am certain it must appear that way, Georgiana dear, but women of Miss Eliza's ilk are cunning and subtle. She will bring your brother nothing but misery and regret, should this marriage proceed." Miss Bingley turned back to Darcy. "I am certain you can extricate yourself from this, sir. The Bennets are greedy enough that you could likely pay them off instead of throwing your future away on such an artful trollop."

With a shaken head and a mirthless chuckle, Darcy said: "That is nonsensical, Miss Bingley. Even if I was compromised, as you say, why would Miss Elizabeth forgo the status and wealth for a mere pittance? I *am* a wealthy man, after all."

The reminder of his position had been deliberate, if not completely gentlemanly. Miss Bingley certainly understood the point, as her expression turned sickly at the thought of that which she had never been able to obtain. But she shook off the reminder.

"I understand grasping women such as Miss Eliza. The greed which will overwhelm her at the sight of so much money will be enough to accept it." Miss Bingley sneered. "She will no doubt understand her error later, but it is nothing less than she deserves. I am certain you must agree."

"Your certainty is misplaced."

Darcy's tone provoked a gasp of surprise from the woman. He shook his head — she had always assumed he would simply fall in with her opinions just because she spoke them. She truly was an odd sort of woman.

"I will speak bluntly, Miss Bingley, so there are no misunderstandings. There was nothing underhanded in my engagement to Miss Elizabeth. I proposed, and she accepted, and I did so because I wish to have her for my wife. Nothing less than inclination prompted my actions. Furthermore, as a man, I may not — under any circumstances — break off an engagement. If I were to do so, the scandal would be such that I would become unmarriageable, at least until talk of it died down. I will not do it — not to Miss Elizabeth, nor to my sister.

"Furthermore," continued he, his tone harsher, "I will hear nothing against my betrothed, from you or anyone else. If you find this neighborhood is not to your taste, then I recommend you return to London, or wherever the Hursts wish to go next. I am quite comfortable here, and Georgiana has made several friends. We will not depart as long as your brother will have us."

"You are welcome to stay as long as you wish," said Bingley. "I find I am fond of this neighborhood as well, and I have no intention of departing."

"Oh, I would not think of leaving," interjected Hurst. "I am certain our residence here will be quite amusing, indeed."

While Darcy did not truly appreciate Hurst's sense of humor, he could see Miss Bingley was on the edge of delivering a stinging retort.

He would not allow it, for he had no wish of listening to her continuing disparagement of Elizabeth.

"Please desist, Miss Bingley. I have no wish to discuss this. If you feel some measure of disappointment because of my choice, I apologize. I will, however, remind you that I never gave you any reason to hope for anything else."

"Of course, I will not speak of your betrothal any further," said Miss Bingley. "You are, of course, free to act in whatever manner you see fit."

The sickening sweetness of her false smile masked undertones of rage, and poorly at that. Her insinuation that he was making a terrible mistake he ignored completely. But for the moment, Darcy decided to be content.

"But I think it may be time for us to depart and return to London," continued Miss Bingley, turning her attention on her brother. "Mr. Darcy may do whatever he sees fit, and his reputation will not suffer much. But for the Bingley family, it would not do to continue to keep such company."

"And what company is that, Caroline?" asked Bingley. Darcy peered at his friend, noting Bingley's barely concealed anger. Seeing him in such a state was rare, indeed, for Bingley was more apt to avoid any hint of disagreement.

"Why, the Bennets and others of their ilk who inhabit this neighborhood. If you continue to pay Miss Jane Bennet such attention, it will raise her expectations, which have already been increased by her sister's . . . good fortune." Her glance at Darcy left no one in any doubt of her meaning. "As we are still establishing ourselves in society, it is imperative you choose properly. Miss Bennet is a handsome girl to be sure, but that is her only virtue, and I am absolutely certain she has a mere pittance for a dowry."

The look with which Bingley regarded his sister was amused. "You may be correct as to their dowries, Caroline. I cannot say, for I have not been so gauche as to ask about them. But you are entirely incorrect about Miss Bennet's connections."

"Oh?" asked Miss Bingley. "Has she an uncle who keeps a shop in Cheapside? Or perhaps she is connected to a parson of a small parish, for I cannot imagine she has any connection *we* would know."

"In fact, she does — or she soon will." Bingley stood and drained his glass, setting it down on a side table. "You see, her sister will soon marry Fitzwilliam Darcy, and thus, she will be Darcy's sister. I know of no one in town who would discount such a connection or declare it unsuitable."

With those words, Bingley excused himself and left the room, leaving his sister fuming where she sat. Knowing another outburst was imminent, Darcy also rose and excused himself and Georgiana, leaving with what he felt was an almost unseemly haste. They managed to walk almost to the end of the hall before Georgiana finally lost the battle to restrain her mirth.

"Did you see the look on Miss Bingley's face, Brother?" asked she amid her hiccupping laughter. "I thought she would expire when her brother reminded her of Miss Bennet's future connections."

"I did, for I was busy watching the snake," replied Darcy, chuckling along with her. "I thought at some point she would transform in front of us, revealing venom-coated fangs."

"She *was* angry," said Georgiana, her laughter giving way to concern. "We will need to take care, William. She will be desperate now."

"I will take care, Georgiana. But I do not think it likely she will try anything. She is aware of my inability to break off my engagement. She has a supreme confidence in her own abilities and an arrogance which leads her to believe she cannot fail."

"I hope you are correct, William. I hope so, very much."

Later that evening, Georgiana's apprehensions were put to the test when the Bingley sisters gathered in the younger sister's room to discuss the events of the evening. Caroline Bingley was a woman who was not accustomed to disappointment. She had firmly believed she was destined to marry Fitzwilliam Darcy, and the news of his engagement had filled her with a rage which could not be dispelled.

"How dare that trollop steal my future husband!" cried she as she stalked the sitting-room of her suite. Caroline felt the urge to throw things about the room, vent her rage and frustration on what was on hand since she could not reach the one who truly deserved her bile. But Caroline Bingley was a lady, and a lady she would remain. She would not resort to such gauche acts as if she were a commoner.

"It is beyond belief," lamented Louisa, who was with her. "I cannot imagine what Mr. Darcy was thinking. I was certain you were so close to obtaining him for a husband."

"This is all Charles's fault! If he had informed us of Mr. Darcy's presence, we could have come at once and prevented it. Now it is a disaster: Mr. Darcy has been caught by that scheming adventuress and her elder sister has her claws sunk into our brother.

"Well, I, for one, will not allow this to stand. I will not be defeated by the likes of those inferior Bennets."

"Oh, Caroline," said Louisa, "do not do anything foolish. Mr. Darcy is correct—he is engaged, and there is nothing to be done."

While Caroline had wondered if that was the truth, she was forced to agree with Louisa's assertion. At least for now. Perhaps something would present itself. But since Louisa was the naturally more hesitant of them, Caroline decided she would not speak of that.

"There is no engagement between Charles and Miss Bennet. And there never will be. We will make certain of it."

"What do you mean to do?"

Caroline shook her head. "I do not know yet. But I will not give up. It is still important for Charles to marry an heiress, and I will do anything to ensure he does. And you will help me."

"Of course," replied Louisa. "I shall consider the matter and let you know if anything comes to mind."

As Louisa departed the room, Caroline watched her go. Louisa was a good sister and a willing confederate, but she had always followed Caroline's lead, rarely contributing her own designs. But she thought in a similar manner as Caroline, and she always did as she was asked without complaint. It was enough.

But Caroline would not give up. Charles would not marry Miss Bennet, and if there was anything to be done about Mr. Darcy's engagement, she would do it. Caroline Bingley would not be defeated!

CHAPTER X

*M*iss Caroline Bingley was a woman who was used to having her own way. While she was naught but the daughter of a tradesman—a fact which she assiduously attempted to forget, desirous as she was to inhabit the first circles—she had been, as the youngest, indulged with everything she desired, cooed and exclaimed over as the prettiest, and able to obtain anything she wanted due to the family wealth. Since her father's demise, her influence over her brother and his preference for avoiding conflict had resulted in his giving in to her demands with little question or hesitation. All these advantages had given her a sense of entitlement, leading her to believe anything she wanted was hers by right.

The night at Lucas Lodge and subsequent discussion at Netherfield after had badly disturbed her equilibrium. It was true she had not managed to induce a proposal from Mr. Darcy, but she had always known it was a matter of time. When he told her he was engaged, she had disbelieved at first, until his familiarity with the hussy had convinced her it was the truth. The knowledge had stung, provoking disappointment like she had never experienced.

But Charles's defiance was the greater of the two shocks, even though Mr. Darcy had been her path to everything for which she had ever wished. Mild-mannered Charles had been so easily led, so simple to control, that she could hardly recognize her brother. Though he did not realize it, Caroline had been how some of his infatuations had ended prematurely, when she had not approved of the woman. He was so eager to move on to the next pretty face, that he had been easy to manipulate. A part of Caroline thought this time would be the same, but a sliver of doubt had entered her mind, lodged there by his defiance the previous evening. She was still confident in her success, but she knew it might not be as easy this time.

Unfortunately, when she met Louisa that morning, she learned her usual confederate would be denied her. Not for the first time, she wished she had been blessed with a more cunning sister.

"Hurst has forbidden me from attempting to dissuade Charles," said Louisa, almost the first words out of her mouth.

"Why should he concern himself?" demanded Caroline.

"I do not know," replied Louisa. "But he informed me that Charles is his own man and able to make his own decisions. I am not to attempt to persuade him."

"He just wants a closer connection with Mr. Darcy," sneered Caroline. "Or more precisely, with Pemberley's wine cellar."

"Possibly," agreed Louisa, "though it may also be because of his twisted sense of humor. I have no choice, Caroline."

Though she wished to tell the drunken sod what she thought of him, Caroline was forced to agree. While Hurst was not of the first circles himself, he was, at present, their only entry into gentle society at all. Thus, prudence was the order of the day.

"I understand, Louisa. Leave it to me."

The sense of relief in Louisa's face was not to be mistaken, and Caroline smiled at her, attempting to put her at ease. Caroline could very well execute her plans by herself. But first, she would need to endure the indignity of a visit from those artful Bennets, for they arrived at Netherfield that morning, looking for all the world like the greedy, grasping supplicants she knew they were. How was this to be endured?

Elizabeth had been of two minds concerning the proposal to visit Netherfield the morning after the assembly. But as her mother would not hear of anything else, to Netherfield they were to go.

"Perhaps it is best to refrain," argued Elizabeth when her mother suggested it. "We were all late returning home last night, and I am sure they will wish for solitude to rest."

"Nonsense," said Mrs. Bennet. "I am certain elegant ladies such as Mrs. Hurst and Miss Bingley must expect good manners from their neighbors. Besides, you will see your Mr. Darcy, and Jane will once again be in company with Mr. Bingley."

Mrs. Bennet's eyes lit up at her own mention of their neighbor of the last two months. "I have never seen such a promising inclination as his for our Jane." Mrs. Bennet paused and directed an apologetic smile at Elizabeth. "Other than Mr. Darcy's for you, of course. But I am confident that if he should only be in Jane's company, Mr. Bingley will fall in love with her and propose.

"Two daughters married!" cried Mrs. Bennet, falling back against her chair and fanning herself. "I am certain I shall go distracted!"

It was the fact that Elizabeth agreed with her mother concerning Jane and Mr. Bingley that prompted her to relent. Of course, her desire to see William again was no small part of it. Soon, the Bennet ladies had entered the coach, and they made the short journey to Netherfield. Unfortunately, they were not to see the gentlemen.

When they were led into the sitting-room, they were greeted by Mrs. Hurst, Miss Bingley, and Georgiana, though greeted might be considered a strong word. Georgiana was, of course, happy to see them, welcoming Elizabeth with enthusiasm, not the least of which, Elizabeth thought, was because she had been alone with the two harpies. Mrs. Hurst was distant, but she at least showed herself to be well-bred when she greeted them with composure, if not enthusiasm. From Miss Bingley, they had little more than contempt, though she managed a short and unintelligible word in greeting.

It was Mrs. Hurst who sent for tea, though Elizabeth knew it was Miss Bingley who was Mr. Bingley's hostess. It seemed the woman was not interested in paying them even a hint of civility. Elizabeth decided at once that she was not about to concern herself with the woman's ill humors. Consequently, she sat down with Georgiana to begin speaking with her future sister, while Mary, Jane, and her mother took seats closer to the Bingley sisters.

"I am happy you are here, Elizabeth," said Georgiana, speaking softly, almost as soon as she was seated.

"Have they been difficult?"

"Mrs. Hurst usually does not say much," replied Georgiana. "But Miss Bingley . . ."

The girl shot a look at Miss Bingley, who was staring at them, not a hint of friendship in her eyes or posture. Though the woman surely knew they were speaking of her, Georgiana turned her attention back to Elizabeth and blithely spoke of the woman as if she was not there.

"This morning she has been behaving much as she ever has to me." The girl snorted. "In other words, she flatters and simpers and attempts to ingratiate herself with me, all the while speaking in patronizing tones and claiming that I am too young to understand certain matters."

"And has she made any specific comments?" asked Elizabeth, knowing the woman had almost certainly had choice words to say about her engagement to William.

"Not this morning, though she has spoken of helping me make my way in society and protecting myself from the unworthy. Last night, however, she actually attempted to convince William it would be best to break off his engagement to you. She is also no friend to her brother's interest in Jane."

Elizabeth could not help but shake her head, a movement which produced a scowl from Miss Bingley. "She almost seems delusional. Does she not understand what would happen if William were to break our engagement?"

"She is blind. She sees only what she wishes to see. She has convinced herself that in a society such as this, there would be little consequence."

"She *is* delusional," said Elizabeth.

"I dare say she is. But William put her in her place, though I think we will need to take care when he is in her company."

"That is likely for the best." Elizabeth paused and glanced about the room. "Where is William? I cannot imagine he would have left you to the sisters' tender mercies willingly."

Georgiana giggled. "Some matter of one of the tenants arose, and William accompanied Mr. Bingley when he departed. Mr. Hurst returned to his rooms after breakfast. I would have had Mrs. Annesley for company, but she was feeling ill this morning, and she also returned to her room."

"Poor Georgiana," said Elizabeth. "You have been left to fend for yourself. I shall provide you with relief, but alas, I can only stay for thirty minutes!"

"Even that would be welcome. When you and your family depart, I think I shall also take myself to my room."

Elizabeth nodded, knowing it was likely for the best. For the balance of the visit, Elizabeth remained with Georgiana, and neither gave the objectionable presence of Miss Bingley any further notice. Mary eventually joined them, and as she and Georgiana were friendly, due to their shared love of music, the girls greeted each other with enthusiasm. Soon, Georgiana drew Mary to the nearby pianoforte to show her some music she had purchased only a few days before in Meryton.

As she was interested herself, Elizabeth rose along with them, but before she could proceed to the instrument, she was confronted by none other than Miss Bingley. The woman seemed determined to provoke an argument, but Elizabeth, knowing it would do no good, was less interested in defending herself. The woman's first words, however, changed her mind.

"You must be proud of yourself, Miss Eliza."

"I am not sure to what you refer," replied Elizabeth. "And I would appreciate it if you did not use that moniker—my name is Elizabeth."

Miss Bingley sneered and leaned in to speak a little more softly. "You are well aware of my meaning. Do not try to deny it. You have somehow managed to pass yourself off as a woman of quality. But I know the truth."

"You do?" asked Elizabeth, disdain for this harpy welling up within her. "I am sorry, Miss Bingley, but I believe we have just met for the first time last night. As such, you cannot know anything about me."

"Of course, I do," snapped Miss Bingley. "I have seen your kind many times before. Raised in squalor and intent upon rising up from your insignificant beginnings, you pass yourself off as something you can never be."

"I suppose you would know about this," said Elizabeth, injecting every bit of scorn she could in her voice. "After all, you were born the daughter of a tradesman. Is that not what you have been attempting to do since making William's acquaintance?"

Though her eyes blazed with affront, Miss Bingley held tightly to her composure. "I will not be drawn into an exchange of words with the likes of you."

"It seems to me you *initiated* this exchange of words. If you will allow me to pass so that I may join my sister and Georgiana at the pianoforte, we may put this unpleasantness behind us."

"I am not finished with you." Miss Bingley leaned in closer. "I do not mean to allow you your victory, Miss *Eliza*. You may think you have won, but I assure you that you have not. I will know what is to be done."

"You mean to interfere with our engagement? We have both done no more than exercise our own free wills. The announcements have been made and the articles signed. I welcome you to try, Miss Bingley. There is nothing you can do to break us apart."

The way the woman stared at her, Elizabeth wondered if she truly had some thought of attempting to pull them apart. Surely, she could not be so foolhardy.

"It is futile to attempt to reason with you," said Miss Bingley after a moment. "I have no wish to speak with a witless worm. Only remember, little Eliza, that I am not accustomed to being bested by the likes of you."

The woman turned on her heel and stalked away, leaving Elizabeth watching her retreating back, pensive thoughts of Miss Bingley embarrassing herself and, consequently, her brother, working their way through her mind. It was true that having such a harpy of a sister was a point against Mr. Bingley, making Elizabeth wonder if it was in Jane's best interests to make a match with him. But while Elizabeth worried for her sister's future happiness, her larger concern was for Mr. Bingley, of whom she thought very highly.

In the end, she sighed and made her way to the pianoforte to join Georgiana and Mary. If Miss Bingley was determined to make herself foolish, there was nothing Elizabeth could do about it. Perhaps Mr. Bingley could control her behavior. If he could not, Elizabeth was forced to acknowledge that any embarrassment would be on his head as well.

"I saw Miss Bingley approach you," said Georgiana as Elizabeth moved a chair near the pianoforte. "I suppose it was not to exchange pleasantries."

Mindful of Mary, who sat nearby playing, but listening to every word they said, Elizabeth replied: "She had little to say which anyone would wish to hear. I do not think it bears repeating."

Mary listened with wide eyes, even while she continued playing the piece Georgiana was showing her. Georgiana, however, understood Elizabeth's inference of not wishing to speak further of Miss Bingley and allowed the subject to drop. The rest of the visit was spent with the two younger girls and blessedly free of Miss Bingley's contempt.

While Elizabeth had avoided any further conflict with Miss Bingley while at Netherfield, her short discussion with Miss Bingley had not gone unnoticed by the rest of her family. She had hoped it would have appeared unremarkable, like a short exchange of pleasantries between two women who were not well acquainted. But sadly, it was not to be, for as soon as they entered the carriage, her mother directed a pointed look at Elizabeth.

"What were you thinking, Lizzy?"

Nonplused, Elizabeth stared at her mother. "What do you mean, Mama?"

Mrs. Bennet's returning glare was fierce. "Do not claim a lack of understanding, Lizzy, for I will not have it. I clearly saw your conversation with Miss Bingley, and I could see that it was not cordial. You have obtained your happiness — I will not now have you interfere with Jane's."

Elizabeth gaped at her mother. "You saw what you believe to be a confrontation between your daughter and Miss Bingley, and you immediately assume that it was *I* who was at fault?"

A rosy glow came over Mrs. Bennet's cheeks, and she stammered for a moment. For her part, Elizabeth was not amused. She had long known that she was her mother's least favorite daughter, and a month as her darling, due to her engagement with Mr. Darcy, had not erased the memory of her mother's disapprobation.

"I am sorry, Lizzy," said Mrs. Bennet after a moment. "It is just . . . Well . . . You have always possessed such a quick tongue. I thought you said something impertinent to Miss Bingley and she reacted accordingly."

"Mama," said Elizabeth, praying for patience, "I would never endeavor to ruin Jane's happiness. Though I do say things, at times, which you think I should not, I am always aware of when I should speak and when I should not.

"And did it escape your attention that it was *Miss Bingley* who approached *me*, rather than the reverse?"

"Are you suggesting that Miss Bingley said something offensive to you?" demanded Mrs. Bennet.

At once Elizabeth wished she had not been quite so open. Regardless of her mother's censure at various times, Mrs. Bennet was a fierce mother bear protecting her cubs at any sign of real or perceived criticism. She would not put it past Mrs. Bennet to attempt to call Miss Bingley to account for such a slight, which was something Elizabeth was eager to avoid.

"We did exchange some words, Mama," said Elizabeth, intentionally downplaying the conversation. "I think Miss Bingley and I did not begin our acquaintance on the best foot, and as such, she does not find me much to her taste."

Jane frowned as Elizabeth was speaking. "She did seem to be a little aloof."

"That she did," said Mrs. Bennet, still clearly not understanding, which was what Elizabeth wished.

"She was not aloof," said Mary, her words coming out in a rush, as if she could not hold them in any longer. "She was unkind and jealous."

Mrs. Bennet gasped and gaped at Mary, while Jane frowned. Elizabeth, however, shook her head at Mary, asking her silently to allow the matter to pass.

"No, Lizzy," said Mary with shaken head, "I will not allow Mama to censure you when you have done nothing wrong. It is best that Mama and Jane understand exactly what kind of woman Miss Bingley is."

Then without waiting for Elizabeth's response, Mary turned back to her mother. "I spoke with Miss Darcy a little while we were sitting at the pianoforte. Miss Bingley has wished to be Mrs. Darcy since she first made his acquaintance four years ago."

Shocked, Mrs. Bennet turned to Elizabeth and demanded: "Is this true?"

With a sigh, Elizabeth nodded, reflecting that Mary might be correct. "It is, Mama. She is disappointed that Mr. Darcy is no longer within her reach. The short conversation we had today was not the only time we have exchanged words. She was no friendlier last night than she was this morning."

"And did Mr. Darcy give her any encouragement?" demanded Mrs. Bennet.

"No, he did not. But that has not had any effect on Miss Bingley."

"Well, your engagement now must have an effect on the woman," declared Mrs. Bennet, looking at once smug and assured. "There is little she can do but focus on some other gentleman now that he is no longer available."

Elizabeth sighed. "Of course, you are correct. But I suspect she is not content to simply give up and depart, and I am certain she is no friend to Mr. Bingley's attentions to Jane."

Again, shock colored Mrs. Bennet's features. "Surely you are mistaken."

"She all but told me, Mama. It is clear from her words today, to her behavior last night, Miss Bingley considers herself to be quite above us. Everyone in Meryton is insignificant, and no one can meet her standards of gentility and breeding."

The insult Mrs. Bennet felt was well beyond anything Elizabeth had ever witnessed. "How dare she? Is she not the daughter of a tradesman? Who is she to think herself above the daughters of a gentleman?"

"She is a woman who has benefited from her father's wealth," replied Elizabeth. "She possesses a fine dowry, has attended a seminary, and furthermore, has a brother who was befriended by a member of the first circles in Mr. Darcy. All these advantages have induced her to think very well of herself."

"Then she is a fool," snapped Mrs. Bennet. "She may have the benefit of wealth, but her origins are decidedly common. You girls all know *I* was not born to a gentleman, but at least I am the daughter of a solicitor, which is an honorable profession, and am descended from gentle stock. I cannot begin to fathom such willful blindness as this woman has shown. I have half a mind to inform her exactly what I think of her."

"I beg you do not," said Elizabeth at once, desperate to stop her mother from making a scene. "There is little reason, for our words will not change the woman she is. Furthermore, there are other considerations, not the least of which is the fact that Mr. Bingley is a very good man, regardless of *his* origins."

It seemed Mrs. Bennet understood the hint at once, for her eyes darted to Jane, who was watching them all with no little astonishment. For a moment, Elizabeth thought her mother would still insist, despite Elizabeth's words. In the end, however, she responded with a curt nod.

"Perhaps you are correct, Lizzy. Though this woman's behavior offends me, I shall ignore it. Perhaps she will improve with time."

Mary's snort of disbelief mirrored Elizabeth's own feelings on the matter. It was not, however, quite resolved with that.

"Perhaps there is some misunderstanding," said Jane, speaking for the first time. She was wringing her hands, her voice pleading. Jane had ever seen the best in others—her distress upon hearing the truth about Miss Bingley was nothing Elizabeth had not seen before.

"I am sorry, Jane," replied Elizabeth, grasping her sister's hand in compassion. "But there is no mistake. I have not only William and Georgiana's account, but the woman's own words convict her."

"But he is such a good man!" Jane's words were practically wailed.

"Perhaps Mr. Bingley's attentions are not so good for our Jane," said Mrs. Bennet. Jane only looked at her, wide-eyed and fearful.

"Mama," said Elizabeth, "I have never seen such a promising inclination as that Mr. Bingley shows to Jane. While I would not, at this early juncture, expect more from Mr. Bingley than he is willing to give, *should* he propose to Jane, she would be marrying *him*, not his sister. Mr. Bingley is of a pleasant disposition, but I cannot imagine he would allow his sister any disparagement of his wife."

Mrs. Bennet seemed pensive for a moment before she nodded slowly. "I suppose you must be correct, Lizzy. He *is* a good man, and we would not wish to paint him with the same brush as his sister. Perhaps it is best to simply allow matters to evolve as they will."

"I could not agree more."

The rest of the journey to Longbourn was passed in silence. Though she had wished to avoid the conversation altogether, Elizabeth supposed it was best that Mary had forced it, for they all knew to be on their guard with respect to Miss Bingley. Mary appeared a little smug—which was unusual, as she tended more toward strictly upright behavior—while Mrs. Bennet was contemplative. It was clear Jane was still distressed. Elizabeth knew it likely Jane would approach her again.

Her supposition was proven correct when later that evening, as Elizabeth was preparing for bed, her sister knocked on her door and entered the room at Elizabeth's call. Noting Jane's mood throughout the day, she was not surprised to see her sister looking at her with more than a hint of consternation.

"What do you think I should do with respect to Miss Bingley?"

Elizabeth beckoned Jane to sit beside her, which her sister did without hesitation. "I think there is little you can do other than accept any overtures she might offer. There is no reason to shun her, even if I do expect her to behave badly."

"You will not tease or vex her, will you Lizzy?"

A laugh escaped at Jane's plea, at which her countenance grew darker. "No, I have no intention of it. I suspect Miss Bingley will give me a wide berth, and I have no desire to hear her continue to disparage my family and friends.

"Feel free to continue to act in a friendly manner with her, Jane. But do not let your guard down. I know you wish to believe the best of her, but she is no friend to you. She means to do everything in her power to interfere with your relationship with her brother and, if she can, to interfere with my engagement."

"But, Lizzy, that is not sensible. She must understand there is nothing she can do about your engagement."

"I am sure she must. But she is angry and disappointed, and those who feel as she does are rarely rational. But do not worry for me—I fear nothing she can do. It is best you concern yourself for whatever interference she means between you and Mr. Bingley. His inclination is still in its infancy, which makes it much more vulnerable."

Jane nodded, though distracted, and after a few moments she returned to her own room. Knowing Jane as she did, Elizabeth knew that while Miss Bingley would not now be in a position to deceive Jane concerning the strength of her affection, Jane was not the kind of woman to put herself forward. She needed a champion, someone to push back at the machinations of Miss Bingley and foil her when she made her attempt. Having her sister's best interests at heart and having been Jane's advocate for years, Elizabeth knew there was no one better positioned than she to take up the role. Miss Bingley would not succeed, Elizabeth vowed. Jane would have her happiness with Mr. Bingley if that was what she desired.

CHAPTER XI

When one encounters a wild animal, it is prudent to watch it carefully. But when one has cornered a wild beast, the vigilance must be doubly increased, for it then becomes unpredictable and more dangerous. Though he knew it was not polite to think of his host's sister as a caged animal, Darcy could not help but feel that way about her.

For a time after she learned of his betrothal, Darcy had instructed his valet, Snell, to be on his guard for any plotting in which the woman might engage. He wondered if she meant to attempt a compromise, for he would not put anything past her. But a few days passed where nothing happened, and rather than attempt to flatter and ingratiate herself as she had done in the past, she remained largely aloof, watching and doing nothing. It was readily apparent that she had nothing but contempt for the Bennets, as was amply shown any time they were in company. But even so, her behavior, while not friendly, was at least acceptable.

It was the comportment of the Bennets which surprised Darcy. Elizabeth, he knew, was aware of her character and treated her accordingly. But Miss Mary watched the woman with barely concealed disgust, Miss Bennet was friendly but more reserved than even she was normally, and Mrs. Bennet, the most surprising of all, seemed to have little patience for Miss Bingley. This was odd, as he had heard the woman speak of Miss Bingley in glowing terms at least once, making it clear that she thought of Miss Bingley as a fine woman, indeed.

"My mother's eyes may have been opened," said Elizabeth when Darcy made this observance to her.

"Oh?" asked Darcy.

"Yes. You see, my mother does not take kindly to ladies of Miss Bingley's background considering themselves better than her daughters. We, after all, are daughters of a gentleman, though my father is naught but a country squire."

"I cannot but agree with her," said Darcy, considering the matter. "I *am* surprised, however, that your mother has interpreted Miss Bingley's behavior. She does not strike me as a woman who is adept at divining the intentions of others."

"No," replied Elizabeth, her eyes dancing in amusement. "But she was assisted to this conclusion. And before you ask, I was not the one who forced it."

Darcy thought for a moment. Surely Miss Bennet, as self-effacing a creature as ever existed, would not have done so, and Mr. Bennet seemed more amused than anything. Miss Mary, therefore, was the likely candidate, though he might have thought she would simply preach at Miss Bingley.

"I see you have come to the right conclusion, William," said Elizabeth, drawing Darcy's eyes back to her. "But do not fear we will attempt to censure Miss Bingley. We Bennets understand her and will take care in our dealings with her, but we have no desire to embarrass Mr. Bingley."

"My dearest Elizabeth," replied Darcy, "I would not have expected it of you. I do, however, expect it of *her*."

"That is why it is best that my family has been warned. I had thought to keep it to myself, but I have been persuaded this is for the best."

Darcy could not but agree with her. Having known Miss Bingley for some years, he knew of what the woman was capable. She would have no compunction in doing her utmost to ruin the Bennets should the opportunity arise, for nothing more than spite.

The days passed, and Miss Bingley did nothing but remain watchful, and while Darcy did not relax his guard, he thought she might have given up her pursuit of him. Georgiana also watched her but was able to report no more than Darcy had already observed.

"She says very little about the Bennets and nothing about your engagement with Elizabeth. It is almost as if she is waiting for something."

"That may be true," replied Darcy. "But what it might be, I cannot say."

The day after his conversation with Georgiana, Darcy was treated to a little of Miss Bingley's usual venom, though it was mild in comparison to what he might have expected. Darcy had made an effort to avoid being alone in the same room as she or even giving a hint of the appearance of impropriety. As Miss Bingley had not attempted to force the issue, he felt it had been successful. That did not stop her from making her little jabbing comments when the opportunity presented itself.

"Mr. Darcy," said she, "have I informed you how happy we are to have you in residence with us? And your charming sister, of course."

"I thank you, Miss Bingley. I appreciate your willingness to host us, for I am desirous of being in Hertfordshire at the present."

Though Darcy had not intended it to be a jab at the woman, it was apparent she took it as such, for it was a reminder of *why* he wished to be in the country. That it was nothing less than the truth was of no consequence, for Miss Bingley should already have understood that fact.

"Oh, I understand, of course," said she, which Darcy knew was true. "We are quite happy to be of service." That, Darcy knew, was patently false, at least from Miss Bingley's perspective. "Indeed, we are fortunate to have such prominent personages as you and your sister in our midst, for you are both overflowing with gentility and refinement. We are all uplifted by the example you show us and cannot help but strive to approach your level."

Miss Bingley was truly laying it on thick, but Darcy decided it was best to simply thank her and end the conversation. He did, but Miss Bingley was not to be put off so easily.

"There is no need to thank me, Mr. Darcy, for saying nothing more than is your due. I have no doubt you will continue to uphold your position in society, and generations will look on the Darcys as the standards to which all polite society must aspire. Of course, the road will be more difficult in the future, but I have every confidence in your abilities."

"I am sure I have no notion of your meaning, Miss Bingley," replied Darcy.

"Why, in your choice of wife, of course," replied she. "Miss Elizabeth is . . . Well, let us simply say that she has no familiarity with the level of society she will inhabit when your marriage is solemnized. But I am certain you are equal to the task, sir. With instruction and close supervision, she *may* yet do you proud."

Darcy was amused at the woman's words and did not hesitate to show her, though he did not respond. It appeared Miss Bingley had no stomach for his mirth, for her countenance soured, and she soon excused herself, muttering as she went. For Elizabeth's part, it seemed she was equally diverted by Miss Bingley's mean-spirited attack.

"Had it come from anyone other than Miss Bingley, I might have felt some offense," said she when Darcy had related the matter to her. "As it is, I shall refrain and instead take delight in her ridiculous behavior, knowing that what *she* would consider proper, *I* would find offensive."

"A prudent choice," replied Darcy, his heart swelling with affection for this rare and beautiful woman. He grasped her hand and held it down where no one could see, saying: "I have no doubt of your success in town. And if there are naysayers, we do not need to care for anything they say. Anyone admitted to the pleasure of knowing you must find you as estimable as I."

"Thank you, William." She glanced down shyly before looking up at him. "She is correct in one way—I have no experience with London society. I would be lying if I said I am not a little apprehensive."

"And yet your courage will rise, I have no doubt."

For the rest of their time together that day, they were attached to each other's side, whispering between them, speaking of their future and other matters. Miss Bingley, who was present in Longbourn's sitting-room, where they had paid a call, could not but notice. Darcy, who habitually watched the woman, saw her countenance darken as they stood close together. It was at that moment he thought her dream of marrying him finally came to an end, as she looked away and seemed to wilt before his eyes. But that did not end her plans to keep her brother from Miss Bennet. Quite the contrary.

The very next day at least part of her stratagem became apparent, for the early afternoon saw a carriage arrive at Netherfield. Darcy, who had been closeted in the study with Bingley, discussing a matter of the estate, heard the sound of a carriage rumbling its way up the drive. Bingley noticed it also, for he frowned and went to the window.

"It is late for a visit, and I was not expecting anyone. I wonder who it could be."

"Has your sister invited anyone else to stay at Netherfield?" asked Darcy. "If they left town before noon, they would just be arriving now, assuming they made good time."

Bingley's countenance darkened. "If she has, I was not informed of it. I suppose there is little to be done except to go to the sitting-room and discover it for ourselves."

Agreeing with his friend's assessment, Darcy rose and followed him from the room. As they walked, he reflected that this had to be some sort of ploy of Miss Bingley's. While he was confident she had given up all pretense of breaking him away from Elizabeth, she was not likely to accept defeat from her brother with any sort of equanimity.

When they entered the room, they were immediately arrested by the sight of two women, in addition to the Bingley sisters. They were both friends, confederates of Miss Bingley, though their level of society was quite different. They were also known to Darcy and Bingley both: The taller of the two was Lady Diane Montrose, the daughter of a baron, and the other was Miss Jessica Cartwright, the daughter of a wealthy landowner.

The lady was blond and willowy, possessed of a handsome face, which Darcy had always thought was rendered less appealing by the expression of disdain which often adorned it. In other words, she was a perfect match for Miss Bingley. Miss Cartwright was, by contrast, smaller of stature, buxom, with a pretty face and a darker shade of golden locks than Lady Diane's. She was also much quieter of temperament, kind and thoughtful, and Darcy had often wondered why the woman would be the friend of a virago such as Miss Bingley.

Bingley stopped at the sight of them, his face carefully blank. His sister, however, took no notice of it and rose at the sight of him.

"Charles, I am glad you have come. As you can see, we have been blessed with additional visitors. You must remember my friends, Lady Diane and Miss Cartwright."

"Indeed, I remember them very well," said Bingley, his manners overcoming what Darcy was certain was a rising fury. "How do you do, Lady Diane, Miss Cartwright?"

The women both curtseyed to Bingley's bow, which Darcy mirrored. "I welcome you to Netherfield," said Bingley. "We are happy to have you here with us."

There truly was nothing else Bingley could say. If he chastised his sister for inviting them without informing him, he would be opening himself up to ridicule for not being in control of his estate. But he could hardly turn them away, especially the daughter of a baron, no matter how much he wished it. Darcy was aware of what was happening here, and he knew Bingley did too. It was clear he was not happy about it in the slightest.

"I am certain we shall be a merry party, indeed," cried Miss Bingley. "For I remember when we were all together in London for the season. We were pleased with each other, I think, and my friends were especially eager to greet you gentlemen."

"Were they?" asked Bingley, holding his anger in by the barest of threads. "I hope, then, you have planned for their amusement, Caroline, for I am much engaged with other matters."

Miss Bingley frowned. "I am certain such engagements may be put to the side. Our friends are, after all, most important."

"Yes, they are," replied Bingley. "Both those friends of longstanding and those of a newer variety. I would not wish to offend either."

"Of course not."

"Then I shall leave you to it," said Bingley, once again bowing to the ladies. "I will see you again at dinner, for Darcy and I were in the midst of an important discussion."

Though Miss Bingley frowned at how quickly Bingley excused himself, she could say nothing, for they left at once. As they walked back to the study, Darcy was not certain Bingley would make it there without some outburst. He had rarely seen his friend in such a state.

Once they had gained the privacy of his room, Bingley went to the sideboard, poured himself a finger of brandy, and tossed it back at once, grimacing at the burning in his throat. Darcy decided it would be best to simply allow Bingley to have his say, for it appeared his friend was bursting at the seams.

"Of all the underhanded, audacious, malicious devices!" snarled Bingley. "How dare she invite her friends without informing me?"

"As mistress of the estate, she may invite whomever she pleases," replied Darcy. "Though, I will grant you, she should have informed you."

"I understand the proprieties of the situation, Darcy," said Bingley. "But that is not the point. I am certain you know why she has invited Miss Cartwright and that termagant, Lady Diane to Netherfield."

"Miss Cartwright is obvious," replied Darcy. "It is Lady Diane who confuses me."

Bingley snorted and threw himself into the armchair next to Darcy's. "Had she had a willing confederate in Lady Diane, I have no doubt she would have done everything in her power to marry me off to the woman years ago. She fits Caroline's notion of a proper sort of wife to raise my—*her*—fortunes in society. This, of course, was only after Lady Emily Teasdale, who is the daughter of an earl, laughed in Caroline's face at the suggestion I would make her a good husband."

"But why invite her now?" asked Darcy. "She has already made her sentiments known."

"Perhaps she hopes to persuade her," replied Bingley. "Or perhaps she merely means Lady Diane to distract me."

"And Miss Cartwright? It seems to me she is more likely to push you toward Miss Cartwright, given your past with her."

Bingley grimaced and turned away. "I feel nothing for Miss Cartwright now. She is a good sort of woman, but the regard I possessed for her in the spring has quite mellowed to the extent that I consider her a friend, but not a potential partner in marriage."

"But you did pay significant attention to her. There has not been anyone else since, as I recall."

"No, there has not. Miss Cartwright and I decided mutually we would not suit, Darcy. We remain friendly—that is all. Miss Cartwright, of course, possesses enough dowry to make her acceptable to Caroline, but she is not high enough in society. Had she been higher, I have no doubt Caroline would have pressed me to offer for her."

"Since you know of Caroline's intentions, that makes them much less likely to succeed."

"They have no chance of success," was Bingley's short reply. "I do not intend to allow Caroline to interfere with my happiness, and the more time I spend in Miss Bennet's company, the more I am convinced that she is integral to it."

Bingley fell silent, brooding over the situation. Darcy allowed him his thoughts. Miss Bingley's audacity was truly beyond anything he had ever experienced in any other person of his acquaintance. Bingley would need to plan carefully to avoid any entanglement with either of the two women. And he would have Darcy's support.

While Netherfield saw a pair of visitors arrive, Longbourn was also welcoming its own. True to his usual custom of teasing his wife and family, Mr. Bennet had not informed them of the matter until that morning, then dropping the information and watching for the response. It seemed his cousin, Mr. Collins, who was also his heir, had been invited to stay with them for a fortnight. But Mr. Bennet was destined to be disappointed, though Elizabeth could not imagine why he had not expected it himself.

"Mr. Collins, you say," said Mrs. Bennet when her husband unceremoniously dropped the information on them.

"Yes, Mrs. Bennet," said he, frowning a little at his wife's lack of the expected reaction. "He wishes, as he states in his letter, to heal the breach between us. He also mentions some other recompense, which I suspect concerns our daughters, but I shan't sport with your nerves by reading his comments to you."

Elizabeth thought Mrs. Bennet might erupt in her usual paroxysms at the mention of the odious—in her mind—Mr. Collins. But she glanced at Elizabeth, the meaning of which was not lost on her second daughter, and was able to respond with composure.

"I might wonder why he wishes to heal the breach after so many years. Does he mean to apologize for his father's behavior?"

"He mentions no such thing, Mrs. Bennet. I expect he has heard of the matter from his father's perspective and does not feel the elder Mr. Collins had anything for which to apologize."

Mrs. Bennet huffed. "Perhaps you are correct. I am not excited at the prospect of his presence, to be sure. His father behaved in an infamous manner, and I have little hope the son will be any better. But I suppose it is not unusual that he would wish to visit the estate he will inherit. We will do our best to welcome him since there is little other choice."

Such a tepid resolve could not help but make Elizabeth smile. Her mother set about instructing the maids to air out the spare bedroom for Mr. Collins's residence with them. Her father watched with a faint sense of disappointment, and he had no compunction in informing Elizabeth of his feelings.

"I must say I am disappointed in you, Lizzy," said he. "You have deprived me of a source of amusement, though I will say that I am shocked your mother remembered that she is protected from the hedgerows by her daughter's engagement to a wealthy man. I would have expected her to shriek first and remember later."

"You should be happy instead, Papa," replied Elizabeth. In fact, she was feeling a little insulted by her father's manner—his teasing of his wife in this instance was beyond cruel. "Mama's nerves affect her much less now, which means more peace and quiet in your home."

"Well, when you put it that way, I suppose I must agree. I will say that I *am* happy for you, Lizzy, for Mr. Darcy appears to be a very good man. I believe you shall be quite happy with him, despite the fact that I shall be left with your mother and, when the two youngest return, three silly sisters."

Before Elizabeth could make a reply, he turned and departed for his sitting-room. Though she still felt disappointed and annoyed with his manner, Elizabeth decided to ignore it. She still loved him, regardless of his faults.

Mr. Collins arrived in due time, but rather than discover him to be objectionable, Elizabeth found him to be merely silly. He was, perhaps, the most servile specimen Elizabeth had ever met, and his obsequious nature was punctuated by his possession of a weak understanding and an overly formal manner. He was tall and portly, his hair thinning and greasy, his eyes a dull brown, and he was altogether homely. Suspecting as she did that he had come to Longbourn to look for a wife, Elizabeth was happy she was not available for him to pursue.

The next day, she was informed that her suspicions had been correct. Mr. Collins had said nothing in her hearing, though the first evening at dinner he had looked at both Elizabeth and Jane with some interest. But the following day his interest seemed to disappear, and at the same time, Mrs. Bennet appeared a little melancholy. Though Elizabeth would not have expected her mother to commiserate with her in particular, it seemed the absence of her favorite, coupled with Elizabeth's recent elevation in her eyes, provoked her mother to speak with her.

"It appears Longbourn is lost to our family forever, Lizzy. I have done my best, but we shall not have any hold on it once your father passes."

Surprised at the sudden words from her mother, Elizabeth—the only one of her sisters present in the sitting-room—looked at Mrs. Bennet askance. The question must have been evident, for Mrs. Bennet was eager to share her misfortune.

"Mr. Collins asked me concerning you all this morning, you see. It seems he is interested in procuring one of Longbourn's daughters for a wife." Unsurprised, Elizabeth nodded for her mother to continue. "He looked to Jane first, but when I informed him of Mr. Bingley's interest, he was forced to give way. Then he made some suggestion that you might be a good substitute. I was obliged, of course, to inform him of your recent engagement."

"Of course," replied Elizabeth quietly, relieved for William's proposal.

"Lydia and Kitty are not present—"

"And are too young anyway," interjected Elizabeth."

"Yes, yes," was her mother's impatient reply. "I had thought to direct him to Mary, but he does not favor her. Thus, when all the possibilities were exhausted, he asked if we would be offended should he find some other woman for a wife. I had no choice but to give him my blessing."

"That is an . . . interesting way to put it," said Elizabeth.

"I suppose it is, but it is no less than the truth. I suppose we cannot direct him in this. I *had* hoped, from your father's words yesterday, that we might keep Longbourn in the family through marriage. But it is not to be."

Mrs. Bennet shook her head and announced her intention to retire for a time. Elizabeth wished her mother a good nap and allowed her to depart. It was fortunate, indeed, that Mr. Collins had not decided to pursue Mary, for the girl in question did not favor Mr. Collins.

"Mama wished to set that odious man on me?" demanded Mary when Elizabeth mentioned the matter to her.

"It seems to be so," replied Elizabeth.

"Then I am grateful Mr. Collins had the sense to balk at such a suggestion, though I wonder if he possesses any other sense. Though I have no compunction toward marrying a parson, Mr. Collins is far too sycophantic for me. Why, with his talk about his patroness, I have no doubt any wife of his would hardly be mistress of her own home!"

Elizabeth laughed. "I am sure you are correct, Mary. But all is well. You shall not be forced to cause an uproar by refusing him. I suppose he shall be required to return to Kent and find a wife there."

"Good riddance," muttered Mary. "I have no desire to become Mrs. Collins."

Mary's sentiments matched Elizabeth's with exactness. It was fortunate, indeed, that Mr. Collins had been redirected. Elizabeth could not imagine being the focus of his ineffectual courting, especially not after being the recipient of William's ardent interest.

CHAPTER XII

*T*he evening at Netherfield after the arrival of Miss Bingley's two friends was strained. While Bingley treated the two ladies with respect and kindness, he had little to say to his sister which was not short and clipped, and under normal circumstances, Darcy might have thought him unkind. But the situation, being what it was, engendered nothing more than compassion. At least Darcy himself had a sister who was mild and kind and governable. None of those three adjectives could be used to describe Miss Caroline Bingley.

Dinner passed in an unremarkable manner—or perhaps it was remarkable in what it lacked. In the past, Darcy, being the only male guest in residence, would have sat by Miss Bingley, listening to her unceasing conversation while they were at the table. On this evening, however, he was surprised and pleased to note that the woman ignored him altogether. Instead, by a maneuver of Miss Bingley's, Lady Diane and Miss Cartwright ended up seated on either side of Bingley, where Miss Cartwright should have sat further down the table. Throughout the entire meal, he could see Bingley sneaking dark glances at his sister, while she watched the scene with satisfaction. After what seemed like the hundredth such scowl from his friend, Darcy shook his head.

Though he had intended it to be unnoticeable, his hostess proved to be more observant than he thought. "Is there something that displeases you, Mr. Darcy?"

Darcy turned to her, noting her regarding him with a malicious sort of smirk. "Nothing more than a random thought, Miss Bingley."

"Ah," said the woman. Her eyes almost seemed to glow with intensity. "I believe I understand. I hope you enjoy these few days at Netherfield, Mr. Darcy. After all, you will have few meals spent in polite company after you leave."

A flat glare was Darcy's response. "I am afraid I do not understand your meaning, Miss Bingley."

The woman speared a bite of her pork, chewing slowly while seemingly thinking of her response. Darcy, for his part, hoped she would just remain silent, for he was certain she had nothing to say he would wish to hear. In this, he was to be disappointed.

"Perhaps I misspoke. Your future wife is not of your circles, so her lack of knowledge is to be expected. It is *possible* you will be able to mold her into the proper wife. Until then, however, it would likely be best if you simply kept her from the rest of society, lest the Darcy name and standing be reduced as a consequence."

"Miss Bingley," said Darcy, his tone harsh, though even, "you have spoken in such terms of my future wife on several occasions now. If you can speak no good of my fiancée, then I would appreciate it if you would keep your observances to yourself."

"I apologize, Mr. Darcy," said Miss Bingley, feigning surprise, though it was undone by the glittering hardness of her eyes. "I only meant to dispense some advice which I think would be beneficial for you."

"It is not. I have every confidence in Elizabeth's abilities and no doubt she will not only be acceptable to society but will excel in anything to which she puts her mind. Experience in society may be gained. Elizabeth has a natural intelligence, and while some might not think much of my wife, those who matter will love her as much as I do."

Miss Bingley's eyes narrowed at Darcy's assertion of those who mattered to him, but he stared at her, daring her to speak further. In the end, she chose the sensible course of saying nothing, though she turned away from him in anger. A moment later she had returned to her satisfied glances down the length of the table. Georgiana, who sat on Darcy's other side, regarded him with pity.

"Since you have been so free with your advice," said Darcy,

drawing her eyes back to him, "perhaps you would listen to mine."

While it was clear she was not eager to listen to him, she gave him a short nod. The contrast between now and what would have ensued should they have been together without Darcy already being engaged nearly caused him to break out in laughter.

"Your purpose is quite transparent, Miss Bingley, and your brother sees it too. Do not push him too hard, for I suspect you will not like the result if you do."

Miss Bingley gazed at him, her expression revealing no hint of her thoughts. "That is . . . interesting advice, Mr. Darcy. I will certainly take it into consideration."

Darcy knew she would do no such thing, more was the pity for her. The problem, he decided, was that they were outnumbered. Miss Bingley had Lady Diane and Miss Cartwright—though that lady's cooperation, in Darcy's eyes, was not at all guaranteed. Mrs. Hurst could be counted on to support her sister, though she had been surprisingly quiet since their arrival. Hurst would do nothing but watch and chuckle at their antics. On Bingley's side, he had only Darcy himself; Georgiana he wished to keep above the fray.

Perhaps there was merit in the Bard's words when he said: "Be stirring as the time; be fire with fire." And Darcy thought he knew exactly how to counteract Miss Bingley's schemes. As soon as dinner was over, Darcy would suggest it to his friend. He had no doubt Bingley would agree.

When the Netherfield party arrived the morning after Mr. Collins's arrival, Elizabeth was interested to see there were two new members among their number. Contrary to her previous behavior at Longbourn, Miss Bingley floated into the room, her head held as high as a queen's, seemingly eager to be in their company. The truth of the matter, however, was soon revealed.

"Mrs. Bennet," said Miss Bingley, "please allow me to introduce my friends to the acquaintance of you and your family. This is Lady Diane Montrose, daughter of the Baron of Redfields, and my close friend, Miss Jessica Cartwright. They have come to Netherfield to enhance our party and stay with us for a time."

"The daughter of a baron!" said Mrs. Bennet, eyes wide. Miss Bingley's responding grin was positively smug. "I will say I had never thought to host a member of the nobility. Of course, Mr. Darcy has been among us frequently of late, and he is the grandson of an earl, and one of the best men of our acquaintance. Welcome, Lady Diane,

Miss Cartwright. Please allow me to introduce my family to you."

It seemed Miss Bingley had not enjoyed the introductions as much as she might have thought, and that was likely a direct result of Mrs. Bennet's behavior being less mortifying than Elizabeth expected. Mrs. Bennet introduced all her family, as well as Mr. Collins, who was present with them that morning, and soon they sat down to visit.

"Can I suppose Miss Bingley's purpose in inviting her friends to be what I suspect?" asked Elizabeth of William when he had taken his place beside her.

"If you suspect her of attempting to distract her brother from your sister, then you are correct."

"And what do you think of her chances of success?"

William's grin relieved much of Elizabeth's concern. "Miss Cartwright was Bingley's last 'angel' in the spring. As for Lady Diane, Bingley suspects Miss Bingley would have had him married off to her the moment he left university had she had her way. But she is far too proud to consider marrying him, and according to Bingley, he and Miss Cartwright jointly decided they would not suit."

"Does Miss Bingley not know this?"

"I do not know," replied William with a shrug. "It is possible she believes he was distracted from Miss Cartwright and she may easily redirect him. Or it may be that she believes he will be led by her regardless."

It was beyond Elizabeth's ability to fathom, so she contented herself with simply watching Miss Bingley, alert for any obvious ploys, with the intention of interfering if necessary.

As it turned out, it was not necessary for Elizabeth to do so on that day. Miss Bingley was her usual scheming self, and she arranged for Miss Cartwright and Lady Diane to sit in a group with Jane, with Mr. Bingley nearby. As Elizabeth was also close, she was able to hear what was said and participate in the discussion, little though she might have wished to associate with such supercilious women as Lady Diane and Miss Bingley. Miss Cartwright was another matter, as Elizabeth soon discovered when she spoke to the woman.

"I hope your journey passed with tolerable ease, Miss Cartwright," said Elizabeth, intending to show the woman she was not to be intimidated. "Miss Bingley never dropped a word of your coming. I assume it must have been a sudden decision."

Miss Cartwright shot a look at Miss Bingley, who was currently watching all like a queen surveying her realm before she turned back to Elizabeth. "It was sudden, I suppose. I had not seen Caroline in some time when her invitation arrived. I was surprised, but as the little season is mostly dull, it was no difficult decision to accept."

"Have you known Miss Bingley long?"

"We were friends in school," replied Miss Cartwright.

"Oh, Jessica and I have been famous friends for years," spoke Miss Bingley. She displayed a smile in which Elizabeth comprehended a measure of hidden nastiness as she glanced at Jane. "Charles and I have both been so fond of Jessica, and of Lady Diane too! I dare say they are both as welcome at our home as anyone. It is almost as if we are dear relations."

Two things caught Elizabeth's attention at that moment. The first and most important was how Jane slumped a little, crestfallen at Miss Bingley's statement, as the woman had no doubt intended. The other was how Miss Cartwright's mouth tightened at Miss Bingley's declaration, showing she, at least, understood Miss Bingley's inference and did not agree with it. It seemed William's information, gained through Mr. Bingley, was entirely correct.

"Yes, we have known *your* friends for some time," said Mr. Bingley, speaking up before Elizabeth could. "They are both estimable ladies, indeed. I am just as happy with our new acquaintances here in Hertfordshire, both for Miss Elizabeth's friendship, which I have enjoyed these last months, and with that of your sisters and the other good people of the neighborhood."

Mr. Bingley's firm gaze in Jane's direction spoke more than words could, and she blushed in response. Miss Bingley was not happy, and she scowled even more when Elizabeth directed a smug look at her.

The conversation continued in more acceptable subjects for some time. On the far side of their little group, Elizabeth could see Lady Diane and Miss Bingley whispering between themselves, but as they said nothing, she decided it was best to ignore them. Mr. Bingley paid much of his attention to Jane, and she responded in kind, but there was also an opportunity to learn more of Miss Cartwright, who seemed more willing to engage with them.

"Do you live in London, Miss Cartwright?" asked Elizabeth.

"I have been there this autumn," replied the woman. "But my home is in Oxfordshire. My father owns an estate not far from Swindon."

"Jessica's father is a *very* wealthy man," interjected Miss Bingley. "And she has the distinction of being his only child."

Miss Cartwright reddened, but she did not respond to Miss Bingley's gauche observation. Elizabeth, deciding it was best to redirect the conversation, did so at the first opportunity.

"Is your father in London at present?"

"Father prefers his estate to London," said Miss Cartwright, smiling her gratitude at Elizabeth. "When I was in town, I was staying with some cousins. It is only on rare occasions that I can tempt my father to come to town, especially since my mother passed several years ago."

"That is a sentiment I can well understand," said Elizabeth. "My father detests London and does not like to travel. We sometimes stay in London with my uncle, but usually, it is Jane or I who go stay with them."

"Ah, yes," said Miss Bingley, the light of malevolence evident in her eyes. "I have heard you speak of your uncle before. Why do you not inform us of him? Is he well known among certain circles?"

"I believe the Bennets have spoken of their relations many times," said Mr. Bingley, now glaring at his sister. "In fact, unless I am very much mistaken, I believe Mr. Gardiner was known to our father."

Though she glared at her brother, at the same time Miss Bingley paled and would not continue in the same vein. Elizabeth grinned at her, prompting another glare from the woman.

"Yes, Mr. Gardiner is a good man, and he has a very good reputation in London. I would not be the least bit surprised if he knew your father, Mr. Bingley. From what you have informed me of him, it sounds like he was a good man."

"He was," said Mr. Bingley. "I miss his guidance exceedingly." Then Mr. Bingley laughed. "But then again, I now have Darcy to look to for assistance whenever I should require it. There are certain matters for which Darcy possesses even more knowledge than my father, eh Darcy?"

"If you refer to my assistance with the estate, you must know I am happy to help."

"I know it and appreciate it, Darcy. Your help has allowed me to learn to stand on my own." Mr. Bingley affixed a sly look on both Darcy and Elizabeth. "As you are soon to be occupied with other matters, it is a good thing, indeed."

Miss Cartwright turned to Elizabeth. "I am sorry, Miss Elizabeth, but I was not aware. Am I to understand that you are engaged to Mr. Darcy?"

"I am," replied Elizabeth, feeling a little heat rise in her cheeks. "We are to marry early in the New Year."

"Then I offer my congratulations. Mr. Darcy is very highly thought of in town; I am sure you will be happy with him." The woman then paused and grinned. "I hope, however, that you have a greater tolerance for society than your father, for Mr. Darcy holds a high place in society."

Elizabeth laughed and nodded, rapidly beginning to think that she could esteem Miss Cartwright tolerably well. "I am quite comfortable in society, Miss Cartwright. I believe I shall be happy with whatever level Mr. Darcy inhabits. And if he prefers his estate more than the crowds of London, I believe I would be very happy there too."

"That is eminently sensible," said Miss Cartwright with a laugh. "It is best to be comfortable in both locations, is it not? A gentleman's life will, of a necessity, be divided between his estate and his duties in society."

"I have never made it any secret that I prefer life in the country," added William.

"A diligent master of an estate is always to be respected, sir."

At that moment, their discussion was interrupted by the two ladies at the other end of the company, however. Miss Bingley was still regarding Elizabeth was some measure of hate for interrupting her plans. But it was Lady Diane who proved to be the spokeswoman between them, and her astonishment rang out through her voice.

"I beg your pardon, Miss Elizabeth," said she, "but have I heard correctly? Am I to understand that *you* are engaged to Mr. Darcy?"

"I am, Lady Diane," replied Elizabeth with no hint of embarrassment or hesitation. Should this proud woman be her first test among the supercilious of society, she was determined she would pass it with dignity.

Lady Diane's eyes found Mr. Darcy, and she said: "Miss Elizabeth is a . . . singular choice, Mr. Darcy." She turned back to Elizabeth. "I know not if you are aware of this, Miss Elizabeth, but Mr. Darcy is highly sought after, being connected to an earl, and possessing an old and respected name. It has long been *expected* that he would take a wife who is his equal in society. Why, I have even heard it said he could aspire to marry the daughter of an earl!"

"I have heard much of Mr. Darcy's position in society, Lady Diane," said Elizabeth. "I believe it is much more important to find a spouse with whom one can be happy, who shares the same values, and with whom one may pursue complementary goals. I believe I have found that in Mr. Darcy."

The eyebrow the lady arched spoke to her belief in Elizabeth's simple-mindedness, but William also spoke at this moment. "And I have found the same in Miss Elizabeth. I have no doubt we will do well together, as I could not imagine offering for anyone else."

"Then I am happy for you, sir," said Lady Diane. "I only hope others in society will accept your choice with as much enthusiasm as you have made it. Your uncle, the earl, for example."

"Lord Matlock is, indeed, happy for me," replied William. "I received a letter from him only the other day, in which he congratulated me and informed me of his intention to be in attendance at our wedding."

"Your uncle is to be present for your wedding with my Lizzy?" asked Mrs. Bennet, the edge of hysteria evident in her tone.

"He will, Mrs. Bennet," replied William in a kindly voice. "I hope it will not be too much trouble to endure him. He is rather eccentric and seems to think he must make a joke of everything."

Mrs. Bennet, clearly incapable of understanding how an *earl* might not be welcome anywhere he wished to go, assured William that she was quite anticipating his visit. Then she fell silent, no doubt pondering how she could plan a wedding breakfast grand enough to honor an earl's attendance. Elizabeth caught William's eye at that moment, and they shared a grin, each knowing they were in accord with their thoughts.

For her part, Lady Diane only sniffed with disdain and turned to Miss Bingley, resuming their whispering. Jane and Mr. Bingley were once again focused on each other, while Elizabeth and William were left to their own devices. Miss Cartwright was close by, and in deference to her, not wishing to leave her without a conversation partner, Elizabeth included her in what she was speaking of with William. But their conversation could not proceed without another interruption.

While she might not have been able to credit the notion, given how voluble the man had already proven himself to be, Mr. Collins had remained on the fringes of the group, largely silent. He was so unobtrusive that Elizabeth had almost forgotten he was present, as strange as that must seem. When he approached them, however, and spoke, she was witness to a curious wildness about his eyes, almost as if he had suddenly become terrified.

"I beg your pardon, Cousin Elizabeth," said he, "but am I to understand that your companion here is Mr. Darcy? *The* Mr. Darcy of Pemberley in Derbyshire?"

"I do not know that I would refer to myself in such terms," replied William. Elizabeth caught a flash of amusement from her betrothed at Mr. Collins's manner, but she did not think the man himself perceptive enough to have noted it himself.

"I apologize, Mr. Darcy. I meant no disrespect. Am I to suppose, then, that you are *the* Mr. Darcy who is connected to Lady Catherine de Bourgh of Rosings in Kent?"

This question seemed to provoke William's interest. "Yes, I am connected to Lady Catherine. She is my late mother's sister. May I ask how you know her?"

"Yes, of course. You see, Mr. Darcy, I have recently received my ordination last Easter. As your aunt was coincidentally searching for a replacement for the parson of her parish, who had passed only weeks earlier, I was sent to her as a possible candidate. It is, thus, my privilege and honor to serve her ladyship as the parson of Hunsford, of which I am certain you must be familiar."

"You are my aunt's parson," said William, clarifying the man's longwinded explanation.

"I am, sir."

"I see." It seemed new understanding of Mr. Collins had resulted in William's wariness. Elizabeth could not quite account for it, as William now looked on her cousin with what she could only term as circumspection. It was as if he expected the man to suddenly make a scene in her mother's sitting-room.

For her part, Elizabeth wondered if he was not about to do just that. He said nothing after he confirmed his connection to Mr. Darcy's aunt, but the way he opened his mouth several times, only to close it again in indecision, struck Elizabeth as rather odd. When he looked over at Elizabeth, his expression darkened, but when he looked back at William, again he seemed to retreat into himself, as if not quite knowing what to say.

But it is impossible to expect a man of Mr. William Collins's vociferous disposition to remain silent for long, and at length, he spoke, though quickly, as if wishing to say it before his courage failed. "But what of your cousin, Miss Anne de Bourgh?"

Once again, William's amusement returned. "I assume my aunt has told you that tired old cradle betrothal story?"

Mr. Collins's mouth gaped open like a fish, but he said: "She has informed me that you are engaged to her daughter. Indeed, she has stated she expects the marriage to take place before another year has passed."

"It seems I shall be forced to have another word with Lady Catherine," muttered William, much to Mr. Collins's shock. When he noticed the other man's reaction, he further explained: "My aunt has often told this story of an agreement between sisters, but as far as I can determine, it has no basis in truth."

"Mr. Darcy!" exclaimed Mr. Collins, clearly appalled. His outburst drew the attention of the rest of the room, and he colored because of it.

"You have my apologies, Mr. Collins," said Darcy. "I did not mean to accuse my aunt of falsehood. In fact, I suspect she and my mother *did* speak on the matter. But my mother did not mention it to me as any wish of hers, and my father declined to enter us into a betrothal agreement. Considering such facts, you can hardly blame me for not feeling bound by my aunt's wishes."

It was clear Mr. Collins was not in full agreement with Mr. Darcy's assessment, but he seemed to draw on some well of discretion Elizabeth would not have believed he possessed. After struggling with a response for several moments, Mr. Collins finally sighed and nodded.

"I suppose you must be correct, sir. I congratulate you for securing my cousin for a wife. I have no doubt she will be a credit to you. Had I arrived a few weeks earlier, I might have snapped her up before you had the chance. I can only lament my tardiness."

With those final words, Mr. Collins bowed and walked away, leaving Elizabeth and Mr. Darcy grinning at each other. Even Miss Cartwright, who had been sitting nearby, could not contain her mirth at what had just happened.

"Well, Elizabeth?" asked William in a soft voice. "Are you downcast at the opportunity you have missed due to Mr. Collins's late arrival?"

"Perhaps I am," replied Elizabeth. "But I am sure I shall rally tolerably."

Miss Cartwright giggled, and William laughed. Elizabeth glared at them both, before turning to Miss Cartwright and saying: "I could put in a good word for you with Mr. Collins, should you desire. I am certain he would find you quite fascinating."

Hearing the tease in Elizabeth's voice, Miss Cartwright only laughed again. "I thank you for my part, Miss Elizabeth. But I think I shall decline. I do not think Mr. Collins and I would suit."

CHAPTER XIII

*R*espect. It was the one thing Caroline Bingley had always craved. The respect of her peers, the respect of the masses, respect for her intelligence, her person, her status as a rational woman. It was also something she felt she had not been accorded — or at least, had not received in the abundance she thought she deserved.

Caroline Bingley was no fool. She was aware of her origins, despite how she attempted to forget at times or to avoid acknowledging it. In a society such as Meryton, where the gentry was countrified and unfashionable, she could pass herself off with a high degree of credit. But the adulation of savages was not what Caroline craved — it was that of a higher strata of society.

In her mind, the path to respect, and everything else she had ever wanted in life, was assured should she only induce a man of a sufficient level of society to offer for her. A man of Hurst's level and questionable character would not do — only a member of the first circles would ensure she received all that she had ever wished. Mr. Darcy had been the easiest path to that end. But that chit Eliza Bennet had snapped him up when Caroline was not looking, had somehow — and through underhanded means, Caroline was certain — provoked a proposal. And now Caroline was left to find another man who fit her requirements.

But esteem from a man was not the only thing she desired — in fact, that consideration paled next to her real motives. From the time she had been in school, she had been looked down on for her common origins, made to feel inferior to the heiresses of society. It was these women from whom Caroline craved the acceptance of an equal. Caroline had worked hard to shed, as much as she was able, the stigma attached to her name due to her father's profession and lack of an estate. And now, unfortunately, she was in a position again where a woman of quality looked down on her without regard. It was enough to make her scream in frustration.

"Caroline, dear," said Lady Diane as soon as they alighted from the carriage. "I require a moment of your time if you will oblige me."

Recognizing it for the command it was, Caroline obliged her guest, also noting the insolence in Lady Diane's tone when she used the endearment. Mr. Darcy and her brother were oblivious to her plight, and Caroline scowled at Miss Cartwright for her almost unseemly haste in retreating from them with Mr. Darcy's insipid sister in tow. Knowing she had little choice, Caroline led her guest to a small, little-used parlor, hoping this discussion would not devolve to a fight.

"It seems, my *friend*, that you invited me here under false pretenses," said Lady Diane the moment the door was closed behind them. "When you informed me that Mr. Darcy was in residence, I naturally thought there was some possibility of attracting his attention." The lady's eyes raked over Caroline's form. "I will own it seemed a little strange, considering how assiduously you have attempted to attach yourself to him. But I thought perhaps you had finally come to your senses and realized you had no chance of securing him."

Caroline's lips tightened as the latest evidence of disrespect was presented to her. But she carefully kept her expression blank, knowing Lady Diane was not perceptive enough to have noticed her slight reaction. Indeed, the woman did not, for she continued to speak.

"How surprised I was, therefore, to learn that Mr. Darcy is already engaged, and to a country miss of no significance in the world! It is curious that you neglected to include this information when you tendered your invitation."

"It was not my intention — "

"I am aware of your intentions. It seems I was not clear enough to you before, so I will state my feelings again. I will not marry your brother. *I* am a daughter of the nobility and have a much more illustrious match in my future. You have wasted my time in inviting me. Have I made myself quite clear?"

Before responding, Caroline paused and considered what she would say, knowing if the wrong thing came out of her mouth, Lady Diane would board her carriage and depart that very day. It could also see the end of their friendship, and that was too important for Caroline's place in society to lose, especially since she had lost Mr. Darcy.

"Lady Diane," said she, trying to show as much deference as she could, "I am quite aware of your position in society and had no intention of attempting to throw you into my brother's path."

The baron's daughter regarded Caroline, suspicion liberally oozing from her in waves. "Then why did you invite me, if this was not your intention?"

"I will own that the situation was part of my reason," replied Caroline. She smiled, knowing the lady was susceptible to flattery. "You have often provided excellent counsel, and I suspected you could now assist me in extricating him from his current entanglement. Furthermore, as Netherfield is such a pretty estate, I thought you might enjoy some time in the country."

A grunt was the woman's response. "In that, I suppose you are correct. I have friends who live in the north of Hertfordshire, and I have always found it to be a pretty county."

Caroline nodded, serenity returning to her breast — the woman was preening under the force of Caroline's fawning, as she had known she would. It was a useful tool, and one she had employed many times in the past, despite how much she detested it.

"As I said," continued Caroline, "I knew you would enjoy some time in the country. Furthermore, I cannot countenance my brother tying himself to a penniless fortune-hunter and knew you would know what is to be done. With your help — and that of Jessica — I thought we could devise a stratagem to release him from his infatuation."

Lady Diane paused and tapped her lips in thought. "As I recall, did your brother not shower Jessica with his attention during the last season?"

"He did," replied Caroline. "He is always interested in a pretty face and can be distracted rather easily."

"That does not speak well to his character, my dear. Though all women wish for a man to listen to them, none want one who can be made to roll over like a dog."

Caroline snorted. "Unfortunately, Charles has a streak of iron in him when he puts his mind to it. I have at times had occasion to tempt him away from unsuitable ladies. In this instance, however, he has been stubborn."

"Thus, Jessica's inclusion in your plans."

"Yes," replied Caroline. "She is a friend, she is easily led herself, and with a handsome dowry and a position in society which is above reproach, she is the ideal woman to marry my brother."

In reality, though Jessica would have been acceptable to Caroline, she still had dreams of Charles marrying into the minor nobility, at the very least. But she would never say that to Lady Diane for obvious reasons.

"I suppose she is. Then you wish for my help to bring this about."

"Yes," replied Caroline. "Though, perhaps, a little distraction provided by you would also assist. I know you mean nothing by it," Caroline hastened to say, "but Charles can be easily flattered by a pretty woman. With your presence and character, I have no doubt you can turn him away from Miss Bennet. Then we may work together to transfer his affections back to Jessica."

Lady Diane regarded Caroline for a moment, her expression unreadable. "Have you considered that perhaps Miss Bennet might be acceptable?" When Caroline tried to protest, Lady Diane held up her hand. Caroline subsided, but not with any grace. "I say this only because the girl is quiet and well-mannered, I suspect she is weak-willed, and she *will* be the sister of the future Mrs. Darcy."

Bile rose in Caroline's throat, but she suppressed it, knowing from Lady Diane's scrutiny that the woman was looking for it. Mastering herself quickly, Caroline essayed to respond.

"You are correct about Miss Bennet. To the woman herself, there is little to object. But other than Mr. Darcy she has no connections worth mentioning, and I suspect her portion is small, if not nonexistent. Furthermore, her mother is silly and intolerable, the future Mrs. Darcy is impertinent, and the whole family is not what I believe my brother should aspire to obtain in marriage. There are more suitable ladies aplenty for him to choose from. I will not have him tied to the Bennets if I can avoid it."

"Very well. It seems you have thought this through carefully. You have my support."

Caroline breathed a sigh of relief. Not only had she managed to placate her friend, but matters could now be put to rights regarding her brother. The two women stayed in the parlor for nearly thirty minutes planning their strategy. And when they left, Caroline felt more optimistic than at any time since she had arrived at this miserable hole.

Jane's reaction to Miss Bingley's intrigues was not surprising to Elizabeth. In fact, Elizabeth could have predicted it in advance, had she thought to do so.

"I am simply not convinced in Mr. Bingley's regard for me," said she when they spoke of the matter not long after the departure of the man in question. "Miss Bingley believes he favors Miss Cartwright, or perhaps Lady Diane. As she is much more familiar with her brother than any of us—even you, Lizzy, though you got on well with him—we must accept her opinion as the one most likely to be correct."

"The fallacy with your belief, dearest Jane, is your confidence in Miss Bingley's opinion. It allows for no possibility of the woman manipulating events for her own purpose, nor does it take her character into account."

A sigh escaped Jane's lips, and she passed a hand over her forehead. "I understand you do not think well of Miss Bingley, Lizzy, and your concerns for her character are not unfounded, it seems. But must all her doings be suspect? Can you not allow for the possibility that she simply wishes the best for her brother?"

"I could allow it if I saw any hint of it. But her behavior gives the lie to any such belief and renders any attempt to vindicate her futile."

It was clear Jane was reluctant to be persuaded. Fortunately, Mary was of like mind with Elizabeth and not hesitant to share her opinion.

"You should listen to Lizzy, Jane."

"Are you to add your voice to our sister's? I do not know why you both seek to persuade me in this matter."

"I *will* add my voice to Lizzy's," said Mary. "I trust Miss Bingley no more than our sister does, and I believe you should not either. Elizabeth's account of Miss Bingley's words to her, the way she views us all in contempt—these things speak to her intention to direct her brother by any means possible."

"I am convinced she brought her friends here as a means to distract her brother from you, Jane," added Elizabeth.

"And what of her assertion of her brother's interest in Miss Cartwright?" demanded Jane.

"Yes, Mr. Bingley himself has owned that he previously had some interest in her. But Mr. Darcy told me they agreed together that they would not suit.

"Jane, dearest," said Elizabeth, forestalling what she knew would be another protest, "there is no reason to argue. Mr. Bingley's future behavior will prove our opinion correct, or he will prove it wrong. I have little doubt which it will be, but if you are not convinced, simply watch him and make your own judgment."

A pause ensued, in which Jane seemed to be having difficulty in mastering her emotions. Though she had not known Mr. Bingley long, Elizabeth knew her sister did not do anything by half measures. Though Elizabeth did not think Jane in love with him, she was convinced that Jane esteemed him highly and, even now, was in danger of losing her heart.

"I would not wish to be hurt should he not behave as you suggest."

Her heart going out to her sensitive sister, Elizabeth reached out and put an arm around Jane's shoulders, drawing her close. Mary was not a girl who tended toward overt displays of emotion, but on this occasion, she mirrored Elizabeth's actions on Jane's other side, though more stiffly.

"Then guard your heart, by all means. But do not push him away, and do not hide so much of yourself that he feels you do not care. Trust my judgment, and trust what you can see of his actions, the way he regards you, how he attends to you and no other. I think you will not be disappointed, Jane."

The subject was not canvassed between them again. But Elizabeth knew her sister was thinking about her advice—indeed, it seemed she rarely thought of anything else. It was odd, Elizabeth decided, but while William's account of his previous behavior had caused Elizabeth to pause, she now trusted him to deal well with her sister. Elizabeth was certain it would all turn out well. But someone needed to keep Miss Bingley in check and prevent her interference, and Elizabeth had appointed herself to that task.

Wary as she was of Miss Bingley's motives, when the invitation arrived the next day to a dinner at Netherfield, Elizabeth assumed it was to try to forward Miss Bingley's schemes with respect to her brother. The dinner was to be held some three days hence, and they soon discovered that the Lucases and certain other families in the district had also been invited. But while Mr. Bingley came with Mr. and Miss Darcy to visit Longbourn the first day after the invitation arrived, the two days before the dinner, he did not accompany them. While Jane appeared to keep her serenity, Elizabeth, who knew her best, could see that she was suffering from a lack of confidence in his feelings.

"Can I assume Mr. Bingley has not come for reasons beyond his own wishes?" Elizabeth asked of William on that third day.

"You are correct," replied William. "Though I will own to relief that she no longer harbors hope of attracting me to her, Miss Bingley's focus on her brother is unrelenting. She is determined to pair him with one of her friends, and as such, has dominated every free moment he has."

Elizabeth sighed, hoping she had not misread the situation entirely. "I knew how it would be. How do you think Miss Bingley is getting on then? Will he be drawn in by her efforts?"

"Not well at all," replied William with a smirk. "Lady Diane, regardless of how she behaves, has no intention of accepting his regard. And while Miss Cartwright does not openly protest, it is clear she is being made uncomfortable by the situation."

From uncertainty to relief, Elizabeth beamed at her fiancé. "Then I was not incorrect. I should think this upcoming dinner party will be very interesting, indeed."

"I believe, my dear Miss Bennet, that is a rather severe understatement."

When the day arrived, the Bennets made their way to Netherfield, Elizabeth afire with anticipation for the evening. Jane was also excited, but her eagerness was tempered by her continuing uncertainty. When they arrived, Mr. Bingley's close attention to Jane put a smile back on her sister's face and seemed to hearten her.

"Miss Bennet, how wonderful it is to see you here," said Mr. Bingley when the Bennets stepped from the carriage. "You are all welcome, of course," continued he, speaking to the rest of the family. "If you will follow me, I shall lead you to the sitting-room."

Then Mr. Bingley took Jane's hand in his own and placed it firmly on the arm he offered her, guiding her into the house. Elizabeth, who had been greeted by William at the same time, followed along behind with her own gentleman, grinning at the scene Mr. Bingley was making.

"Your friend appears to be staking his claim at the outset, sir," said she. "With such an overt inclination, it will be difficult for Jane to doubt his intentions."

"He has not spoken to me," replied William. "But I have sensed more determination about him, even as his sister's manipulations have multiplied."

Content with what he was telling her, Elizabeth settled on watching them, especially eager to see how Miss Bingley would react to her brother's statement. She would not be disappointed.

"Charles!" called Miss Bingley as soon as they entered the room. There was a note of shrillness in her tone, a fact which set Elizabeth to grinning even more. "I see you have greeted the Bennets and brought them hither. I daresay the housekeeper could have performed the office well enough."

"Perhaps she could have," replied Mr. Bingley unperturbed. "But the Bennets are our close friends, and I wished to welcome them myself."

It was clear from the faces of those of the neighborhood—the Lucases, Robinsons, and Longs were all present—that he had not chosen to greet *them* at the door. Many looked between them with an air of knowing. That did not meet Miss Bingley's approval, but it appeared that Mr. Bingley did not care. The host took Jane to the side of the room, and when she saw she would not entice him away from Jane, Miss Bingley led her two friends to where he stood.

"Now we are all here together," said the woman. "I, for one, could not be happier."

Though Elizabeth could not quite see what happened next, she thought Miss Bingley had almost forcibly elbowed Jane to the side. In her place, she attempted to put Miss Cartwright, who was looking rather uncomfortable. But Mr. Bingley was not about to allow his sister her way.

"Have a care, Caroline," said he, shifting adroitly and moving Jane to the side until she was once again equal with the other two ladies.

"Oh, Miss Bennet," said Miss Bingley, her look all that was insolent. "I see you are here too."

Then she proceeded to ignore Jane altogether, directing the conversation and allowing little for any of the others to say. Elizabeth, who saw her actions, was on the verge of going over and giving the woman a piece of her mind, but the hand holding hers would not allow her to move away.

"Allow Bingley to respond to his sister's poor behavior, Elizabeth," said William, speaking in a low tone. "I can see his determination. I think you will be pleased with his reply."

Though Elizabeth wished for nothing more than to put Caroline Bingley in her place, she knew it was best to stay away and avoid making a scene. That did not mean she did not keep a close watch on what was happening. As Mr. Collins was near them, however, and he had not yet been introduced to the neighborhood, Elizabeth took on the office of performing the introductions. Elizabeth could not respect the man or even like him, but the grateful way in which he looked at her told her she had made the correct decision. Her mother or father should have taken on the office, but her father had gone to speak with Sir William, while her mother was closely watching Jane and Mr. Bingley.

The most interesting part of introducing Mr. Collins was, perhaps, the introduction to Charlotte. While the Longs and Robinsons all greeted him with good cheer and Mr. Collins was verbose in his response, as was to be expected, nothing seemed to pass between them which suggested anything out of the ordinary. Mrs. Long's two nieces, Elizabeth thought, might be of some interest to him, given his avowed reason in coming to Hertfordshire to secure a wife. But he did not pay them much attention. When he was introduced to the Lucases, however, that all changed.

"Sir William?" asked Mr. Collins, finally seeming to show some interest. "Am I correct in assuming you are a knight, sir?"

"Indeed, I am, Mr. Collins," replied Sir William, as always eager to speak of his experience at court. "It was presented to me because of an address I made to the king some years gone."

"Ah," replied Mr. Collins. "Then I think you would be acceptable to my patroness, Lady Catherine de Bourgh. She is, as you must understand, the daughter of an earl, and while she is affable to all, she insists upon the distinction of rank."

"She sounds much like many with whom I am acquainted," was Sir William's jovial reply. "The very great are among the best people that I have ever known. This Lady Catherine sounds like a truly refined lady."

A soft snort by her side told Elizabeth that William was not at all of Sir William's opinion, but he carefully schooled his countenance. Sir William and Mr. Collins continued to speak, and it seemed like each was attempting to outdo the other in their tales of the condescension of the higher classes. Sir William spun tales of St. James's court and the many men and women he had met there, but Mr. Collins did not fall behind simply because he could only speak of Lady Catherine. In the end, Elizabeth and William left them to their boasting conversation, content that Mr. Collins had been introduced to all with whom he wished to make an acquaintance.

Sometime later the company was called in to dinner, and while William, being the highest man in society was to escort Miss Bingley and sit by her, he chose the simple expedient of escorting Elizabeth on his other arm. When they were seated, he reserved most of his attention for Elizabeth. This seemed to suit Miss Bingley quite well, for she all but ignored them both. Instead, her gaze was fixed down the length of the table, where Mr. Bingley had done the same with Lady Diane and Jane. While Lady Diane seemed intent upon pulling Mr. Bingley's attention to her, Mr. Bingley had little for anyone other than Jane. As the meal went on, Miss Bingley's countenance darkened considerably.

It was after dinner when the fun truly began. A member of society since her seventeenth birthday, Elizabeth thought she was familiar with the proper behavior in a drawing room. She was also familiar with the steps of all the dances which were in vogue at present. But though some of them were complex, she had never engaged in any that were as complex a dance as she was about to in the next days and weeks in her attempts to thwart Miss Bingley's schemes.

"Oh, Charles," said Miss Bingley as soon as the gentlemen rejoined the ladies in the sitting-room, "I must have you come and lend us your assistance, for dearest Jessica and I cannot agree."

Without giving him any choice in the matter, Miss Bingley grasped her brother's arm with a grip which Elizabeth would not have been surprised had left bruises. Soon, she had him boxed in with Miss Cartwright and Lady Diane, though the former did not appear any happier about it than Mr. Bingley did himself.

"Better him than me," a mutter caught Elizabeth's attention, and she turned to see William watching them carefully. When he noted Elizabeth's scrutiny, he gave her a wry grin. "I cannot count the number of times Miss Bingley has clasped onto my arm with those claws she calls hands. That I have been at Netherfield with her for two weeks and she has not attempted to do it since the first day is rather refreshing."

"Perhaps that is so, sir," replied Elizabeth, sniffing with disdain, which she then ruined with a wink at him. "But this is not helping Jane, and I do not intend to allow it to continue."

With a determined step, Elizabeth approached the small group. When Bingley looked up at her with pleading eyes and stood abruptly to greet her, Elizabeth could only grin.

"Miss Elizabeth!" exclaimed he. "I am sure you already know Lady Diane and Miss Cartwright. Of course, you must. We were just engaged in a conversation of the McIntosh ball we all attended last season."

"I dare say it must have been a sight to see, indeed," said Elizabeth, winking at him before turning to the three ladies. "Perhaps you could describe it to me, Miss Bingley. I hazard a guess there was no little finery in evidence that evening."

As Elizabeth had known Miss Bingley would, she lost no time in regaling them all with tales which were of little interest to Elizabeth. The woman was predictable, after all—she would lose no opportunity to press her supposed superiority over Elizabeth. But as she was speaking, Elizabeth noticed that Mr. Bingley made himself scarce, though it appeared Miss Bingley had not.

Summoning a well of patience she had not thought she owned, Elizabeth listened to the woman's boasting claims, replying with the appropriate responses when she thought necessary. As such, it was some moments before Miss Bingley noticed her brother had left the vicinity, and it was when she turned to him for corroboration for her account.

"Is that not so, Charles?" said she, casting her eyes to where her brother had been standing earlier. "Charles?"

At that moment, Mr. Bingley was on the other side of the room, standing in close proximity to Jane, speaking in low tones. An expression of fury came over Miss Bingley's countenance, and she began to rise in pursuit of her recalcitrant brother. She was neatly forestalled when Elizabeth excused herself.

"Thank you, Miss Bingley, for this fascinating glimpse into London society. I will be certain to compare it with my own experiences when I attend with William after our wedding."

Then, with a smug nod at the woman, who was fuming by now, Elizabeth stepped away and returned to William's side. As she was leaving, however, she happened to notice that Miss Cartwright was looking at her with laughing eyes, though Lady Diane's expression was much more difficult to read. Elizabeth did not care for her opinion.

"You are an evil woman, Elizabeth Bennet," said William when she returned to him.

"My evil nature is only displayed when another deserves it," replied she, affecting airy unconcern. "I suggest you remember that, sir, for it may be the key to your future happiness."

They exchanged a look and soon were laughing merrily. "I would not have it any other way, my dear," said William. "I shall ensure you are properly directed in the future, for I would not wish your wicked wiles to be fixed upon me."

Elizabeth laughed again and put a hand on her betrothed's arm, an affectionate gesture. "I am so very fortunate to have you here, William. I had thought it unlikely that I would ever find someone to whom I could tie my life."

The way William's hand rose of its own accord to touch her cheek informed Elizabeth how much he cared for her. He was not a demonstrative man, and he adhered strictly to propriety—Elizabeth had never concerned herself with the worry that he would behave in an inappropriate manner with her, though at times she almost wished he would! But that only made these spontaneous displays of affection all the more to be cherished.

"I doubt you would have remained unclaimed for long," said William, his voice husky with emotion. "I am certain there are any number of men who would see your incomparable worth and snap you up without a second thought."

"You have more confidence in these unnamed gentlemen than I. But be that as it may, I am happy it was you. I cannot wait to start our lives together."

"Nor can I, Elizabeth. Nor can I."

The two lovers stayed together for the rest of the evening, basking in their shared intimacy. The others of the party, recognizing their intimacy for what it was, looked on indulgently but allowed them their privacy. Mr. Bingley was firmly ensconced by Jane's side and would not be moved, so that situation was well for the time being. And if Miss Bingley glared at them, both for their happiness with each other and the meddling in her plans, neither of the two lovers cared for her opinion.

CHAPTER XIV

One of the only things marring Elizabeth's happiness during this time was the deterioration of her friendship with Charlotte. While it should be noted that no one saw anything amiss between the two friends, Charlotte's encouragement for Elizabeth to feign love to induce Mr. Bingley to propose had never sat right with her. Elizabeth had managed to work past her disgust for such a suggestion, but much of their interaction together since had been done under a cloud of reserve.

On the morning after the dinner at Netherfield, Charlotte came to call on Elizabeth, as she had many times in the past after such an activity. While Elizabeth had not been able to forget her friend's words, she was more successful in pushing them to the side, so she could converse with Charlotte in an easy fashion. Of course, Charlotte was an intelligent woman and, as such, had seen what Elizabeth was attempting to do the previous evening. Thus, that was the main topic of their conversation.

"You were in fine form last night, Lizzy," said she, showing Elizabeth a knowing smirk. "With an opponent as clever as you, it is a wonder why Miss Bingley does not simply quit the field of battle altogether."

This was more the kind of conversation she had come to expect from Charlotte over the years of their friendship, and Elizabeth responded in kind: "Perhaps it would be best if she did. It would almost certainly be less strain on her dignity."

Charlotte laughed. "I treasure your friendship so, Lizzy, for your observations are so delightfully irreverent."

It struck Elizabeth that she treasured Charlotte's friendship too, regardless of what had come between them these past months. While she had been surprised and had held Charlotte's words against her, those ill feelings had lasted long enough. It would be best now to simply forget them. Many times were words spoken which were regretted later, and while Charlotte did not seem to regret them, Elizabeth had seen no indication she would behave as she had suggested. And it was not Elizabeth's place to judge her friend.

With these thoughts rolling around in her head, Elizabeth said without thinking: "I appreciate your friendship too, Charlotte. More than I can say."

"Then perhaps I can assist you in your struggle against the dastardly Miss Bingley?" Elizabeth laughed at her friend's characterization of the supercilious woman. "Surely you could use more foot-soldiers to do your bidding."

"Then I shall make use of your prowess should the opportunity arise. I am sure you will be a great assistance in our struggle." Charlotte grinned. But a moment later she became serious again. "On another subject, you and Mr. Darcy generated quite a lot of interest last night."

Unable to help it, Elizabeth blushed. "Surely we were not so very open."

"No, you were not. You were perfectly well behaved for a couple engaged and besotted with each other. I do not mean to insinuate that you acted improperly. Rather, I think there were many who perhaps saw you as grasping for the man with the larger fortune. Last night, however, after you rescued Mr. Bingley, it was clear to anyone with any wit at all to see that you positively doted on each other."

"I should hope so," replied Elizabeth. She had known there were some who would see her actions in such a way, as one could not please everyone at all times. But she had never thought of it in the terms Charlotte suggested.

"And it seems you were correct to maintain only a friendship with Mr. Bingley. His inclination for Jane is clear for all to see."

"Most of all his sister!" exclaimed Elizabeth, appreciating her friend's subtle and understated apology. "Remember, you have agreed to assist. I shall be calling on your assistance at some time or another."

"And I shall not fail you, my lord general!"

They laughed together, much of their former closeness restored. Thereafter, more general conversation ensued, with Elizabeth's sisters also sharing in it. Mr. Collins was also present, but while he normally commanded the course of any conversation in his ponderous tones, he seemed to think better of it on this occasion, contenting himself with a few observations here and there, usually at inopportune times.

When Charlotte rose to depart, she issued an invitation to Mr. Collins to dine with them that evening, claiming her father had asked her to do so. As the Longbourn family was more than a little fatigued with the man, they were eager to relinquish his company for an evening. Charlotte seemed to notice this, for she winked at Elizabeth, and then departed, after setting a time by which Mr. Collins was expected to attend them at Lucas Lodge.

For his part, Mr. Collins seemed well pleased with the invitation and took himself to his room, though Elizabeth judged it much too early to prepare for his evening out. Left with little to occupy themselves, the remaining three Bennet sisters decided to walk into Meryton. As Kitty and Lydia were safely ensconced in their school — and their infrequent letters to the family suggested they were actually enjoying the experience — such an endeavor could be undertaken without fear of being embarrassed by their antics. Soon, they were dressed in bonnets and pelisses, strolling down the lane which led to the town, swinging their arms and speaking in lively tones.

Meryton was much as it ever had been, not that she had expected anything different. The Bennet sisters all had their own favorite shops, the younger tending toward the haberdashery and milliners, while the eldest were fond of the bookstore. The sweet shop was a favorite of them all, and no walk to Meryton was complete without partaking of one of Mr. Graham's sugar sticks.

While the town was a bustle with activity, it was the presence of several red coats which caught the sisters' attention. With their sisters' absence, the Bennets had not had much contact with the militia, a matter of which Mrs. Bennet still lamented at times. Of course, the young ladies of the neighborhood could not gather together without speaking of them incessantly, and as such, Elizabeth knew more of them than she ever wished to.

One particular officer came to their notice that day, though the meeting was not without embarrassment, on one side at least. Lieutenant Denny, though he had made himself scarce whenever any Bennets were present, appeared on the street that morning in the company of another man not wearing regimentals, and as he was situated only a short distance away when he caught sight of them, to turn around and depart would be rude. Therefore, he put the best face on it that he could and stepped forward to greet them.

"Lieutenant Denny," said Elizabeth, her tone friendly. "It has been some time. I trust you are well?"

It seemed Denny was relieved that Elizabeth had chosen to simply ignore what had happened in the past, for he smiled. "Quite well, Miss Elizabeth. I understand your family has been much engaged with the Netherfield residents of late."

Though Elizabeth caught his slight emphasis on the word "engaged" she did not think he meant anything by it. "Yes, we have. Mr. Bingley and his friends are a welcome addition to our neighborhood."

"And soon you must leave the neighborhood," said Mr. Denny. "I wish you joy, Miss Elizabeth. Your future husband appears to be a good man."

At this moment, Elizabeth's attention was caught by the man at Mr. Denny's side, for he looked on her with some interest. He was a handsome man, well-favored, his bearing erect, and in person and manners appeared to be as attractive a man as she had ever seen. Had she not already been in love with William, she might have found herself under his power, for he was the most gentlemanly man she had ever seen. Should he remain in the neighborhood, he would undoubtedly command the attention of the masses of young girls by the force of his dashing smile alone.

"Ah, yes," said Mr. Denny, turning to his companion. "You have my apologies, Miss Elizabeth. Please allow me to introduce my friend to your acquaintance—George Wickham, lately of London. Wickham, this is Miss Bennet, Miss Elizabeth Bennet, and Miss Mary Bennet, of Longbourn estate quite nearby."

Mr. Wickham bowed and favored them all with an easy smile. "I am happy to make your acquaintance. I hope we become the best of friends."

"Do you mean to stay long in the neighborhood?" asked Jane.

"All winter, in fact," replied Mr. Wickham. "I am to accept a commission in Colonel Forster's regiment. I dare say from Denny's tales that I shall receive a welcome such as is not common, for the people of this neighborhood are very obliging."

While Elizabeth thought to say they were obliging only so long as their daughters were not trifled with, she decided to spare Denny the mortification such an observance would cause. "I believe we are as friendly as the next neighborhood, Mr. Wickham. I hope you find ample amusement to distract you when you are not on duty."

It may have been a trick of the light, but Elizabeth thought she caught a glimpse of Mr. Wickham's distaste when she mentioned his duties. As it was, however, he turned a charming smile on her and spoke, while Denny was speaking with Jane and Mary.

"If you will excuse my saying so, Miss Elizabeth, I am already disposed to appreciate this neighborhood. I have rarely seen such gentility and welcome for a poor soldier, such as I am set to become. You and your neighbors should be proud—it is not every day that people welcome outsiders with such artless enthusiasm."

"I would like to think newcomers are welcome according to their merits."

"You are wonderfully naïve, Miss Elizabeth," said Mr. Wickham. "In my experience, most people are distrustful of those with whom they are not acquainted. I, personally, know a man who is disdainful of all, incapable of speaking to them as an equal, or even of seeing any good in anyone who is not of his circle or level in society."

"There are always people who are less sociable than others," replied Elizabeth, wondering to where his comments tended.

"Yes, I suppose you are correct." Mr. Wickham paused and smiled, and he edged a little closer to her, speaking in a low tone: "I would be willing to share my experiences with you if you will give me an opportunity. I have a feeling you and I can be exceedingly good . . . friends, given the chance."

"I am always willing to make new friends," said Elizabeth, stepping back to put a little room between herself and Mr. Wickham. This man was far too forward for her liking, and his actions had begun to take on the appearance of flirting.

"Of course, you are!" exclaimed he. "How could any so lovely be anything less? Indeed, I am eager for our acquaintance to blossom into friendship. I have the feeling there will be none closer."

"It would be best if you did not come any closer than you are now."

Elizabeth jumped at the sound of Mary's voice so close by her side. She had been too consumed in fending off Mr. Wickham to note her younger sister's approach.

"I am interested in friendship with you too, of course," said Mr.

Wickham, favoring Elizabeth with an outrageous wink.

"Friendship is one thing, sir," said Mary, her voice as prim as Elizabeth had ever heard. "I am certain you understood your friend's reference to Elizabeth's situation and engagement?"

"I did," replied Mr. Wickham. There was no embarrassment in his response. He simply smiled and nodded, acknowledging Mary's point without hesitation.

"Then I would ask that you cease your flirting, sir," said Elizabeth, before Mary's overly sensitive nature could prompt her to say anything more.

"I am wounded!" exclaimed Mr. Wickham, clutching his heart. "I never meant my actions to be taken in such a way, Miss Elizabeth. I have a friendly, open disposition which is sometimes misunderstood. You have a ready defender it appears. Good for you, Miss Mary."

As he spoke, however, he turned his head slightly to the side and winked at Elizabeth from a position which she was certain Mary could not see. Then he glanced at her and back at Elizabeth and rolled his eyes. Elizabeth was offended in an instant.

Before she could speak up, however, and deliver a stinging rebuke, the attention of the party was caught by the approach of a group on horseback. It was Mr. Darcy, along with Mr. Bingley and Georgiana, as well as two other men Elizabeth had never met.

The moment Darcy spied George Wickham on the street, leering at Elizabeth in a wholly inappropriate manner, he was spurred into action. A glare at his cousin, coupled with a jut of his head toward Georgiana, and his sister was escorted away from the man who had broken her heart. But even before they had begun to move, Darcy vaulted from the saddle and strode forward, intent upon protecting Elizabeth from the libertine.

"Wickham," growled he, noting with satisfaction when Wickham shrank back in fear. "How singularly unfortunate it is to see you here today."

"D-Darcy," stuttered the man. "I had . . . had no idea you were in the district."

"Oh?" asked Darcy, his eyebrow raised in challenge. "Is that why you were attempting to charm my intended?"

"Wickham's brand of charm is like the appearance of a rose," said Fitzwilliam, who came to stand beside Darcy. "It is pretty to look at, but one never sees the thorn until pricked by it."

"A-and Fitzwilliam," stammered Wickham. He swallowed thickly and attempted to regain his control. "A good day to your gentlemen. I had no idea I would be so fortunate as to come across your paths in Hertfordshire."

"Unlikely," said Fitzwilliam, his tone flat and unfriendly. "There is very little about you which can be put down to chance, Wickham. I suspect you learned of Darcy's presence in advance and came here with the intention of trying your usual tricks."

"I assure you—"

"Your assurances are worthless, Wickham," growled Darcy. "I would not trust you if you told me water is wet."

"Do you gentlemen have some issue with Wickham?" asked a new voice. Darcy looked up to see a man dressed in regimentals, watching them with evident confusion.

"You are known to this man?" asked Fitzwilliam.

"I am," replied the man. "He is a friend and has agreed to join the regiment on my suggestion."

Fitzwilliam snorted. "Then your choice of friends is a poor one unless you are of his ilk."

Then Fitzwilliam turned back to Wickham, a gleam in his eye. It was clear that Wickham did not like the look of it, for he blanched.

"But perhaps it is good that you should join the militia, Wickham. It would finally allow me a method of controlling you. I am certain your future commanding officer would be pleased to learn of exactly what kind of man he will have in his regiment."

Wickham, it seemed, had had enough. He shook his head and turned to the officer, saying: "I believe I have reconsidered, Denny. It would be best that I do not take the commission. In fact, I believe I should be on my way."

Then Wickham turned and began to walk away, his steps swift and clipped. But Fitzwilliam was not the kind of man to simply allow him to escape in such a manner.

"Yes, Wickham, be gone. But do not stop when you reach the sea. No man has managed to swim all the way to the New World, but if you keep in mind what I shall do to you should I catch you, I believe you might just make it!"

Fitzwilliam laughed as Wickham's steps quickened, but Denny, clearly distressed, shouted after him: "What of the commission, Wickham?"

"Someone else may have it, for I care not," Wickham's voice floated back to them.

Then he turned a corner and disappeared from view. Fitzwilliam watched him for a few moments before starting forward himself. "I will make sure he is gone. You can never trust a snake like Wickham."

Satisfied Wickham had been chased off, Darcy turned to Elizabeth to assure himself of her wellbeing. She watched him, clearly relieved that the man was gone, yet unperturbed by her encounter with him. By her side, Mary was watching with clear approval. Whatever else had happened, the two young ladies had not been fooled by the man's silken tongue.

"Excuse me, Mr. Darcy," said the militia officer—Darcy remembered Wickham addressing him as Denny. "From your reaction to seeing Wickham, I assume you have no cordial relationship with him."

"And neither should you," said Darcy, his distaste for his former playmate overruling his sense of polite behavior. "He is not a man with whom anyone of good standing in society should associate."

Mr. Denny nodded slowly. "Then I am happy I was warned away. In truth, Wickham is just a passing acquaintance. Colonel Forster will be relieved he did not accept the commission if he is as you say."

Darcy nodded, a clear dismissal, which Mr. Denny seemed to understand. He bowed and excused himself, leaving Darcy in the company of the younger two Bennet sisters. Bingley was standing several feet away speaking with the eldest. Before Darcy could address his fiancée, Fitzwilliam returned, whistling a jaunty tune as if he had not a care in the world.

"He is gone unless he doubles back. I judge that highly unlikely, however, considering his haste to depart."

"Good riddance," Darcy replied. "I know not how he learned of my presence, but I will not have him importuning anyone in the neighborhood."

Elizabeth gasped. "Mr. Denny mentioned my engagement, but he did not mention your name in my hearing. It seemed to me that Mr. Wickham did not seem surprised by it."

"It is possible his plan to join this particular militia company was a coincidence," said Fitzwilliam. "But I suspect that he heard something of Darcy's engagement and planned some devilry based on whatever information he was able to obtain."

"Unfortunately, one never knows with Wickham," said Darcy. "But be that as it may, I believe it would be best if we were to escort the ladies back to Longbourn."

"Mr. Darcy!" exclaimed Elizabeth, laughing at his lapse. "I am afraid you have forgotten the civilities, sir. You have not yet introduced your companion to our acquaintance."

William colored but then grinned at Elizabeth, while directing a teasing grin at his friend. "I am not certain you wish to know *him*. He can be teasing, unserious, and is altogether an unsuitable acquaintance for a young lady of your quality."

Laughing again, Elizabeth turned a raised eyebrow to the second man. He only shook his head at William and grinned at Elizabeth. "He is ever thus. It seems a great estate and an income to make many a man envious leads him to believe he is better than everyone else. I am sure you have seen this in his character."

"You cannot expect me to answer in the affirmative, sir. He is soon to be my husband. I am certain I have never seen such a shade as you describe in his character."

"Thank you, Elizabeth," said William as the other man laughed again. I suppose I have little choice but to introduce him to you." He turned and beckoned Mr. Bingley and Jane to join them, and by this time Georgiana had approached with the final man who had escorted her away during the confrontation with Mr. Wickham. He then introduced the three Bennet sisters to their acquaintance before turning to the two gentlemen.

"Please allow me to introduce my cousins, Lord James Fitzwilliam, Viscount Chesterfield, and his younger brother and reprobate, Colonel Anthony Fitzwilliam.

The colonel protested again, his good humor clearly a match for Mr. Bingley's. William only smirked at him and rolled his eyes at Elizabeth.

"We are happy to make your acquaintances, of course," said Elizabeth, speaking for the sisters—Jane was still distracted by Mr. Bingley, while Mary was in awe at the sight of an actual viscount in their midst. "You are very welcome in Meryton, my lord. But I believe we even have a place for a reprobate if he suppresses his natural inclinations."

"You may be disappointed, Miss Elizabeth," said Colonel Fitzwilliam. "Reprobates are rarely well behaved."

"Then let us hope this will mark a change in your character, sir. We would not wish to be taken in by the appearance of good humor and courtly manners."

They stood on the street speaking for several moments before they began to take some thought of returning to Longbourn, for which the cousins immediately pledged their attendance to walk them there.

Thus, they set out, the viscount and Georgiana hanging back, while Mr. Bingley was by Jane's side as was his custom. When William thought to offer his arm to Elizabeth, the colonel stepped forward with a word of admonishment for his cousin.

"If you will allow me, Darcy, I will escort your betrothed, so I may come to know the woman who has captured your heart."

Though he clearly wished to stay by Elizabeth's side, William readily offered his arm to Mary. And soon they set off.

"I am surprised to see you here, Colonel," said Elizabeth. "I had not thought Mr. Bingley intended to invite any more guests to his estate."

"I do not think he had," replied the colonel. He showed her a devilish smile, continuing: "I understand that Mr. Bingley is having difficulty with his sister. My brother and I are . . . reinforcements, if you will."

Elizabeth laughed. "You have proven your profession, sir. That was a marvelous use of a battle metaphor, indeed. How did you manage to escape Netherfield without Miss Bingley and her friend hanging onto your coattails?"

"We did not. We have not been to Netherfield yet. You see, knowing we were coming, Darcy, Bingley, and Georgiana rode out to meet us out of town. Our carriage has been sent on to Netherfield, which is where we shall go when we have left you at your home."

"Well played then. You have managed to put off the inevitable. I suspect that once your brother arrives at Netherfield, he shall be less than comfortable there."

Colonel Fitzwilliam's eyes positively gleamed in response. "James has never met Caroline Bingley, but I have. I am quite anticipating the spectacle, I assure you."

The walk back to Longbourn was amusing, indeed. Colonel Fitzwilliam was a jovial man, quick with a jest and quick on his feet. He was quite like Mr. Bingley in some respects, though Elizabeth was certain he was the more serious of the two. If asked, she could only state that it was the seriousness of his occupation which led her to suppose that to be so. Elizabeth found she liked him very well, indeed.

When they arrived in the environs of Longbourn, William's party declined to continue any further, instead urging the sisters to return directly to their home. "We would not wish to overwhelm your mother on a day when she is not expecting any more visitors, and we truly must return to Netherfield. We shall return tomorrow when I will be happy to introduce my relations."

"I believe I see what you are doing, William," said Elizabeth in a teasing response to his announcement. "You suspect my mother will be quite out of her wits to have *two* sons of an earl in her sitting-room, and you do not wish to expose your cousins to her without preparing them first."

"I believe I may safely say, my dear Elizabeth, that I would happily brave a hundred such scenes, should it allow me another thirty minutes in your company. But we truly must depart, for I expect Miss Bingley is quite in a tizzy over the appearance of a carriage on her doorstep."

"Then I wish you well. But it *is* shocking the way you are putting your cousins in an unenviable situation, sir. You *know* how Miss Bingley will act. The viscount, in particular, will be an object of prey to no less than *two* young ladies in residence."

"It is nothing to which he is not accustomed," said William, grinning openly. "I dare say it will keep him on his toes."

With that, William leaned over, captured her hand and bestowed a lingering kiss on its back, and then mounted his horse and departed. Elizabeth watched long as he receded in the distance, eventually a turn in the road taking him from her view. She was highly gratified that he had looked back at her several times.

CHAPTER XV

*espite a lack of interest in ascribing anything of good to Miss Bingley, Darcy was forced to acknowledge the woman possessed a highly developed ability to see to her own interests. When they arrived back at Netherfield, it was to find the place in an uproar, with Miss Bingley as the maestro conducting the chorus. Upon spying them, she was quick to approach her brother, the fire obviously in her eyes. It was only because Darcy was nearby that he heard her words, for she had the sense to restrain from shrieking as she obviously wished to do.

"Charles! How could you have neglected to inform me of the imminent arrival of a viscount, no less? Do you not know of the preparations which must be undertaken to meet such a man's expectations?"

"I think, Caroline, you will discover that Lord Chesterfield is not the demanding noble you may have seen in London. In fact, he is quite easy and unpretentious."

They had all climbed the stairs by that point, and Miss Bingley was not able to continue her diatribe, though her glare promised retribution. Instead, she curtseyed and put on her best subservient mask, addressing them all.

"I am happy to see you returned and bid you all welcome to Netherfield."

"Of course, Caroline," said Bingley, no one missing the sardonic note in his voice. "I would be happy to make the introductions."

He did so, though it was done in an almost perfunctory manner. Miss Bingley quivered with excitement, even as she maintained an air of sophisticated calm for Chesterfield's benefit. But he was not so easily fooled, and his glare at Darcy soon spoke to his annoyance.

They managed to make their escape soon after, removing to their rooms, allowing the travelers to change and the others to refresh themselves. The demands of society, however, dictated that they attend to their hosts. Thus, after delaying as long as they dared, they made their way down to the sitting-room and the most uncomfortable afternoon of their lives.

By dinner, it was clear which way the wind was blowing. In the intervening time, Miss Bingley had realized that a viscount was a much greater catch than a gentleman, no matter how wealthy, and had decided to do her utmost to pursue a man who had no intention of being caught. At dinner, she preened at the pleasure of having a member of high society situated by her side, even while Darcy was relieved that he was not obliged to occupy that position any longer.

"Let me inform you again of how honored we are to have you with us. I do hope your chambers are quite comfortable and convenient?"

Darcy stifled a laugh—she knew the only reason why she did not speak of ensuring his cousin received the best rooms in the house was because Darcy himself already occupied them. The woman's glance at him confirmed how she wished she had been able to find some way to eject him so they could be bestowed on the worthier recipient. By his side, Fitzwilliam also grinned, catching the viscount's attention. He declined to respond to them, however, turning his attention back to Miss Bingley.

"They are quite fine, indeed, Miss Bingley. I thank you for doing so much with so little time to prepare. I cannot imagine how your brother forgot to inform you of our coming."

"A simple oversight, my lord," said Bingley, though Darcy knew it was anything but.

For a moment, Miss Bingley seemed to hover between exasperation with her brother and pleasure at the viscount's praise. Eventually, pleasure won out, for she directed what she thought was a beguiling smile at him.

"It is nothing more than a matter of being prepared for any

eventuality. I have personally directed the servants to keep all the bedchambers clean in the event we should have unexpected visitors."

"That is impressive forethought, indeed, Miss Bingley."

Darcy and Fitzwilliam exchanged a look, but neither dared to laugh. It seemed Hurst was not similarly afflicted by discretion, for he chuckled, as he ate his dinner with relish. The rest of the diners carried on conversations quietly, most attempting not to see the blatant attempts by their hostess to ingratiate herself with her dinner companion.

"I understand the society here is quite interesting," said the viscount, seemingly searching for a topic safe to discuss.

"I expect you will be disappointed," replied Miss Bingley, a hint of testiness entering her voice. "I cannot imagine where you might have obtained such a notion. There is little but savagery in the characters of those who inhabit this neighborhood. Were there any other choice, I would not give them even a hint of my attention."

"Is that so?" replied the viscount, a faint hint of a smile on his countenance. "Your brother gave me quite a different account,"

Miss Bingley snorted with disdain. "Well, Charles *does* tend to find himself comfortable with even the most undeserving of any society. I suppose it serves him well at times, though it often means mingling with those who cling to him like a leach."

"You do not say," said Chesterfield. He turned to Darcy. "I hope you have not chosen one of these savages of which Miss Bingley has spoken. We Fitzwilliams consider ourselves open-minded, but there are limits, old man."

"I know you did not speak to her beyond civilities," replied Darcy, his glare at Miss Bingley warning the woman to guard her tongue. "Did she seem to you to be a savage?"

"Point taken, Darcy. In fact, she seemed perfectly charming, a clever sort of girl."

Miss Bingley blanched. "You have already met Eliza Bennet?"

"Yes, we have," said Chesterfield in an offhand manner. "Darcy, Georgiana, and your brother met us outside Meryton, and we met the Bennet sisters while we rode through town. I found them quite agreeable, indeed, though I did not have an opportunity to speak much with them."

While she was silent for a moment, in the end, Miss Bingley was not able to restrain her vitriol. She sniffed and replied: "I am afraid I cannot agree, my lord. I hope for the best for your cousin, of course, but I am afraid Miss Eliza will embarrass him dreadfully in society."

"Oh, you need have no worry of that," said the viscount with an airy wave. "She was perfectly charming. Besides, Darcy is quite capable of embarrassing himself without the assistance of a wife."

By his side, Fitzwilliam only avoided spraying them all with wine by the barest of margins. Hurst, it seemed, was in similar straits, and even Georgiana and Bingley were grinning openly.

"We all have some tendency toward the ridiculous at times, Chesterfield," said Darcy, not offended in the slightest. "I could regale the company with tales of your behavior at the Cavendish ball last year."

Chesterfield laughed. "Touché, Darcy. Touché. I should refrain from trading barbs with you, for you are far too quick."

"You should understand that by now, Cousin," replied Darcy.

"Oh, what excellent cousins you are!" cried Miss Bingley, clearly desperate to have Chesterfield's attention back on her. "Unfortunately, though Mr. Darcy is the epitome of a society gentleman, and his future wife *may* comport herself well in company with copious amounts of training, the rest of her family is a lost cause."

"Miss Bennet is everything that is lovely," interjected Bingley with a studied nonchalance which spoke of a rapidly waning patience.

"Of course!" exclaimed Miss Bingley. "How could I have forgotten the lovely Miss Bennet? She is, indeed, quiet and decorous, of course. And utterly insipid. But at least she is not an embarrassment.

"I am afraid, my lord," said Miss Bingley, turning and leaning toward Chesterfield like a conspirator sharing a secret, "that you will find no one with any of the superior breeding or behavior such as that to which you are accustomed. I believe you should content yourself with Netherfield while you are here."

"In fact," said Lady Diane, speaking for the first time, "there are only two in the room who are of Lord Chesterfield's level of society. Even Mr. Darcy, though he must be acceptable as his lordship's cousin, is naught but a gentleman, regardless of his lineage."

The piercing way in which Lady Diane stared at Miss Bingley informed everyone that she was not disposed to allow her friend free rein in pursuing the suddenly available viscount. For his part, Chesterfield directed a hard look at Darcy, a reprimand for putting him in this situation. Darcy only grinned and raised his glass and Chesterfield, being the good man he was, laughed and shook his head.

The rest of the dinner passed in like fashion with Miss Bingley attempting to ingratiate herself with the viscount, who answered in a blithe and disinterested manner. That did not deter the huntress, of course—her ability to flatter was positively indefatigable. Lady Diane, situated as she was at the opposite end of the table, could hardly vie for his attention where she was. Miss Bingley noted this, of course, and while her glances at her guest were not triumphant, Darcy could see a certain amount of smug satisfaction in them. Fitzwilliam, for his part, relished the absurdity present at the dinner table, but as the meal continued, he began to pay more attention to Miss Cartwright, who was seated on his other side.

After dinner was more of the same, though the two women competing for Chesterfield's attention were in a position to do it in much closer quarters. Darcy sat with Georgiana, speaking quietly, while Fitzwilliam again took his seat next to Miss Cartwright. And Darcy was amused to note that in her zeal to recommend herself to the viscount, Miss Bingley quite forgot her previous goal, which was to recommend her friends to Bingley and turn his attention from Miss Bennet.

In all, Darcy thought it was a nice bit of work he had performed in the service of his future sister. Elizabeth would no doubt have something else in mind to thwart her, but with all the distractions in place, Darcy hardly thought it would be necessary. But he anticipated it nonetheless.

As Elizabeth expected, Mrs. Bennet was by no means silent when the viscount came to visit with the Netherfield party the next day. But her behavior was better than she might have expected, largely, she thought, because her mother was awed at the presence of a member of the peerage in their midst.

"Mr. Darcy's cousin, you say," said Mrs. Bennet, her handkerchief fluttering as she moved it with agitation. "I can scarce believe an actual viscount has visited my sitting-room. You are quite welcome to Longbourn, of course."

"Thank you, Mrs. Bennet," said Lord Chesterfield, smiling to put her at ease. "You have a comfortable house, and I can see you have done much to make it into a home for your family."

"Well . . . I have done my best, and I thank you, sir."

Mrs. Bennet's awe at the man's kind words was such that Elizabeth did not hear her speak more than two words together for the rest of the visit. Mr. Collins, thankfully, was absent, for she doubted he would have been able to restrain himself as her mother did.

With the first visit completed, the neighboring estates once again fell into the routine of visits and society engagements of the area, of which there were a few. Lord Chesterfield continued to be a fixture, and he was given every deference wherever he went. But at times Elizabeth thought he would have preferred that others forget his title and treat him as a simple man.

Mr. Darcy continued to see Elizabeth every day, either at Netherfield, Longbourn, at any events they jointly attended, or in Meryton. Mr. Bingley's attentions to Jane continued apace, and while Miss Bingley was distracted by her design to attract Lord Chesterfield, she soon remembered her now secondary design, throwing Miss Cartwright in his direction whenever she had the chance.

Unfortunately for Miss Bingley, Miss Cartwright was more often seen in company with Colonel Fitzwilliam in those days and had little interest in being paired with Mr. Bingley. Still, the woman kept at it with dogged determination, necessitating Elizabeth's intervention at various times. And as for Lady Diane, she was also vying for Lord Chesterfield's notice, seeming less interested in whatever schemes Miss Bingley designed as time wore on. And so, the next week past in this fashion.

The following week, Monday, the day after church, saw a new piece of information come to Longbourn which surprised Elizabeth exceedingly. Mr. Collins, much to the relief of everyone in the Bennet family, was largely absent those days, and while Elizabeth soon learned that he spent much of his time at Lucas Lodge in the company of the Lucases, she had not thought much of it. The possibility of his having an interest in Charlotte had crossed her mind, but other than a shudder at the thought of what form such a repulsive man's lovemaking might take, she concerned herself with other matters.

Thus, it was a surprise when Charlotte arrived early that morning to relate a piece of momentous news to them all. When she entered, it was easy to discern that Charlotte was nervous, though Elizabeth did not understand why. When her friend asked her for a moment in private, Elizabeth wondered what could possibly be amiss.

"I suppose you must wonder why I have asked to speak to you, Lizzy."

"I will own that I am curious, my dear Charlotte. Has something happened at Lucas Lodge to cause you distress?"

Charlotte released a nervous laugh. "No, it is not that. We are all very well. Rather, this concerns you, Lizzy. Or perhaps it is more appropriate to say that it concerns me, and I hope very much you will be happy for me when you hear my news."

"Then, by all means, share it with me! You have my curiosity afire."

Again, it appeared Charlotte was more than a little anxious. But she squared her shoulders, raised her chin, and looked Elizabeth directly in the eye.

"I wished to inform you, Lizzy, before you could hear by any other means. I am certain you are aware that Mr. Collins has been at Lucas Lodge much of late?"

"I *am* aware, Charlotte. And I thank you for seeing to his amusement while he is in Hertfordshire. Unfortunately, there is too much activity at Longbourn, and I am certain Mr. Collins would not have found the interest here he would have expected, having been long sundered from the family."

"In that, I believe you are correct," exclaimed Charlotte. "But I must inform you, Lizzy, that Mr. Collins's purpose in visiting us was not simply because he desired the attention of others. It is actually for me that he has been coming these days. Yesterday, after church, Mr. Collins made me an offer and I have accepted him"

After the event, when Elizabeth had an opportunity to take some time to herself and think on the matter, she would realize that she had not been surprised that Mr. Collins had proposed to Charlotte. Indeed, the signs were all there, from his focus on the Lucases in particular to the times she had seen them talking together in company or even one occasion when Elizabeth had visited Lucas Lodge herself. Rather, it was that Mr. Collins had been so precipitous as to propose less than a fortnight after meeting Charlotte that shocked her. Elizabeth's own courtship of about a month was far and away the quickest she had ever heard of, and even then, she had wondered many times if they had not proceeded too expeditiously!

"Will you not say something, Lizzy?" asked Charlotte, a plaintive note in her voice. "Can you wish me happiness?"

A multitude of thoughts passed through Elizabeth's mind at this time, and most of them centered on her belief that her friend was too good for such a sycophantic toad as Mr. William Collins. But while Elizabeth would think this privately and acknowledge to herself that she could never have made Charlotte's choice had she been in her friend's place, on the other hand, she realized that to rail against that choice or otherwise criticize it would be to change forever—and perhaps end—their friendship. And as altered as it had become, she found she could not reconcile herself to it. She valued it too much.

"Of course, I congratulate you!" said Elizabeth, drawing her friend into an embrace. "I only hesitated because I was surprised at the suddenness of your announcement. You have not known him for two weeks!"

"Well do I know it!" replied Charlotte, her relief evident in the tremble of her voice. "But you should not talk, my friend. You only knew Mr. Darcy a month, after all."

"That is true," said Elizabeth, resisting reminding Charlotte that *she* was not marrying a repulsive man. "It is just all so sudden. I will own that I have had some inkling that Mr. Collins possessed some partiality for you. But I would have thought he would return to stay at Longbourn, continued his wooing over the course of several visits."

"Perhaps he might have," replied Charlotte. "But I will confess I encouraged him. I am not romantic, and I do not see the point in becoming more acquainted with his character when all I wish is a good home and the protection of marriage. It is, you know, best to know as little of your partner's faults as possible. What I do not know now cannot vex me before our marriage. And it is possible I may even be pleasantly surprised."

Again, Elizabeth was forced to bite her tongue, lest she say something which would offend her friend. Instead, she chose the simple expedient of repeating her congratulations.

"I have heard much of your future husband's patroness," said she. "It will be interesting to see how you manage her, especially since I expect she will be extremely angry in the near future."

"Oh?" asked Charlotte, fixing Elizabeth with a quizzical look. "In what way?"

"On the day they first met, Mr. Collins asked Mr. Darcy about a supposed engagement between my betrothed and Miss de Bourgh. It seems that Lady Catherine has long hoped for their union."

"And she will be displeased when she learns of your engagement to him," said Charlotte, at once understanding Elizabeth's point.

"Yes," replied Elizabeth. "Mr. Darcy means to inform her of the matter, but he does not wish to do so until the time before our marriage is almost accomplished."

"Thus limiting her ability to interfere."

"Exactly."

Charlotte nodded, distracted. "I can see where such a woman as I am led to believe she is would react with fury over her nephew's supposed defection. If you will excuse my asking, what was Mr. Darcy's response?"

"That there was never any engagement formalized and that his aunt's wishes did not constitute a binding contract. Mr. Darcy informed Mr. Collins that neither he nor Miss de Bourgh had any intention of marrying the other."

"I might wonder why Mr. Collins has not written to Lady Catherine of the matter. It seems out of character for him to keep this from her, considering his continual veneration of her character."

"I have nothing more than conjecture," replied Elizabeth. "I suspect, however, that he did not wish to offend Mr. Darcy, who will soon be a relation, albeit a distant one. It is also possible, though I hope you will forgive me for saying as much, Mr. Collins realizes that Mr. Darcy is in a position to do more for his career than Lady Catherine."

"That is quite possible," replied Charlotte, nodding her head, though still distracted. "But he runs the risk of offending Lady Catherine. If she becomes aware that he knew of it and did not speak to her, she will react badly."

Elizabeth chewed her lip in thought. It was a possibility she had not considered. While she had little esteem for Mr. Collins, she certainly had for the future *Mrs. Collins*. She would not make Charlotte's life difficult, especially when she thought it likely living with Mr. Collins would be difficult enough.

"Then I shall have a word with Mr. Darcy. I am certain he will know what is to be done to temper her anger when she discovers it. Perhaps he can announce it to her when Mr. Collins is to return to Kent, thereby making it appear as if Mr. Collins did not know of the matter in advance. Then, if Mr. Collins gives the appearance of supporting Lady Catherine, suspicion will not fall on him."

"Thank you," said Charlotte, once again seeming overcome by emotion. "I cannot tell you what your support means to me. I hope we shall continue to be friends, though we shall be situated a great distance from each other."

"I hope so too, Charlotte."

Their conversation concluded, Elizabeth led Charlotte back down the hall to the sitting-room in which her mother entertained guests. When they entered therein, only Mrs. Bennet, Jane, and Mary were present. Mrs. Bennet peered at them, interest written upon her brow, no doubt eager to know why her daughter had been ensconced for the past fifteen minutes with Charlotte. Elizabeth judged it best that her mother be told at once, though after Charlotte departed. But her friend had other ideas.

"Mrs. Bennet," greeted she. "I suppose you are wondering why I asked for a private audience with Lizzy."

"Y-Yes, that is true," stammered Mrs. Bennet, surprised by Charlotte's forthright manner.

"Then your curiosity will be assuaged, for my news will affect this estate in the future. You see, Mr. Collins has been at Lucas Lodge much of late, and he has come for a particular purpose. Yesterday he proposed to me, and I have accepted him."

While Elizabeth might have expected a loud outburst from her mother, she surprised them all by remaining silent. Her eyes practically bulged out of her head, and her mouth opened wide, but though her jaw moved, she did not speak. A moment later her mouth closed with an audible snap, and several emotions passed over her face. Mrs. Bennet had known Mr. Collins would marry a woman who was not her daughter. This was only confirmation of what she had already known.

"I am . . . happy to hear of it, Charlotte my dear," said Mrs. Bennet, rising to catch Charlotte's hands and squeeze them gently. "If the next mistress of this estate cannot be one of my daughters, then I am happy it will be you, for I know you will cherish it as my husband's family has for many years."

Resignation was not what Elizabeth had expected from her mother. It was clear Charlotte was no less surprised by Mrs. Bennet's actions than Elizabeth, but she held her composure and thanked Mrs. Bennet.

"Of course, I will, Mrs. Bennet. You have my word."

Mrs. Bennet smiled at her, a tremulous gesture, and then announced her intention to retire to her rooms to rest. They watched her as she departed, Elizabeth with bemusement, while she suspected Charlotte felt nothing but relief.

Soon Charlotte made her own apologies and returned to Lucas Lodge, leaving Elizabeth alone with her sisters. She did not miss the curious looks they both gave her, but she did not intend to begin the conversation herself. She was saved the trouble of it when Jane spoke up.

"That *is* a surprise, is it not Lizzy? I had no notion that Mr. Collins was partial to Charlotte."

Though she wished to say something to the effect that any partiality at this early stage was entirely in Mr. Collins's imagination, she refrained. She had not spoken such venomous words to her friend — she would not now to her sisters.

"No, but for practical Charlotte, I suppose it is a prudent choice." Elizabeth laughed. "She even told me it was best this way, as she did not wish to vex herself with her husband's faults before they were married."

Mary wrinkled her nose at Elizabeth's jest, and Elizabeth could not say that she disagreed with her sister. Jane, however, sighed.

"I would not wish to make such a dispassionate choice. It would be far better to have a man's esteem before I agree to marry him."

"You know I agree with you, Jane. But I understand Charlotte's position and have supported her choice. It is now in her hands."

The three sisters fell silent after that, each lost in her own thoughts. For Elizabeth's part, she could only hope that Charlotte did not learn to regret her choice.

Chapter XVI

*I*t was fortunate that William agreed with Elizabeth concerning the matter of Mr. Collins.

"It is astute of you to think of it, my dear," said he when she raised the matter with him. "I had never considered Lady Catherine's response to our news and certainly not in conjunction with your cousin."

"Had it not been for my friend's engagement, I may have been content to allow him to face Lady Catherine's wrath himself." Elizabeth paused and grinned. "I have no doubt his groveling would soon win her over."

William laughed at Elizabeth's sally. "Perhaps it would."

"But I would not wish for my friend to begin her marriage under such a cloud of ill feelings and your aunt's fury, which I have been led to believe can be legendary. To protect Mr. Collins, I think we should inform her as soon as possible."

"Very well," replied William. "I shall write to her today. I cannot predict what form her displeasure will take, but I will warn her against taking matters into her own hands."

"You need not fear for me. I can handle angry aunts if necessary."

William smiled and grasped her hand, raising it to his lips. "I know you can, my love. Your fortitude is truly a sight to be seen. But I will do everything in my power to protect you, regardless. My uncle knows of our engagement. I shall also write to him. He can control her if anyone can.

"But, Elizabeth," continued William, his countenance turning grave, "a shadow over your countenance when you informed me of your friend's engagement suggests you are not happy with her choice."

"I *was* shocked," replied Elizabeth with a sigh. "Though it was more due to the speed of their engagement rather than that Charlotte chose to accept his suit. I understand her choice, but I could never have made it for myself. "

"And that is one of the things I love about you. I know that I am gaining the best wife, one who is marrying me for nothing more than inclination. There are many men who marry for prudence and many more who remain uncertain of their future wives' feelings. I am blessed, for I *know*."

Embarrassed at his praise, Elizabeth ducked her head, only to become aware of his soft chuckling. They stayed together for some time until Elizabeth finally shooed him away to write his letter.

So matters continued for the rest of the week. Miss Bingley's schemes continued apace, and Elizabeth thwarted them whenever they were in company, though at times she hardly thought it was necessary. Miss Bingley's initial distraction with Lord Chesterfield was soon tempered with her desire to keep her brother from Jane, and as her attention was divided, it often happened she accomplished neither objective well.

Certainly, her friends were not the confederates she hoped they would be. Lady Diane paid less and less attention to Mr. Bingley, focusing more on the viscount, her manner becoming ever more supercilious the longer she was in Hertfordshire. As for Miss Cartwright, she seemed pleased with Colonel Fitzwilliam and could rarely be found away from his side, except when Miss Bingley attempted to pair her with her brother.

The beginning of the next week saw another event on the schedule of Meryton's social calendar: an assembly at the local hall. They were held monthly in the town, but this month's edition drove interest due to the new arrivals at Netherfield, and, in particular, Lord Chesterfield.

"I had intended to hold a ball at Netherfield," confided Mr. Bingley on the day before the event. "But Caroline flatly refused, saying she was far too busy to organize a ball and had not been in Hertfordshire long enough." Mr. Bingley grimaced. "She claimed it was my own fault for not inviting her to stay earlier."

"As I recall, did you not inform her of your coming and extend an invitation in September?"

"I did," replied he. "But you must translate my sister's words to understand them. You see, in saying I did not invite her, she truly means that I did not inform her of Darcy's presence, which would have necessitated her immediate cessation of whatever she had been doing in London in order to hurry to Hertfordshire."

"I thank you for it, Mr. Bingley," said Elizabeth with a laugh. "I imagine my courtship with Mr. Darcy might have been quite different had your sister been present for it."

"There is little doubt of that. I shall wait until the New Year, I suppose. Should Caroline still balk at it, perhaps Louisa will consent."

Perhaps she would, thought Elizabeth, though she could not hope to discern Mr. Bingley's other sister's feelings on virtually any subject. Mrs. Hurst was almost always found at the periphery of any gathering, and while Elizabeth thought she had seen evidence of her disapproval of Mr. Bingley's action toward Jane, the woman had not raised any explicit objections. She was grateful for the other woman's forbearance, though she had little desire to become better acquainted.

On the day of the assembly, the Bennet sisters dressed with their usual care. Or perhaps it was more correct to say their mother fluttered about them, ensuring her daughters would be shown to their best advantage. All the while, she fluttered about them, flitting from one topic to the next, most of which concerned her hopes for her yet unattached daughters.

"You are looking very good tonight, Lizzy," said Mrs. Bennet, as she touched one lock of hair which refused to be tamed, attempting for the third time to push it back into place. "Mr. Darcy will not be able to keep his eyes from you."

"I certainly hope so, Mama," replied Elizabeth. "I *am* betrothed to him, after all."

"You are, and he is not shy about showing his appreciation for your charms. I would never have thought you would be the first to marry, Elizabeth, but I am happy with your choice. He is a fine man."

"I believe he is."

"Now, Jane," said Mrs. Bennet, turning to her eldest daughter, "I believe Mr. Bingley is very close to proposing to you, should you only give him some encouragement."

"I will not behave improperly, Mama," said Jane.

Mrs. Bennet clucked at her. "Of course not, my dear. No one would wish you to be too forward. But a man likes to know when his attentions are appreciated. Be certain to leave him in no doubt of your feelings and I suspect all will turn out well."

Mary's turn was next. "And you are looking very pretty this evening as well, Mary. It is a shame there is no man here for you tonight. But it is of no matter—I am certain your sisters' future husbands will wish to introduce you to all their wealthy friends. You may find a husband from among them."

The sisters shared an amused glance and stifled laughter when their mother turned to gather her wrap. Mrs. Bennet would never change. While her mother's antics had often frustrated her, Elizabeth knew she would not wish to change her.

Their arrival to the assembly rooms was accomplished early, as was the Bennets' wont. They entered the rooms to find them sparsely populated, which Mrs. Bennet used to her advantage. Elizabeth was reminded, as her mother herded them to prime locations within full sight of the doors, of another assembly earlier that autumn. She would miss these gatherings when she was in Derbyshire, Elizabeth decided. Surely there would be similar activities near her new home, but they would not be the same.

Given what they knew of Miss Bingley's character, it was, perhaps, surprising when the Netherfield party entered the room almost fifteen minutes before the first dance was scheduled to begin. The woman's sulky frowns at her brother informed them that it had not been by her choice. She soon recovered, however, and grasped her brother's arm. While her voice could not be heard from where the Bennet sisters stood, her purpose was clear when they turned and accosted Miss Cartwright. The latter woman's own suppressed annoyance informed Elizabeth that she was also becoming frustrated with Miss Bingley's actions.

"I begin to think you are entirely correct, Lizzy," said Jane from where she stood by Elizabeth's side. "Miss Cartwright clearly does not want Mr. Bingley's attentions, and Mr. Bingley is as unwilling as you suggest."

"Thank you, Jane, for coming around to my way of thinking," said Elizabeth, smirking at her sister. "I knew I could count on you to see things my way."

"Stop it, Lizzy," said Jane. "The question is, what shall we do to foil her designs?"

"That, my dearest Jane, you should simply leave to me." Elizabeth winked at her and turned away.

"Elizabeth," greeted William as he approached. He caught her hand up and kissed it, lingering over it. Elizabeth flushed at the exquisite sensations he was provoking in her, but she reminded herself she had a woman to thwart. As such, she caught William's eye as he raised his head.

"Your entrance is, indeed, shocking, my dear William. Surely you are not of the fashionable set you claim. Why, your party has come *before* the festivities have begun."

A grin formed on William's countenance. We would have been late tonight if certain elements of our party had gotten their way. In the end, Bingley informed his sister he would be on time, and that she could come in the second carriage if she wished. She, of course, could not allow it, for she would not be in a position to control the situation."

Elizabeth huffed. "That woman possesses an oversized notion of her own abilities."

William grinned at her. "I suppose you mean to do something about it?"

"Watch and learn, William," replied Elizabeth, arching a brow at him before moving off.

As she approached Mr. Bingley, she noted Colonel Fitzwilliam standing nearby, watching her, clearly expecting some mischief, if his amusement was any indication. Another thought entered Elizabeth's mind, and she stopped close to him.

"Wait for my signal, Colonel. I believe your assistance is required."

His grin growing ever wider, Colonel Fitzwilliam replied: "Of course, my lady. I am ever ready to enter the fray at your command."

With a regal nod, Elizabeth stepped away and approached her target. Miss Bingley was situated between Mr. Bingley and Miss Cartwright, and from her vantage, Elizabeth could see she had a tight hold on the arms of both, keeping them in place. Meanwhile, she was prattling on about some subject or another, while the other two searched for some means of escape.

They all caught sight of her at exactly the same moment, and their reactions could not have been any more different. It was more correct to say Miss Bingley's could not be any more different from the other two, as, while Mr. Bingley and Miss Cartwright looked on her as if she were their personal salvation, Miss Bingley regarded her with unfriendly wariness. Elizabeth ignored her, however, approaching Miss Cartwright first.

"My dear Jessica!" said she, stepping forward to clasp the other woman's hands. "How happy I am to see you tonight! I hope you have come ready to dance. These events are always lively affairs, though in general, gentlemen tend to be scarce. But as an unknown, I am sure you will be a popular partner!"

"Thank you, Elizabeth," said Miss Cartwright, bemused at Elizabeth's greeting. "I am interested to see if there are any differences between your assemblies and the ones I attend near my home."

"Well, I am certain there are many similarities, though perhaps our customs are a little different. I should very much like to sit and compare notes if you are amenable."

Miss Cartwright responded with pleasure, and Elizabeth winked at her before turning to Miss Bingley. If there was one person on the face of the earth Miss Bingley wished to see less than Elizabeth herself, she could not imagine who it might be. In response to Elizabeth's scrutiny, Miss Bingley' tightened her grips on the arms of both her companions—though Elizabeth was almost certain it was unconsciously done—and directed a thin smile in Elizabeth's direction.

"I can see you are in fine form already this evening, Miss Eliza. Have the organizers of this affair already laid out the punch?"

Elizabeth laughed unfeigned—it was a paltry attack, more amusing than insulting. "How droll an observation, Miss Bingley. I have not seen a punch bowl yet, but when it is served, I would be happy to sample it with you."

Then Elizabeth turned to Mr. Bingley, noting the beseeching way in which he was regarding her. "And Mr. Bingley too! You are very welcome here, sir, and I know I am not the only young lady to consider you so. Your brother, Miss Bingley, has become quite a favorite at these events, due to his cheerful demeanor and excellent knowledge of the dance steps."

"I thank you, Miss Elizabeth, for your praise," said a harried Mr. Bingley.

"It is no more than deserved," said Elizabeth warmly.

"Of course, it is," replied Miss Bingley, an airy note in her voice. "My brother is appreciated wherever he goes. He has an open and engaging character, which must be valued."

"Oh, I cannot disagree, Miss Bingley. Before the rest of your party arrived, your brother was my constant companion at any event we both attended. I consider him to be one of my dearest friends."

Mr. Bingley beamed, but Miss Cartwright looked on Elizabeth with a quizzical frown, likely not having heard this before. "That is interesting, Miss Bennet. And yet you are now engaged to Mr. Darcy?"

"Yes, well, when you put it that way, it does seem strange." Elizabeth laughed. "While I have no doubt Mr. Bingley will be an excellent husband one day, I knew from early in our acquaintance that he would not be *my* husband. We were and are good friends, but nothing more."

"Of course, you were, Miss Eliza," said Miss Bingley, a malevolence in her eyes and voice which did not surprise Elizabeth in the slightest. "I would not have thought anything else of you. When Mr. Darcy arrived, anyone could see that he was a member of high society, and as such, few would compare them on such a simple scale.

"But there are others who appreciate my brother for the man he is. Miss Cartwright, for example, has long thought him among the best of men. Is that not correct, Jessica?"

Miss Cartwright appeared abashed at Miss Bingley's insinuations, and she allowed quietly that Mr. Bingley was a good man. For his part, Mr. Bingley was glaring holes through his sister, though Miss Bingley was too busy sneering at Elizabeth to notice. For her part, Elizabeth was not the least offended by the woman's poor manners.

"As I said, Miss Bingley, I knew quickly that Mr. Bingley was not the one for me, and I am certain he knew the same of me."

"I did," was Mr. Bingley's quick interjection. Elizabeth, who had been counting on it, smiled at him and nodded.

"No, I am aware of my own character, and I knew Mr. Bingley and I would not suit. I am happy with Mr. Darcy, and I have no doubt Mr. Bingley is happy to be free of my impertinence as well. I am certain he could do much better than I for a wife."

"Of course, he could!" said Miss Bingley, sneering at Elizabeth. At the same time, Mr. Bingley's eyes darted to where Jane stood with Mary not far away, clearly longing for her presence. While Elizabeth knew he would need to develop a little more fortitude to counter his sister, she was happy to help him along.

"Jane!" she called, turning to catch her sister's eye. "Come here, Jane, for Mr. Bingley was looking for you."

Though Jane was uncomfortable with the display, she readily came, as she wished to be in his company as much as he wished to be in hers. Caroline Bingley drew in a hissing breath, no doubt to make some abrasive comment which would embarrass them all. Mr. Bingley, however, forestalled it by the simple expedient of speaking before she could.

"How do you do, Miss Bennet?" asked he, bowing hastily and

pulling away from his sister's grasp. Then, without drawing breath, he blurted: "May I have the first dance?"

"You may," replied Jane, a rosy blush spreading over her cheeks.

Mr. Bingley grinned as the tension was dispelled, and he offered her his arm, guiding her to an empty space next to the dance floor, where they could exchange quiet words. Elizabeth turned back to the two ladies to two entirely different reactions. Miss Bingley was sputtering with fury, appearing as if she wished to claw Elizabeth's face with her fingers, while Miss Cartwright was on the verge of bursting into laughter.

"Oh, Miss Cartwright!" exclaimed Elizabeth, as if in shock. "Has my sister stolen away your partner for the first dance?"

"Mr. Bingley did not ask me to dance, Elizabeth."

"But he has been attending you here. Please, allow me to be of service in correcting my unwitting error."

Turning, Elizabeth beckoned to Colonel Fitzwilliam, who had been watching the scene with barely concealed hilarity. The man came with alacrity.

"Colonel Fitzwilliam," said she, turning to Miss Cartwright, "allow me to present Miss Cartwright as an eligible and beautiful young woman who has not yet found a partner for the first dance."

"Indeed, she is that," replied Colonel Fitzwilliam with a grin. He bowed low to Miss Cartwright and said: "May I have the first?"

"Of course," replied Miss Cartwright, and she gave Elizabeth a smile as she was led away from Miss Bingley.

Having divested the woman of her two companions, Elizabeth was certain she would be required to withstand her vitriol. But before Miss Bingley could bring it to bear, Mr. Darcy stepped up to them and bowed.

"I believe the dancing is about to begin, Elizabeth."

"I think you are correct, William."

And she turned with him and walked away, leaving the fuming mistress of Netherfield standing alone. As they walked, William cleared his throat several times, as if something had become lodged in it. Elizabeth turned to him with a raised eyebrow.

"I hope you are not catching a cold, William."

"No, Elizabeth, I think I am quite well. It is only that we are in company now, and I am unable to vent my mirth without appearing the fool."

Knowing that if she looked back at Miss Bingley, as she was sorely tempted, she would burst out laughing, Elizabeth kept her eyes on her betrothed. "Then you should keep that feeling at hand, William. I am certain there will be an opportunity to release your pent-up amusement later."

William chose wisely in favor of changing the subject. "I believe this is the first opportunity I will have to dance with you at an event such as this. I am anticipating it keenly."

"As am I, William, though it will not be the first time we dance together."

"I hardly count the previous opportunity, though I did enjoy it. Tonight, however, I shall have you all to myself for half an hour."

"Only half an hour?" asked Elizabeth feigning surprise. "You only mean to dance with me once?"

"No, Elizabeth. I will also have your last set if you please. Then I may end the evening with the prettiest girl in attendance."

Elizabeth colored, but refrained from asking if he required spectacles. It was clear from his looks that he considered his words to be nothing less than the truth, despite Jane's presence.

They stood speaking for several moments, waiting for the music for the first dance to begin. It was then that she heard an interesting piece of news concerning a matter of which they had spoken the previous week.

"I received a letter from Lady Catherine today."

"And was she as offended as you expected?" asked Elizabeth.

"Less," replied William. "In fact, I expected her to attempt to abuse you to the point where I would be forced to break all connection with her. It seems, however, that my appeal for assistance from the earl has borne fruit, for Fitzwilliam tells me his father informed Lady Catherine that if she did not wish to have a breach in the family, she would temper her remarks to me. Furthermore, Anne told her that she would not have agreed to a marriage regardless, which quite took the wind from Lady Catherine's sails."

Elizabeth laughed at his characterization of his aunt's response. "Surely she did not receive the news without making *some* protest. If she did, I believe it must cast doubt on your account of your aunt as one of England's most fearsome dragons."

It was William's turn to laugh. "Indeed, she did not. But instead of focusing on you and your arts and allurements in distracting me from my duty, she dwelt on the intransigence of the younger generation and how disappointed my mother would be in me. I found that I could bear her remarks quite cheerfully, though I would have been offended had she chosen to vent her spleen upon you."

"Then I am happy your family still retains some harmony. I would not wish to be the means of a schism."

Only moments before the first dance began, Elizabeth happened to glance to the side. She noticed Lord Chesterfield, bracketed by Miss Bingley and Lady Diane, looking ill at ease. Stifling a laugh, she nudged William's arm and pointed toward the scene. William looked and grinned. His cousin, seeing their amusement at his expense, scowled and stormed away from the two women, eliciting protests in his wake.

"Your poor cousin. Our plotting has left him quite at the mercy of those two viragos."

"Chesterfield will persevere. He is quite used to such attention."

None of them could have guessed how he would endure, however. In stepping away from Miss Bingley and Lady Diane, he stalked toward where Mary was standing beside Mrs. Bennet, surveying the dance floor, likely wondering if anyone would ask her to dance. She was thus astonished when the viscount approached her.

"Miss Mary," said he, "I would like to solicit your hand for the first dance of the evening."

Mary gasped and squeaked: "Me?"

"Yes," was his firm reply. "I see in you the only rational person I can withstand this evening, for you are not beset with a need to display yourself, nor are you prone to descend to scheming. I would very much like to dance with you."

Though Mary stared wide-eyed, Mrs. Bennet was not about to allow the moment to pass without her daughter offering an answer, while she appeared quite as astonished as Mary. She pushed her daughter forward a little and instructed her in a low tone, which was the only reason, Elizabeth thought, that Mary was able to respond at all. Having obtained her agreement, the viscount took her hand and tucked it in her arm, leading her past the two dumbfounded women and away toward the dance floor, leaving silence in his wake.

William eventually summed up what Elizabeth thought they were all feeling. "Well, that was something I could not have predicted."

CHAPTER XVII

Soon after Lord Chesterfield led Mary away, the music for the first dance began. The first dance Elizabeth shared with William was as sublime as she had expected. He was as graceful gliding through the steps of a ballroom dance as he had been light on his feet during their previous effort at Lucas Lodge.

"It seems you had an excellent dance instructor, William."

"As did you, Elizabeth."

"Oh, we learned by ourselves, you know," replied Elizabeth. "As sisters, we stood up with each other whenever the opportunity presented itself"

He smiled. "Then I am even more impressed, for you dance as if the premier dance master in the kingdom himself taught you."

Elizabeth laughed. "I had no notion you were a flatterer. But I must own it is an interesting sensation. By all means, continue."

"You must trust my word, Elizabeth. Without trust, where will we end in our marriage?"

"I *do* trust you, William. But I am also certain of your regard and know that such great regard colors a person's perceptions."

"I speak nothing but the truth, I assure you. I must also say, Elizabeth, that your actions with respect to Miss Bingley and my friend were rather smooth."

"Thank you," replied Elizabeth. "But it was nothing. I am merely promoting what is obvious to all—even Miss Bingley if she could confess to it. Miss Bingley is the one who has the more difficult task."

William smiled, and they were separated by the dance. When they came together again, William did not speak. Instead, he contented himself with just watching Elizabeth as they twirled around each other in the steps. For herself, Elizabeth was happy to simply return his regard, knowing that in this instance, words were not required.

When the set was complete, he led her to the refreshment table and obtained a cup of punch for her. They spent the time before the next sets speaking softly with each other. While they were situated thus, Elizabeth glanced about the room, taking in the lay of the land. Jane and Mr. Bingley were situated close together in much the same manner as Elizabeth and Darcy, while Miss Cartwright and Colonel Fitzwilliam were on the other side of the ballroom with the viscount and Mary, who seemed more than a little shocked to be included in such company.

By contrast, it was clear that Miss Bingley was not enjoying the evening, and Elizabeth knew it would only get worse for her. She was standing not far from the entrance, glaring at all and sundry, having sat out the first dance. Given her expression warning everyone away, Elizabeth doubted many would have the courage to request her hand. Lady Diane was not far from Miss Bingley, and the two women were studiously ignoring each other. At least Lady Diane had danced the first, as one of the local men had asked, and she had, at least, showed some good breeding by accepting. Even Mr. Collins and Charlotte were standing together, though Elizabeth could not remember if they had danced together.

When William left to find his partner for the second dance, Elizabeth took the opportunity to have a word with Charlotte, as Mr. Collins had stepped away for a moment. Charlotte noted her approach and smiled in welcome.

"I am sorry I did not see you before, Charlotte. Did you dance the first with Mr. Collins?"

A faint redness arose in Charlotte's cheeks. "We have not danced, Lizzy. When Mr. Collins spoke of his delight for the assembly this evening, I asked him further concerning his previous experience, only to discover he has rarely attended. As such, he has little understanding of the steps. I did not wish to embarrass him, so I suggested we refrain from dancing."

"That is prudent, indeed," replied Elizabeth, not surprised in the least that Mr. Collins did not possess this particular skill. "Dance steps may be learned if the learner has a patient instructor."

Charlotte beamed at her, her appreciation for Elizabeth's understanding shining from her eyes. "That is exactly it! I do not think there will be another opportunity to attend an assembly before we are wed, so I have promised to teach him when we arrive in Kent."

"Then I wish you luck, Charlotte. With you as a teacher, I have no doubt he will learn quickly."

They exchanged some few words before Mr. Collins returned, and Elizabeth excused herself, noting that Charlotte had decided not to dance if her betrothed was to sit out. Then again, Charlotte had always been a little ambivalent about dancing, like Mary, but not nearly to Mary's extreme. It would be no hardship for her, though in her place, Elizabeth would not have been eager to spend an entire evening in the company of William Collins.

It was not long before her next dance partner arrived to claim her hand. She had been fortunate in that the other three gentlemen at Netherfield had claimed her for the next three dances in succession. As she did not yet consider Miss Bingley defeated, Elizabeth planned to use those dances to her benefit. A glance at the side of the room told her that Lord Chesterfield had managed to secure Jane's hand for the next set of dances, ensuring he was once again removed from the presence of Miss Bingley and Lady Diane. Elizabeth might have laughed at the two women if she thought she could do so without drawing their attention.

"Miss Bennet," said Colonel Fitzwilliam when they were safely away from listening ears, "I must say that I have rarely been more impressed."

"Oh?" asked she, arching a brow at him. "I am not aware I have done anything noteworthy."

"And modest too!" exclaimed the colonel with mock astonishment. When she glared at him, he only grinned. "Truly, Miss Bennet—if you were a man, I would fear for my general's employment, for I have rarely seen a campaign so meticulously planned and carried out. You have my congratulations."

"You think it is complete?" asked Elizabeth coyly.

Colonel Fitzwilliam chuckled, though it was clear he was holding back a more visible display of mirth. "No. In fact, I believe you have something more up your sleeve. If I was playing cards, I might suspect you had a full complement of aces hidden on your person."   "What a shocking suggestion!" cried Elizabeth. "That would be cheating, sir, and I never cheat. I have used no underhanded means tonight—I have simply used what resources I have to their fullest."

"Perhaps it was not the most suitable metaphor," conceded Colonel Fitzwilliam. "But I have often played cards with men I could have sworn were cheating, they performed so very well. I dare say you would be one of those individuals."

"Then perhaps we should sit down to whist some time. But I do not mean to speak of that now."

"And what *did* you wish to speak of?"

"What of your party at Netherfield?" asked Elizabeth, keeping her tone innocent. "I understand you have not met most of those in residence before?"

"Ah, there you would be incorrect. Though I am not well acquainted with Mr. Bingley and his family, I have met them all before coming to Hertfordshire. And Lady Diane is well known in society. The only resident whose acquaintance I had not previously made was Miss Cartwright's."

"Dear Miss Cartwright!" said Elizabeth. She had known in advance of this and had led the discussion in such a way that he would bring her name into the conversation. "She is a lovely woman, is she not? She is pretty, intelligent, and witty, though it is understated. I might almost say she is like my dearest sister, though Jane is even more reticent than she. I am happy I have made her acquaintance, for I find her to be a wonderful friend, indeed!"

"As do I," replied Colonel Fitzwilliam. "If your purpose is to elucidate me to the charms of Miss Cartwright, then you need not bother, for I have already discovered them for myself."

"That is good news, indeed," said Elizabeth. "It is, perhaps, difficult to carry out any sort of courting at Netherfield as those in residence are currently constituted. Perhaps you will continue in the spring?"

Colonel Fitzwilliam laughed and put his hands out in surrender. "Enough, Miss Bennet! It is far too early to speak of such things, though I will own that I am not disinterested."

"Very well, Colonel. That will suffice for now. I do wish you the best and hope you find your happiness with Miss Cartwright. She truly is a good woman, who I think would make you happy."

"I hope very much you are correct." Colonel Fitzwilliam paused and then gave her a conspiratorial wink. "As a second son, I must marry with some attention to money, and I understand Miss Cartwright's situation is no impediment. That I may gain a wife with whom I may share affection would be welcome, indeed."

"I am happy for you, sir. I hope it works out to your advantage."

"I believe it will. I must say, Miss Bennet, I am happy you have come into my cousin's life. I believe he will benefit from your liveliness."

Elizabeth thanked him. Soon the set ended and they parted ways. Elizabeth was pleased to see that he sought out Miss Cartwright and stood beside her until the next dance began. As for Elizabeth, her next set was with a man she considered to be one of the dearest in the world, and one she hoped to soon be in a position to call "brother."

"It seems to me you have been busy tonight, Miss Elizabeth," observed Mr. Bingley when they had found their positions in the line.

"Is there something particular of which you accuse me?" asked Elizabeth. The playful note in her voice was noted by her companion, and he returned it with a wink.

"Accuse you? No, I have no intention of accusing you. Not when it has worked out to my benefit. But I am curious. You have not known my sister long, yet you seem to have divined her purposes with exactness."

"It was not difficult, Mr. Bingley," replied Elizabeth. She stepped away from him, circled another dancer, and when she drew near him again, said: "If I had not had her opinion of both myself and my sister from her own mouth, I still would have noticed. Why, it was clear Miss Cartwright and Lady Diane were invited to Netherfield solely to attempt to distract you from Jane."

Mr. Bingley absorbed this with a distracted nod. Elizabeth knew he knew all this, for he had experienced it since the ladies' coming. But he was so good-natured that he was more apt to allow his sister to do as she would and ignore her, rather than reprimanding her.

"Caroline told you of her designs?"

It was at this point Elizabeth thought to demur. "Perhaps it is best not to speak of such things. I would not be the means of fomenting discord between you and your sister."

With a sigh, Mr. Bingley said: "Which speaks very well of you — Caroline would have no compunction whatsoever of doing exactly that if it promoted her cause. You will not be promoting disagreement between us, Miss Elizabeth. I believe that already exists."

"Very well, then," said Elizabeth. "I do not remember exactly what she said, but in essence, she told me how she was certain that I had managed to 'capture' Mr. Darcy through some underhanded means and that she meant to prevent a similar result between Jane and yourself."

As the steps took them away from each other, Mr. Bingley was given several moments to think on Elizabeth's words. When he returned, therefore, his frustration had built to a greater degree than had he been allowed to simply respond without hesitation.

"I apologize to you, Miss Elizabeth," said Mr. Bingley, though it was clear he wished to have a word with his sister. "I was witness to the entire courtship between you and my friend, and I know there was nothing underhanded on the part of either."

"I did not take offense, Mr. Bingley. Having known previously of her efforts with respect to Mr. Darcy, I expected her disappointment."

Mr. Bingley nodded his agreement, but with an air of distraction. "What I cannot understand is why Caroline thought I was already on the verge of proposing to your sister. At the time, I had only just made her acquaintance!"

"That is true, but your preference was clear, even at that early date." Elizabeth looked at him with fondness. "You are a good man, Mr. Bingley, and I think when you do something, you do it with your whole heart. You had not known Jane for five days when I thought I had never seen such a promising inclination."

Elizabeth directed an arch smile and a wink at him. "Are you not now relieved you did not become closer to me when you came? You may have missed out on the angelic Jane Bennet and been forced into a life with her devilish sister!"

Mr. Bingley barked in laughter, and when he came close again, he took her hand and bowed over it in the midst of the dance steps, a curious affectation, indeed. "Any man would be fortunate with you as a wife, Miss Elizabeth— me no less than any other. But, yes, I am happy it has worked out the way it has. My dearest friend Darcy has not only found his heart's desire, but I believe I might have as well."

"Then go to it, sir," said Elizabeth. "If you have need of my assistance, know that I will provide it without hesitation."

"And likely without my even having thought of it," replied Mr. Bingley with a laugh. Elizabeth parted with him, content in the knowledge that he was in good hands.

Her fourth partner was less lively than Mr. Bingley and Colonel Fitzwilliam, and as Elizabeth did not know Lord Chesterfield as well as the other two men, their conversation largely consisted of more banal subjects. The viscount did congratulate her on her betrothal to his cousin, however, which gratified Elizabeth. One of her persistent worries had been her reception by Mr. Darcy's family, regardless of how he assured her of their support.

"It seems to me that you are good for my cousin," observed his lordship. "Darcy has always had a tendency toward dourness, especially since his father passed and he took control of the family estate."

"One can say many things about me," replied Elizabeth. "But dour is not one of them."

Lord Chesterfield nodded. "And that is what he needs. Even Georgiana, shy as she is, requires a sister who will teach her to be more open and confident, and I believe you may be up to the task."

"Thank you, your lordship. I appreciate your approval."

"You need have no fear of us, Miss Bennet. We simply want Darcy to be happy." He paused and then grinned. "Well, perhaps Lady Catherine *is* fearsome after all. But I doubt there is much she could do to disrupt your life with my cousin."

"I have already had a little experience with her ladyship. My cousin is her parson, and Mr. Darcy has already announced our engagement to her, with your father's assistance."

"Then there is nothing to fear."

They continued to dance for some minutes until the half hour had almost elapsed. Then when the dance ended and the viscount took her hand to lead her back to the side of the room, Elizabeth turned to him again.

"I will also say, your lordship, how sorry I am that you have two women who seem determined to fight over you. I am afraid they are an unexpected consequence of certain other activities."

It was clear he was not certain what she was saying, for he turned to her, puzzled. "I will not say Lady Diane, especially, has not been persistent. I have dealt with her like many times before. But I cannot understand what you have to do with it."

Elizabeth only smiled mysteriously at him and thanked him for the dance. She did not know if he was not as perceptive as his brother, or if he had been too busy fending Lady Diane and Miss Bingley away to notice her activities. In the end, she decided it did not signify. She doubted Lord Chesterfield would endure them much longer before he fled back to town. She would apologize to him when she was married.

The evening continued in much the same manner as it usually did. Elizabeth and Jane were popular partners and rarely sat out, though Elizabeth was certain from the looks given them by Mr. Darcy and Mr. Bingley respectively that they both wished their ladies were not in such demand. They acquitted themselves well, however, Mr. Bingley dancing most of the dances, while even William danced more than he did not.

"Thank you, William," said Elizabeth on one occasion later in the evening, feeling certain her heart was in her eyes.

"You are welcome, of course," replied William, "though I am not certain for what you are thanking me."

"For attending to my neighbors and friends. I know you are not at your best in such circumstances as these, and you have shown your respect in your actions, regardless."

William gave her a secret smile. "Of course, I must respect them. These people have all had some influence in your upbringing. Though I am taking you away from them and you shall live three days distant, we will return at times, and I would wish to be welcomed rather than reviled."

"And you are doing very well at it, sir. I believe the entire room approves of your civility and intelligence. You are as popular among them as Mr. Bingley."

The notion seemed a curious one to William, but there was no further time for conversation, for her next partner arrived to whisk her away. To William's credit, he also left to find his next partner, and Elizabeth had all the pleasure of seeing him standing not far from her on the dance floor.

Late that evening during one of the few occasions when Elizabeth sat out, she happened to be standing not far from Lady Diane, while William was dancing with Penelope Long. Now, to any casual observer, it appeared they were not at all friendly. In fact, one might say that no two people could have less to say to each other than Elizabeth Bennet and Lady Diane. But Elizabeth had a purpose and was determined to see to it. It would be the final coup de grâce on Miss Bingley's efforts.

As the lower in standing, it could be termed an impertinence for Elizabeth to speak to Lady Diane without the other initiating the conversation. As they were acquainted and standing close to each other, Elizabeth though the demands of propriety had been met. Furthermore, after ignoring her for several minutes, Elizabeth saw the lady glance at her several times, which gave her all the courage she required.

"Lady Diane," said she, dropping into a low curtsey, hoping it would make her ladyship more disposed to speak to her. "I hope you are enjoying the amusement with us this evening."

A sniff was the lady's only response. She turned away, and

Elizabeth noted her nose was lifted higher in the air than it had been before. But then she seemed to think better of it and turned back to Elizabeth. The cynical thought that the woman had belatedly remembered she was to be the wife of Mr. Darcy, a relation of the Fitzwilliams, and it would not do to offend her, entered Elizabeth's mind. Whatever Lady Diane's reason for deigning to speak to her, Elizabeth was grateful she had.

"It is amusing enough," said Lady Diane. "I do not often attend country assemblies—I am more interested in society events in London."

"What a sight such events must be!" exclaimed Elizabeth, deciding to put on the guise of the disingenuous supplicant. But it would not do to play the part too well, for she knew Lady Diane was not lacking entirely in discernment. "How much I am looking forward to them, for it is an experience I have not yet had."

It worked, for the woman seemed to feel every bit of her superiority. "Yes, the season can be quite splendid." Lady Diane paused for a moment, and Elizabeth could almost see the progression of her thoughts. "When you are in town for the season with Mr. Darcy, I will be happy to guide your first steps in society."

"Thank you, Lady Diane," said Elizabeth, playing the naïve young girl, though taking care not to spread it too thick. "Your assistance will be invaluable. Mr. Darcy, though he obviously has much experience in society, has not the perspective of a woman."

"Of course, Miss Bennet."

"How grateful I am for your presence, and that of your friend too. I am sorry, however, for I understand the visit has not proceeded as you expected."

"Oh?" asked Lady Diane. "Do you refer to anything in particular?"

"Perhaps I should not speak of it," demurred Elizabeth. "It does no good to dwell on it."

"You may be assured that I shall keep whatever you say in confidence. I will not be offended."

"Well," said Elizabeth, speaking slowly, as if considering her words carefully, "I thought you had come to stay with Mr. and Miss Bingley, to become better acquainted with them."

"And so I have," replied Lady Diane, clearly mystified. "I have known Caroline since our school days together, so we are quite familiar. As for her brother, I am not unknown to him."

Elizabeth frowned. "Then you have my apologies, Lady Diane. It appears I have a quite different impression of your visit than I should."

"What do you mean?" asked Lady Diane. She turned to Elizabeth and fixed her with a frown. "I must know your meaning. Has something censorious been said concerning my visit here?"

"Oh, no, not at all. We are all happy to have you, of course. I meant no disrespect. It is only . . ." When Lady Diane tapped her foot, impatience evident in her rigid demeanor, Elizabeth spoke up. "It is just that I had assumed you were here *for* Mr. Bingley. It is no secret that Miss Bingley wishes you for a sister."

"I am not here for her brother," said Lady Diane. "I am here as a friend. If there is anyone here because of an attachment to her brother, it is Jessica."

"It is all so confusing! I have heard it said in the neighborhood that Mr. Bingley is *your* particular friend, which must give me pain, as my sister likes him very much, indeed. And, of course, Miss Bingley's interest in Lord Chesterfield is not precisely hidden."

Lady Diane's head whipped around, and she immediately focused on his lordship, who was at that very moment enduring the conversation of one Miss Caroline Bingley. It was clear Lady Diane understood Elizabeth's point at once, for she was instantly displeased. Elizabeth could see the fire of determination roar up within her, as she turned back to Elizabeth and nodded.

"Thank you for your candid observations, Miss Bennet. I would like to inform you at once that I am no threat to your sister's happiness—in fact, I think she and my friend's sister would make a lovely couple."

"I am so happy to hear it," said Elizabeth, hoping she had not overdone her simpering voice. "I know she could never hope to compete with you, had you possessed a fondness for Mr. Bingley."

"Well, yes, I suppose that is true," replied the woman, preening in feeling her self-importance. "I am happy you possess the wit to see it. I would be highly gratified if there were more young ladies as erudite as you have shown yourself to be."

Then Lady Diane nodded and left, her steps taking her unerringly toward the unsuspecting viscount. In a moment, the woman was speaking to him in an animated fashion, and Caroline Bingley, who had had his unwilling attention, found herself shunted to the side. Lady Diane's actions were so aggressive that his lordship looked at her with unconcealed astonishment.

"It seems to me, Elizabeth, that you have been busy yet again."

Elizabeth turned and gazed on the countenance of her betrothed with unreserved pleasure. "Why do you say that?"

William nodded in his cousin's direction. When. Elizabeth turned back, she noted Lord Chesterfield now looking at her, suspicion alive in his eyes. Unable to refrain, Elizabeth laughed and waved at him. He seemed charmed by her amusement, for he grinned at her and rolled his eyes at his two tormentors.

At the same time, Miss Bingley, who had been growing more annoyed with Lady Diane's actions, happened to look up and see Elizabeth's byplay with the viscount. It did not take her long to divine the meaning of what she was seeing, and she sent a fierce scowl Elizabeth's way. Elizabeth decided the woman had suffered enough, and she only nodded, rather than smirking as she sorely wished to do.

"I would never have taken you for a matchmaker," said William. But while his countenance was severe, Elizabeth could easily see the twinkle of amusement lighting his eyes.

"I believe you will find I am no matchmaker, William. But I will protect my sisters' interests if they are threatened."

"Not that I am complaining, but you involved my cousin unwillingly in your schemes."

Elizabeth laughed. "It was unintended, nonetheless. Remember, William: it was not *I* who invited your cousins to stay at Netherfield. I only used the resources available to ensure Miss Bingley did not ruin my sister's happiness."

CHAPTER XVIII

"What is it, Lizzy?" asked Jane of Elizabeth the following morning.

Elizabeth, who had been lost in her own thoughts, started at the sound of her sister's voice. "I apologize, Jane, but I must have been woolgathering."

"I was merely asking for your thoughts," repeated Jane. "I am sure I have never seen you in quite this state, though I have often seen you impressed with your own cleverness."

"Pardon me?" asked Elizabeth, confused as to her sister's meaning. She did hear the teasing note in her sister's tone, which informed her Jane's words were not meant in censure.

"You have been silent these last five minutes together," interjected Mary, directing an expressive look at Elizabeth. "Furthermore, you appear akin to the cat which has gotten into the cream."

"And that is not all," added Jane. "You have been this way since we left the assembly last night. Are your thoughts so full of your betrothed that you have nothing left to spare for your poor sisters?"

In spite of herself, Elizabeth laughed. No, she had not been thinking of William, though he always hovered around the periphery of her mind. Instead, she had been considering the fruits of the previous night's labors, and particularly the way Lady Diane had taken her hint with alacrity. But she knew Jane would not appreciate her machinations, even if she had only engaged in them in response to Miss Bingley's designs. Thus, she accepted the explanation Jane so

184 ~~&~~ *Jann Rowland*

conveniently provided.

"When you are engaged, Jane, I shall laugh when your thoughts are full of your betrothed." Jane's countenance softened, and Elizabeth grinned. "Or perhaps I am not required to wait, for it seems the very mention of the name 'Bingley' is enough to send you into your own thoughts for hours at a time."

Mary chuckled at Elizabeth's sally, but Jane only blushed and attempted to turn a glare on her sister. "Mr. Bingley has not made me an offer, Lizzy. I am sure I think of him no more than I think of any other man of our acquaintance."

"You must believe us simpletons if you think we will accept such an explanation," exclaimed Elizabeth. For her part, Mary only snorted her amusement and shook her head.

Jane's blush deepened. "Well, he *is* the most amiable man of my acquaintance."

"Indeed, he is. I give you leave to like him and, if it comes to it, fall in love with him. I have long thought he would be perfect for my angelic elder sister."

"Thank you for your approval, Lizzy. I believe I shall."

Then Jane, with a smile and a nod, rose to her feet, announcing her intention to return to her room. Her younger sisters watched her go, and when the door was closed behind her, Mary turned a look of mock severity on Elizabeth.

"Perhaps Jane was taken in by your prevarication Elizabeth, but I was not. If you were thinking of Mr. Darcy, it was only in conjunction with your activities of last night."

"So I was," said Elizabeth. "But I could hardly tell *Jane* that, now could I?"

The sisters burst out together in merry laughter. As they released their mirth, Elizabeth was struck by how much Mary had changed these past months. She could still be the tiresome, moralizing girl she had always been, and she was proper almost to a fault. But the departure of Kitty and Lydia for school, leaving her and Elizabeth alone in the house, had resulted in an increased closeness between them, which had included Jane when she too had returned. The old Mary would have scolded Elizabeth for her actions the previous night, rather than laughing about them.

"No," replied Mary, when their mirth had run its course. "I suppose you could not. I love Jane dearly, for she is almost too good for this world. But she would not understand your efforts on her behalf, and she would not see Miss Bingley for the conniving witch she is."

"Dearest Mary!" cried Elizabeth. "That is positively the most unforgiving speech I have ever heard you make. Good for you! Perhaps there is still hope for Jane after all."

Once again they allowed their amusement full reign. "She is a horrid woman, Lizzy—I know you can see it. She looks down on us and makes love to Mr. Darcy and Lord Chesterfield. But there is not an ounce of goodness in her; she cares only for her selfish desires."

"It is possible this experience will humble her."

"And there is no one of my acquaintance who could use a modicum of humility more than Miss Caroline Bingley.

"But I don't wish to speak of her," said Mary, as if brushing aside a gnat. "I wish to know what you intend to do next."

"I shall do nothing but watch the fun," replied Elizabeth with a wink. "Everything has been set in motion. Though she may not know it, Miss Bingley's plan to divert her brother from Jane has already been defeated. Lady Diane never had any intention of truly offering herself up as a replacement, and Miss Cartwright is more pleased with Colonel Fitzwilliam than interested in Mr. Bingley resuming his interest. Unless Miss Bingley invites more of her friends to Netherfield, I doubt she has anyone to throw in his way, not that it would matter if she did."

"And what of her own persuasion? Do you not think it likely that she will eventually succeed in turning him away from her?"

Elizabeth shook her head. "According to Mr. Darcy, Mr. Bingley has never listened to his sisters when he felt himself to be in the right. I think Miss Bingley overestimates her level of influence with her brother."

"I certainly hope so. He is a good man. Jane deserves to have a husband who will cherish her as Mr. Bingley will."

"I cannot agree more." Then Elizabeth turned to Mary with interest. "But what of you, Mary? Our mother has all but promised that you will marry one of William or Mr. Bingley's wealthy friends. Shall you cut a swathe through the season, leaving broken hearts in your wake?"

"Oh, please do not suggest such a thing!" said Mary with a shudder. "I have no desire to catch a man of society. I am not romantic like you and Jane, and I would be very happy to attract a good man who will support me and any children we may have. If I am not so fortunate as to meet such a man, I will be happy to remain unmarried."

"I hope you will find someone, Mary," said Elizabeth warmly. "You have much to offer as a wife. It would be a shame if you did not have a home of your own and children to share it with."

"Thank you, Elizabeth," said Mary, tears appearing in the corners of her eyes. "I shall rely on you to assist me to find that man."

"And you have it, dearest sister."

The conversation with Mary would remain in Elizabeth's mind ever after. It was the time she would remember as the period she and Mary had finally forged a friendship as all sisters should.

At Netherfield, the atmosphere was not nearly as light as the one at Longbourn. With Caroline Bingley in residence, such a thing was nigh impossible, in Darcy's opinion, and the day after the assembly was not conducive to joviality. After the woman had seen her plans falter the previous night—though Darcy knew, even if she did not own it herself, that her plans had been doomed for some time—she redoubled her efforts.

As a woman who fancied herself a fashionable woman and a candidate to be raised to the first circles, she was careful in keeping the habits common to them. In the time she had been in Netherfield, he had only seen her about the house in the morning a few times, and then it was usually because of some scheme to which she had set herself. That morning was no different, though due to the previous late evening, she appeared less herself than usual. In other words, she clearly wished she was still abed and was snappish as a result.

"How wonderful it is that we are all here for breakfast this morning," said she when she breezed into the room. Even though it was early for her, she was still the last person to arrive, and there were several others who were usually in their rooms as late as she. "Now that we have experienced the *entertainment* of the area, perhaps we may dispense with such things and continue here at Netherfield without subjecting ourselves to the rest of the neighborhood."

As there were more than a few sandy eyes and drooping heads around the table, no one made much more than a grunt in reply to her statement. Even Bingley, the most likely to take issue with the characterization of the neighborhood, remained silent, concentrating on his breakfast.

"Oh, I do apologize, Mr. Darcy," said Caroline, turning to him as if she had just thought of something. "I had forgotten you have tied yourself to your . . . little country miss. Of course, you will wish to visit their modest estate this morning."

"Actually, Miss Bingley," replied Darcy, sipping his tea, "I had thought to allow the Bennets this morning to recover from the late night, though I know Elizabeth will be up and about early this morning. Perhaps Georgiana and I shall go toward the end of visiting time."

Miss Bingley tittered into her hand. "You are so free with her Christian name, Mr. Darcy. It seems you are becoming less of the staid and proper man you used to be."

"There is nothing improper about a man calling his betrothed by her Christian name," said Bingley, suddenly looking up from his breakfast and glaring down the table at his sister. "I, for one, think very highly of Miss Elizabeth, and will not have anything said against her. Please attend to your breakfast and allow the rest of us to do the same."

More than one set of eyes widened at Bingley's short rebuke, though Miss Bingley's response was to turn red with fury. She did restrain herself from a caustic reply, however. She sniffed instead and picked up her fork.

"I meant no offense, Charles. She is an . . . interesting sort of girl."

"Her liveliness will certainly do Darcy no harm," said Fitzwilliam. "She is exactly the sort of girl I would have hoped for my cousin. You *do* have a tendency toward the morose, Cousin. No offense intended."

"None taken," said Darcy. "I am quite anticipating my life with her. The halls of Pemberley will not be so quiet with Elizabeth as its mistress. It will once again be a home."

Miss Bingley snorted, but Georgiana spoke up. "I could not ask for a better sister than Elizabeth." She shot a grin at Darcy. "Since you are to be married to her, I might simply choose not to marry so that I may stay with you both forever."

Darcy chuckled, even as several others looked on with amusement. Miss Bingley, of course, was scandalized. "You will always be welcome, my dear. But I hope you will not refrain from marrying for such a reason. You have much to offer a man."

Georgiana blushed. "Thank you, Brother. That is one of the things Lizzy has taught me since we became acquainted."

"Nonsense, Georgiana!" cried Miss Bingley. "Of course, you are a wonderful girl, and no girl from the country could have taught you such a thing. You are a Darcy and a Fitzwilliam, and that makes you a force to be reckoned with.

"But why are we speaking of Miss Eliza Bennet? I should much rather talk about other matters much closer to home."

"I believe you were the first to raise the subject of Miss Bennet," said Chesterfield. "For myself, I find her to be an intelligent, pretty, lively sort of girl. I do wonder how you will control her though, old man." His cousin winked at Darcy. "It seems to me she is not above using manipulation to have her own way."

Fitzwilliam swallowed a laugh, though Darcy could hear it clearly, and around the room, several others who had witnessed Elizabeth's activities were also grinning. Hurst, in particular, openly smirked at his sister-in-law and raised an eyebrow in challenge. For Darcy's part, he did not wish to allow this as an excuse for Miss Bingley to vent her spleen again, so he hastened to speak.

"She is determined, to be certain. But then again, so am I."

"You sound as if you are expecting to argue with her, Mr. Darcy," said Miss Bingley, watching him with triumph.

"All married couples argue at times, Miss Bingley. Even those who marry with nothing more than love in mind. Elizabeth and I are both intelligent and strong-willed, and as we are different people, I have no doubt we will experience our share of disagreements. But we will resolve them as any other couple does—through compromise and our shared resolve to do what is best for our family."

"Then she has already won," sneered Miss Bingley. "She will be the inferior in your marriage. She should follow you and allow you to make the decisions as you obviously know best."

"Miss Bingley," said Darcy, a hint of steel injected into his voice, "I wish to have a wife and a partner, not a slave. If you wish to be completely subservient to your future husband, then I invite you to search for such a man. I am not one of them."

This stinging set down provided blessed silence from Miss Bingley thereafter, and Bingley and Hurst smiled at Darcy, nodding their approval. He knew Bingley had attempted to inform his sister many times of Darcy's lack of interest in her, but she had persisted in her own beliefs. Now, for the first time since he made her acquaintance, he thought she realized that he was never the man she had thought him to be. Darcy did not think the woman truly wished to be wholly subservient to a man—that was her disdain for Elizabeth speaking. But his strong words on the matter had awoken her to the fact that she had been more mistaken about him than she had previously confessed.

Unfortunately, while the woman allowed the subject of Elizabeth to rest for the remainder of the breakfast hour, she turned her attention to Chesterfield, who was a captive audience by her side. Chesterfield, as the elder son and heir, had different notions from Darcy concerning marriage, for all that he had not yet married himself. Unfortunately, those notions did not work in Miss Bingley's favor, nor did they for Lady Diane, who was the other player in the drama. Chesterfield would almost certainly end making a stupendous marriage to some society woman to increase the Fitzwilliam family's influence and forge new alliances. Miss Bingley could offer none of those requirements.

When they finally left the dining room, the woman was at it again in the sitting-room. Bingley had not sat down near Darcy for more than a moment when the woman grasped Miss Cartwright's arm and almost forcibly dragged her thither, exclaiming: "Charles, I believe dear Jessica had something of which she wished to speak to you if you will give her a moment of your time."

From the embarrassed expression on the woman's face, it was clear she was being pushed forward unwillingly. It was at that moment that Bingley's temper snapped.

"On the contrary, Caroline," said he, his tone clipped and angry, "I believe I shall pay a visit to Longbourn now."

"Pay a visit to Longbourn?" screeched Miss Bingley. "There is no call for that. I am sure you can go a single day without being required to visit that insignificant speck of an estate."

It was clear that Bingley was on the verge of losing his temper altogether and making a scene. Thus, Darcy took it upon himself to speak before his friend could say something he would later regret.

"I believe Georgiana and I will join you, Bingley. I am sure the Bennets are about by now, and I would very much like to see Elizabeth."

"As would I, Brother," said Georgiana. "I shall go and get my pelisse." Then Georgiana swiftly retreated.

"I will accompany you," added Fitzwilliam. "I believe I would like to come to know my future cousin better."

"As would I," added Chesterfield.

Then, when Miss Bingley's mouth was hanging open in shock, the final member of their party that morning spoke up in support of the plan. "If I may," said Miss Cartwright "I believe I should also like to go. The Miss Bennets are excellent ladies, and I would like to further my acquaintance with them."

"We would be happy to have you, Miss Cartwright," said Fitzwilliam.

Darcy suppressed a snigger—it was clear that Fitzwilliam especially wished to have the company of the pretty Miss Cartwright. A look exchanged with Chesterfield confirmed that his other cousin had seen it too.

Their course set, they began making their way from the room, leaving an astonished Miss Bingley, a silent and watchful Lady Diane, and the Hursts—Hurst amused and his wife unwilling to go against her sister. She *had*, however, been curiously hesitant to speak in her sister's support of late.

When the door closed behind them and they began to walk down the hall toward the entrance, Darcy could only release a sigh of relief. He was not the only one.

"She is truly a special woman, is she not Darcy? I do not know another woman like her." Fitzwilliam paused, as if in thought, and said: "I am very grateful because of it."

Miss Cartwright, who was walking just ahead of them, giggled and turned to regard him, a scowl—which was betrayed to be false by the tremble of her lips—directed at Fitzwilliam. "I will have you know Miss Bingley has been my friend for many years."

"You have my condolences, Miss Cartwright."

Darcy was about to reprimand his cousin when Bingley, who had been walking ahead of them all, burst out laughing. He stopped and turned to Fitzwilliam, slapping him on the back and grinning at Miss Cartwright.

"If Miss Cartwright is to be pitied, then what of me? You have known her for a few short years, yet she has been my sister for more than twenty."

Then Bingley shook his head. "I know it is not proper to speak of her in such a way, but Caroline can sometimes be a trial. She has her good qualities, but these past weeks have left me wondering if they will ever outweigh those which induce me to tear out my hair in frustration. It would be best if I could simply marry her off." He looked at them all with interest. "Any takers?"

"You know I am already engaged, Bingley," said Darcy, while at the same time, Fitzwilliam said: "Ah, no thank you, Bingley, though I appreciate the gesture."

They all turned at once to look at Chesterfield, who had stopped a short distance away and was regarding them. He shook his head at their scrutiny. "You have my apologies, Bingley, but I have no intention of being caught by *either* Lady Diane or your sister."

"Then I simply must endure her for the time being," replied Bingley in a mournful tone. "Perhaps she can find someone next season."

"Cheer up, Bingley!" said Fitzwilliam. "Think of the fact that you are now to go visit your angel. At least you may escape from your sister for a time."

They all laughed and began to walk again. Their laughter at Miss Bingley's expense was, as Bingley had stated, perhaps not the most proper. But the woman was eminently deserving of it.

*   *   *

As those who had declared their intention to visit Longbourn walked through the door, Caroline Bingley could almost hear the sound of her plans crashing to the ground. Where had it all gone wrong? The future had seemed so bright only a few short months ago. She had been sure it would only take another small push and Mr. Darcy would offer for her, after which she could direct Charles to some woman of society, and she would have everything she had ever dreamed. Then Charles had leased this wretched estate without asking her opinion, had introduced Mr. Darcy to that hussy Eliza Bennet, and it had all gone wrong from there. She was left scrambling to prevent her brother from making a disastrous marriage.

Little did Caroline know it was about to become much worse.

"Well, well," the detested voice of her sister's husband assaulted her ears. "That was a bit of entertainment, was it not?"

Caroline turned a glare on the portly man, but he was not cowed by her displeasure in the least. He only chuckled and rose to his feet, extending his hand to Louisa. "Come, my dear. I suspect other events are in the offing. We should absent ourselves lest we are caught in the middle.'

Though Louisa glanced at Caroline, she grasped her husband's offered hand and allowed herself to be led from the room. Caroline watched them go, fuming at her sister who had turned out to be quite the traitor. She was surprised to hear another voice, for she had quite forgotten her other friend was in the room.

"Your sister's husband is an astute man. It is well that he left, for I believe we need to have a word, Caroline."

The last person in the room with her was, of course, Lady Diane, and the way she looked on Caroline reminded her of those looks she had received when she had first arrived at school. Once again, she felt like the undeserving *tradesman's daughter*, inferior of birth and unwelcome in the circles of her betters. The effort to put such things behind her had been enormous. Caroline had never wished to feel that way again. And yet, here she was, a conceited daughter of the nobility, regarding Caroline Bingley as if she was nothing more than the dust on her dainty shoes.

"I wish to thank you for an amusing time, Caroline," said Lady Diane when Caroline did not immediately respond. "I have rarely been so entertained as I have been these last weeks."

"It is no problem, Lady Diane," said Caroline, finally finding her tongue. "I am, indeed, honored to have been in a position to host you.

And I thank you for your efforts with respect to my brother."

"Yes, that is a matter of which I wished to speak to you. It is clear your brother is set in his course. I have decided that Miss Bennet suits him, and as such, I will no longer assist you in attempting to turn him away from her."

Caroline saw red. This was all Eliza's fault! Clearly, the woman had whispered in Lady Diane's ear the previous evening, convincing her that her insipid sister was a match for Charles.

"Whether he favors her or not," said Caroline, "Miss Bennet is still inferior in every way to my brother. I cannot allow it!"

"I am not sure where you obtain your notions of inferiority, Caroline," said Lady Diane with a contemptuous shake of her head. "Your brother *is* the son of a tradesman—that will not change, though he will raise his position in society should he purchase an estate. Whatever you think of Miss Bennet's connections, she is the daughter of a gentleman."

"An insignificant country squire!" snapped Caroline.

Lady Diane only nodded her head, an infuriating complaisance about her which made Caroline want to gnash her teeth. "Perhaps that is so. But a gentleman nonetheless. As such, his marriage to her will raise him in the eyes of society, especially since his sister is to wed Mr. Darcy.

"Regardless, I have no more interest in attempting to keep them apart. You may do what you wish, of course, but I will not be a party to it. I suggest you tread lightly, lest you anger your brother and provoke him to take action."

"Charles is docile as a puppy," sneered Caroline. "I fear nothing he can do."

"That is your choice. But I suggest you watch him. The puppy is developing fangs. If you are not careful, you may end up being bitten.

"But what I am more concerned about is this business with Lord Chesterfield." Lady Diane paused and tapped her lips in a thoughtful manner. "I suppose I should thank you for putting me in his lordship's path, though I am aware it was not your intention. I have noticed, however, that you have fancied yourself a possible match for him and have interfered with my attempts to come to know him better.

"Let me be rightfully understood," continued Lady Diane, fixing Caroline with a glare of bludgeoning steel, "that I intend to have Lord Chesterfield for myself. I will not have some upstart tradesman's daughter ruining my designs. I require you to stay away from his lordship."

Her already blazing anger burned even hotter at this new evidence of disdain from a woman she had thought was her friend. It prompted Caroline to speak without thinking.

"You think he will make you an offer? You are nothing more than the daughter of a minor baron."

Lady Diane returned her glare in full measure. "At least I am not a woman pretending to be something I am not."

They stood this way, the two combatants, hands on hips, heads jutting out in belligerent attitudes. For a moment, Caroline wondered with an idle detachment why there was no ice forming in the air around them.

"Perhaps, then," said Caroline, "I should simply rescind your invitation to stay at Netherfield. Given how he attempts to avoid you, Lord Chesterfield would almost certainly thank me for it."

"Are you witless?" demanded Lady Diane. "Do you not see how I can ruin you and your pathetic family in London? I will see every door closed to you, every voice raised in mocking derision, every soul see you for the grasping social climber you are.

"Do not test me, Caroline *dear*," mocked Lady Diane, as she stepped close and sneered at Caroline. "I will do all of this and more if you continue to cross me."

Then Lady Diane was gone, leaving Caroline fearful and drained. The fact of the matter was that Lady Diane, though she perhaps did not possess the social power she fancied, could seriously harm Caroline in town. And she was vindictive enough to do it. Though Caroline did not know her next move, she knew she would be required to tread lightly.

CHAPTER XIX

As it must, time rolled forward in its inevitable path, a stream winding its never-ending way to the sea. The autumn of that year was significant to many, and many lives were changed, some for the better, some for the worse. Or, perhaps it was the perception of worse which frustrated those who were not satisfied with their new lots in life.

Miss Bingley was, of course, the foremost in the latter category, for not only had she lost Mr. Darcy as a potential husband—many would say she never *had* him—but her increasingly desperate attempts to turn her brother away from Jane Bennet had little effect. Her two confederates—if they had ever actually been her confederates—were little assistance after the assembly, and no one else seemed to see sense in her opinions.

The others were too happy to pay any heed to her annoyance. Elizabeth and Darcy were, of course, happy in their situation, and Jane and Mr. Bingley were not far behind. Charlotte Lucas had made her own match, and if it was not for the same reasons as her close friends, she was contented with her future. As for those others who had joined the Bingleys at Netherfield, that was a subject which came up between Elizabeth and Darcy late that year during a visit to Longbourn.

Several weeks had passed since the assembly, and it was nearing Christmas. Darcy and Georgiana had agreed to stay at Netherfield for Christmas—grudgingly invited by the increasingly irascible Miss Bingley—and were active in the neighborhood. On the day in question, their visit to Longbourn had coincided with a warm day, uncommon in December, which Elizabeth had declared she simply must take advantage of, knowing there would be few such days until March. Mary and Georgiana were huddled about the pianoforte as was their wont, Bingley and Jane were wandering some other part of the estate, while Miss Bingley and the Hursts were sharing a stilted visit with Mrs. Bennet.

"I received a letter from my cousin," noted William as they walked about the back lawn.

Elizabeth directed an arch grin at him. "You have several cousins, William. Should I guess who has written to you?" And then before William could respond, Elizabeth tapped her lip and said: "I know! It is your cousin, Anne de Bourgh, who has written to inform you that she has reconsidered and wishes you to honor her mother's wishes and marry her.

"And well she might," added she, affecting nonchalance. "For you *are* quite the catch. If she should come to her senses, I should not wonder at it." Elizabeth flashed a sly smile at him. "What is it to be, William? Shall your cousin and I meet on the field of honor for the right of obtaining your hand?"

"When I informed you of her warm solicitations, I was not exaggerating, Elizabeth," said William, by now quite accustomed to her sportive manner of speaking. "She has not changed her stance."

"That is a relief! For all I know, she is an excellent marksman!"

William shook his head and seemed to decide it was best to speak quickly. Elizabeth was amused to see he recognized her silly mood, which she was more than willing to own herself. "In fact, it was from Fitzwilliam."

"Ah, the good colonel!" exclaimed Elizabeth. "What has he to relate to you? I hope his sojourn in London has been fruitful."

"I have reason to believe it has been," replied William. "I still reserve the right to tease him for his haste to return to London when Miss Cartwright decided she would return herself. It seems he is in her company as much as he ever was. She has also been introduced to Fitzwilliam's father, who has nothing but praise for her. I suspect they will make a match of it."

"I am happy to hear it," replied Elizabeth.

Her regard for Colonel Fitzwilliam and Miss Cartwright had deepened in the last days of their residence in Hertfordshire before Miss Cartwright was chased from Hertfordshire by Miss Bingley's continued scheming. She had heard that Colonel Fitzwilliam owned a small estate some distance from Pemberley, though she supposed it likely he would eventually become master of her father's estate. Still, she would like to have Miss Cartwright as a cousin, even if she was not situated close to Elizabeth's new home in Derbyshire.

"He also writes of his brother," said William. Elizabeth could see the laughter bubbling under the surface. "It seems Chesterfield has retired to the family estate with some haste."

Elizabeth could not hold her laughter in, and she allowed it free rein, William joining in with her. "Lady Diane became too much for him?"

"The woman is positively a huntress, according to Fitzwilliam. I know not what happened, but Miss Bingley and Lady Diane had a falling out. As a consequence, the lady has become more aggressive in trying to secure Chesterfield for herself. He retired to Snowlock to escape her and swears he will not attend the season if she is still unmarried."

"Poor Lord Chesterfield," said Elizabeth. "I suppose I must take some of the blame for his predicament—it was I, after all, who pointed out to Lady Diane that Miss Bingley had designs in that direction."

"Yes, well there was something in Fitzwilliam's letter to suggest that his lordship is not at all pleased with his cousin's future wife." William winked at Elizabeth. "I have no doubt his annoyance will cool before the time for our nuptials arrive. He was quite fond of you."

"But now all he can see is the woman *I* set upon him."

A chuckle and a shaken head were William's response. They continued in silence for some moments, saying nothing and enjoying each other's company. While there was no snow covering the ground, which was not unusual for Longbourn, the bounty of the trees was lost to the season, and they walked through a landscape of stark greys and browns. Elizabeth missed the summer vibrancy, where the wind rustled the leaves and she and Jane tended to the rose garden in the back of the house. Even that would change, however, for she would now live in the north with William. One of her other sisters would be required to care for the gardens, and Elizabeth knew none of them had the temperament for it.

"Poor Miss Bingley," said Elizabeth, considering the situation in which the woman had landed herself. "I know she does not deserve my pity, but it must be difficult for her."

"I have difficulty summoning any pity for the woman," was William's muttered reply.

"Which I fully understand. But rightly or wrongly, she has had her hopes evaporate like a drop of water on a hot day. I swoop in and steal the man she has been chasing for years, her friends have abandoned her cause, Miss Cartwright seems about to make a match with your cousin, and unless I am very much mistaken, I suspect her brother will offer for a woman she does not believe to be suitable. She must feel as if the world is set against her."

"Perhaps she does," replied William. "But her misfortunes are of her own making. I hope you will acquit me of cruelty when I tell you I have little sympathy for her."

"I am sure her continued attempts to draw you in have slain whatever empathy you might have had for her." Elizabeth smirked. "Poor hunted William. A great tall man such as you has much to fear in a dainty woman, set on finding a husband."

"*This* fox had a few tricks up his sleeve," said William, stopping and turning to face Elizabeth. "Of course, I was not skilled enough to escape *your* siren call."

"My dearest William," said Elizabeth, reaching up to touch his cheek, "Had you been willing to escape me, I have no doubt you would have accomplished it."

"Which makes all the difference in the world, my sweet."

William caught her hand and raised it to his lips, and while Elizabeth was wearing gloves, she fancied she could feel the touch of his kiss. He was such a dear man, his reserve notwithstanding. A woman had only to breach those defenses, which was not an insignificant task, to unleash the passionate man underneath. How lucky Elizabeth was that it was she who had managed to accomplish it!

A sudden sound of someone approaching through the brush alerted them to the fact that they were not alone, and Elizabeth stepped away, putting a respectable distance between them. A few moments later, the color of a blue pelisse, accompanied by a dark man's suit, broke through the brush, and Bingley and Jane stood before them. The jubilant expression on Bingley's face, accompanied by Jane's demure, yet happy smile, told Elizabeth all she needed to know about what had just occurred.

"Darcy, Miss Elizabeth!" cried Mr. Bingley as soon as he caught sight of them. "I must have your congratulations, for I have requested my dearest Jane's hand in marriage, and she has accepted."

"Oh, Jane!" exclaimed Elizabeth, going to her sister and folding her in a tight embrace. "I knew you were destined for each other! How wonderful this is!"

"Thank you, Lizzy," said Jane in her usually quiet voice. She paused and then looked Elizabeth in the eye, saying: "I have you to thank for my happiness."

"Nonsense!" said Elizabeth. "Once Mr. Bingley came into the neighborhood, your meeting was inevitable. He could not resist you once he made your acquaintance."

"But you have helped us all along. You have thwarted his sister's attempts and helped me understand what a good man he is." Jane glanced to where William was now congratulating his friend and, in a quiet tone, said: "Had I not had your encouragement and your insight into Miss Bingley's character, I might have hesitated to accept him, knowing how she does not favor the match."

"Then I am happy to be of service, my dearest Jane. Now I believe the challenge will be for you both to take Miss Bingley in hand and not allow her to rule your marriage, for you are both far too apt to think well of others and too willing by half to allow others their bad behavior."

"I know not what has happened between them, but Charles assures me that his sister will not rule my house. I believe he hopes to marry her off in the next season."

"Then I am happy to hear it."

When the gentlemen had exchanged congratulations and thanks, Elizabeth approached Mr. Bingley and eyed him with an arched brow. "I believe, Mr. Bingley, that I informed you of my sister's perfection long before she returned to Hertfordshire. I am happy to see that you listened to me."

Mr. Bingley released a hearty laugh. "I shall never doubt you, Miss Elizabeth. You are as perspicacious as you are beautiful, and I shall always thank you for leading me to my angel."

"As it should be," said Elizabeth with a grin.

They all laughed and began moving toward the back of the house. Mr. Bingley, as he noted himself, had business with their father which could not be delayed.

"I hope he does not mind this small breach of etiquette," said Mr. Bingley. "I had intended to go directly to the house. But when I saw you both standing there, I could not suppress my great joy."

"Papa will not mind," said Elizabeth. "He has been expecting this for days, and he is aware that Jane and I are the closest of sisters."

They gained the house and shed their outerwear, and while Elizabeth and Jane led William to the sitting-room, Mr. Bingley went directly to Mr. Bennet's study, knocking loudly enough to be heard throughout the entire house. The situation in the sitting-room was uncomfortable, with Miss Bingley and Mrs. Hurst still sitting with Mrs. Bennet. There seemed to be little said between them, however, as the Bingley sisters appeared a little affronted, while Mrs. Bennet was smug. For his part, Mr. Hurst appeared on the verge of breaking into laughter.

"Lizzy! Jane!" said Mrs. Bennet, who appeared relieved, though her demeanor was self-satisfied. "Please, come and sit with us. And you too, Mr. Darcy. You must be chilled. I shall send for tea."

Elizabeth noted Miss Bingley's withering glance at the Bennet matron, but Mrs. Bennet took no notice of her. In the adjacent room, Elizabeth could hear the sound of feminine giggling and the notes of the pianoforte. It seemed Georgiana and Mary, at least, had avoided whatever unpleasantness had occurred in the sitting-room.

"Miss Bennet," said Miss Bingley, fixing her haughty glare on Jane, "it seems you have lost my brother. Has he returned to Netherfield? If so, I believe we should depart also."

"I think you misunderstand your brother's absence, Caroline," said Mr. Hurst. His gleeful expression suggested thinly concealed hilarity, as if he was aware of some joke which she was not. "I have no doubt Bingley will be along soon."

"He has been . . . delayed," said Jane, ever the diplomat. "He will be joining us shortly."

Miss Bingley glared at all and sundry, clearly understanding the inference. There was nothing she could do, however, and at last, the woman seemed to understand it.

In due course, the tea service was delivered and everyone was served. Though Miss Bingley grasped her teacup as if she thought it was a snake, she did not say anything further. Elizabeth, though she knew it was not admirable to enjoy another's distress, could not help doing so at that moment.

When the door opened a few moments later and her father entered the room, accompanied by Mr. Bingley, Elizabeth saw Miss Bingley's countenance fall even further. There could now be no doubt as to the reason for Mr. Bingley's absence. Even she could not doubt it further.

"It seems, Mrs. Bennet, that your second eldest daughter has started a trend, and that furthermore, she has been proven to be positively prophetic."

Mrs. Bennet, who had never truly understood her husband, gazed at him in incomprehension. Mr. Bennet was gleeful in response, and Elizabeth knew from previous experience that he likely considered his objective attained.

"You see, this young buck here accosted me in my library not ten minutes ago, demanding to be allowed to marry my daughter. With due consideration, I have decided to grant him his request. It appears, my dear, you now have another wedding to plan."

What joy flowed from the announcement, and what congratulations were extended to the happy couple! If those of certain members of the party were less sincere than others, it appeared to offend the principals of the celebration not a whit. And even on Mr. Bingley's side, not all the offered sentiments were false — Mr. Hurst was effusive in his congratulations, complimenting Bingley on securing a "damn fine girl" for his wife.

"Now we simply need to determine a wedding date," said Mr. Bingley. He turned to William and said: "I have just the idea. Since you are to marry Elizabeth before long, we may simply make it a double wedding."

"Oh, no, my friend," said William, grinning at his friend. "I would not dream of depriving you of your time of engagement. Elizabeth and I are to be wed in less than a month, after all, which is not nearly enough time to include you. Besides, you must experience being the focus of attention, and I have no doubt Mrs. Bennet will wish to plan a grand celebration in your honor."

Mr. Bingley's crestfallen expression was a perfect counterpoint to the gleam in Mrs. Bennet's eye. Then she turned to Elizabeth, eyes wide, and said: "Mr. Darcy is completely correct, Lizzy. There is still so much to be done!"

Though annoyed with her betrothed for sending her mother into a tizzy in such a way, Elizabeth could not help but laugh when Mr. Bingley's dejection turned to trepidation. William saw it too, for he caught Elizabeth's eye and grinned, which she was only too willing to return.

"William is right," said she. "If you plan it properly, William and I should return from our own wedding trip just in time for your wedding."

"Very well," said Mr. Bingley, though it was clear he did not appreciate the delay.

"And you must assist," said Mrs. Bennet, turning to Mrs. Hurst and Miss Bingley. "After all, this is your only brother. You will, I am sure, wish to ensure the celebration of his marriage is suitably managed. And as you know him best, your assistance in making certain his preferences are met would be invaluable."

Elizabeth had never considered her mother to be particularly manipulative or perceptive, but in that one short speech she had proven herself sly, indeed. The Bingley sisters, seemingly knowing they were caught, agreed that they would be happy to assist, though the elder sister gave her assurances with more warmth than the younger.

The invitation to dine with them that evening was extended and accepted, and the conversation flowed freely and was without exception full of good cheer and happiness. Elizabeth noted that Miss Bingley kept herself out of the fray, but as time wore on, her expression became less forbidding and more resigned. When Elizabeth saw her to be sitting apart from the rest of those present, apparently deeply immersed in her own thoughts, Elizabeth decided it was time to make her peace with the woman. They would be connected, after all, through Jane's marriage.

As Elizabeth took her seat next to Miss Bingley and alerted the other woman of her presence, the cold and haughty look she had learned to expect from Miss Bingley instantly appeared. The woman, however, seemed to reconsider her response, and she became a little more conciliatory, though certainly not friendly.

"I hope, Miss Bingley, you will join me in wishing your brother and my sister every happiness."

Though she might have expected an angry reply or an assertion of superiority, Miss Bingley nodded slowly. "In the end, though I might have wished for different for my brother, I cannot deny that your sister does appear to make him happy."

"As he does for her," Elizabeth was quick to point out. "Jane is not artful, Miss Bingley. She is perfectly honest. One can see her happiness, though I will own that it can be difficult to detect through her reticence."

"Jane is an excellent woman," said Miss Bingley, her statement carrying more weight by the simple fact that it was offered with an absence of mind. "It will be no hardship to have her as a sister."

"I am happy you feel that way. I am certain you can be good friends if you both allow the possibility."

Miss Bingley's gaze once again focused on Elizabeth. "I assume that is a comment directed at *me*. Your sister is the kind of woman who is incapable of *not* offering friendship to another."

"That is, indeed, a faithful representation of my sister," said Elizabeth. "But you must not think Jane is a simpleton. She has not been blind to your opposition to her."

A slow nod was the woman's response. "Yes, well that was not a slight against Jane. I suppose I shall have to make it up to her."

Elizabeth did not reply, and Miss Bingley turned her attention back to her in full. This time, Elizabeth could see a little wryness in her gaze. "I suppose I must congratulate you, Miss Elizabeth. I must acknowledge my defeat. I had not expected you would be such a formidable opponent, but it appears I was incorrect. You have beaten me at my own game."

"It might have been different, had I not possessed every advantage." Miss Bingley's stare turned questioning. "Come now, Miss Bingley, but you have seen the state of their feelings for each other. Mr. Bingley might have singled Miss Cartwright out before, but I cannot think his inclination half so promising as that which he showed Jane."

"I suppose you are correct," conceded Miss Bingley.

"Furthermore, it was obvious the moment she arrived that Lady Diane considered herself far too good for your brother. Her efforts were never more than half-hearted."

Miss Bingley's expression darkened at the mention of her erstwhile friend. But she made no comment. Elizabeth did not think it had been much of a friendship anyway, and she doubted Miss Bingley regretted it, other than the social consequence which must come with the friendship of a baron's daughter.

"In the end," continued Elizabeth, "I did nothing more than nudge their natural inclinations. If you will forgive the metaphor, I was lazily drifting downstream, making an occasional course correction. You, unfortunately, were attempting to paddle against the current. It takes no great insight to understand why I was successful."

"I suppose you must be correct."

Sensing the woman's forbearance was exhausted, Elizabeth thanked her and excused herself. She almost thought Miss Bingley might be a tolerable relation now that she had been humbled. In the end, it did not matter, for she suspected William would be eager to distance himself from her, especially if she should find someone to marry. Elizabeth hoped she did—if nothing else, it would prevent her interference in Jane's married life with her husband.

CHAPTER XX

In the end, Elizabeth's wishes were granted with respect to Miss Bingley. She was introduced to a man of property the following season by the name of Mr. Powell. Though she still tended to be haughty, overly impressed with her own accomplishments and education, and ingratiating to those of a higher social sphere, Mr. Powell thought enough of her to offer for her. Though the Darcys were not close to the Powells and they rarely saw each other, except when in London for the season, Elizabeth offered her friendship, which was accepted by the other woman. They would never be great friends, but they were at the very least tolerable acquaintances.

The new Mr. and Mrs. Bingley were married in March, much later than Mr. Bingley wished, but sooner than Mrs. Bennet hoped. She had taken it into her head to plan a grand celebration on the occasion. Netherfield, unfortunately for Mrs. Bennet's sake, would only be their home for the first few months of their marriage, after which they settled in an adjacent county to Derbyshire. Though their home was some distance from Pemberley, it was closer than Hertfordshire, and thus easier for the two sisters, closer than ever, to visit. While Mrs. Bennet lamented the distance, she soon found another subject on which to focus when Jane gave birth to a succession of three sons. Though one might suspect Mrs. Bennet of being bitter about her daughter succeeding where she had failed, Mrs. Bennet had nothing but praise for Jane, and for all her daughters.

Lydia and Kitty returned from school less silly, though with spirits which were not far suppressed. It was an improvement, Elizabeth thought, though not so much as they had all hoped for. Both eventually made marriages of their own, to two cousins who owned adjacent estates in Wiltshire. As such, the sisters were happy with their lives and continued to be thick as thieves. The cousins, though gentlemen, were not so affluent as Mr. Darcy or Mr. Bingley, and as such, they were rarely in town.

As for Mary, Elizabeth counted her sister as another success, as Mary was introduced to a man of some property not far from Pemberley. Though she was not thrown into the path of a rich man like her mother required, Mary was well pleased with her new situation, which allowed her to be near Elizabeth.

Colonel Fitzwilliam and Miss Cartwright did, indeed, make a match of it, and upon their marriage, Colonel Fitzwilliam resigned his position in the regulars to turn to the life of a gentleman. Miss Cartwright became the best of friends with both Elizabeth and Jane and was often found in their company. It was ironic, Elizabeth decided, that the woman who had been set up as Jane's rival should end in such close friendship with them. But that was a miscalculation on Miss Bingley's part, and as such, neither sister could hold it against their friend.

As for Lady Diane, she did *not* succeed in capturing the viscount, though not because of a lack of effort. She was heard to rail at the man and her former friend when the announcement of his engagement to the daughter of a duke was made public. But since she had made herself ridiculous due to her attempts to garner his interest, her lamentations were largely ignored.

Even Charlotte, Elizabeth found, was content with her marriage to Mr. Collins. They dwelt at Hunsford for many years, Charlotte presenting her husband with two boys, the elder the future heir of Longbourn. Though the Darcys were not in their company much, eventually Lady Catherine's anger cooled enough to allow them to visit. On the occasions they did go, they found that Charlotte managed her husband quite well, wisely choosing to ignore when he said something which was not quite proper. As for Lady Catherine, she largely remained aloof from Elizabeth, though at least she was not abusive, as William had feared.

Elizabeth, herself, was incandescently happy. Pemberley was everything William had ever said it was, and she ever after considered it her home. Georgiana too lived with them until she found her own man without whom she could not live, and before long, the happy chatter and footsteps of children were once again heard through the halls of that hallowed estate. In her husband, she could never be anything but pleased, for in William she had found a true companion and lover. And if, as he had once said, they did not agree all the time, their differences of opinion were usually short-lived.

"It seems I have chosen wisely," said William one morning several years into their marriage. "I have not only gained a rare and beautiful woman for my wife but an intelligent one who can help me bear my burdens."

Elizabeth leaned up against him, sighing at the feeling of his arms securely circling her in his warm embrace. "And I could not have chosen better myself. I can only hope our children make excellent choices as we have."

"I hope so too. But Elizabeth — let us allow them to make their own choices. I would not wish for the repeat of the drama which surrounded Bingley's courtship with Jane."

A smile curved Elizabeth's lips, and she turned her head, accepting his kiss. Then with an arched eyebrow, she said: "I will be perfectly happy to allow them their own freedom to act with respect to their own loves. But if they should encounter another Caroline Bingley, I shall reserve the right to fix everything for them."

The End

It was a little later, when Darcy was beginning to feel like a caged lion, that Bingley approached him. Darcy almost groaned aloud when he saw the man, for he was certain Bingley would importune him to dance, a scene which had played out many times during their acquaintance. For some reason, the man seemed unable to understand that Darcy was not one who could feel comfortable in any company other than family and close friends. It was frustrating, but there was no way out, as to flee from Bingley would be to draw attention.

"Come, Darcy!" said Bingley, confirming Darcy's conjecture. "You must dance. I hate to see you standing around in this stupid manner. You had much better dance."

It was only by force of will that Darcy refrained from rolling his eyes. Bingley was nothing if not predictable.

"I certainly shall not. You know how I detest the activity unless I am previously acquainted with my partner."

"I know you protest as much," replied Bingley, "but I suspect it has more to do with your fastidious nature, which I declare, is a rival for the Prince Regent himself."

"You may think what you like, Bingley. You still shall not induce me to dance."

"Not even with a young woman who is quite pretty, in addition to being someone with whom you conversed quite cordially?"

"Whom do you mean?"

"Miss Elizabeth Bennet," said Bingley, gesturing behind Darcy and a little to his right. Darcy turned and noted the young woman sitting by the side of the room, obviously close enough to overhear their conversation.

"Miss Bennet has been sitting there for some time, having sat out this dance, no doubt due to the fact that gentlemen are scarce. Why, I have even seen her standing up with her sister tonight, as some of the other young ladies have done. I know you think that I do not listen when you drone on about gentlemanly behavior, but would it not be the epitome of such behavior to ask a young woman who does not have a partner to dance?"

"Aye, Miss Bennet is pretty enough to tempt any man," replied Darcy. Then he turned his head slightly and when he was certain Miss Bennet was the only one who could see, he winked at her before turning his attention back to Bingley. "But though she is indeed handsome, I have the distinct impression that she is a bluestocking, and you know it would not do for a Darcy to be seen with one such as she."

Bingley's face fell, and he looked at Darcy with a hint of consternation evident in his mien. Darcy, for his part, felt a savage glee for being able to turn the tables on his friend; perhaps Bingley would think twice before approaching him in this manner in the future.

"Uh . . . Darcy, I believe Miss Bennet is close enough to hear us," said Bingley, shifting from side to side and sneaking glances at Miss Bennet.

"Then perhaps she has received her just desserts for listening to a private conversation. One never overhears anything good about oneself, after all."

"But—"

"Bingley, you are wasting your time with me. Return to your partners and enjoy their flirtatious attentions. I do not intend to dance again tonight."

Though obviously reluctant, Bingley grimaced and walked away, but not without sneaking another glance at Miss Bennet. When he had left and Darcy could see Bingley standing across the room, speaking with several people of the area, he turned and regarded Miss Bennet, allowing a hint of challenge to enter his expression.

FROM ONE GOOD SONNET PUBLISHING

http://onegoodsonnet.com/

FOR READERS WHO LIKED A TALE OF TWO COURTSHIPS

Chaos Comes to Kent
Mr. Collins invites his cousin to stay at his parsonage and the Bennets go to Kent and are introduced to an amiable Lady Catherine de Bourgh. When Mr. Darcy and his cousin, Colonel Fitzwilliam, visit Lady Catherine at the same time, they each begin to focus on a Bennet sister, prodded by well-meaning relations, but spurred on by their own feelings.

Out of Obscurity
Amid the miraculous events of a lost soul returning home, dark forces conspire against a young woman, for her loss was not an accident. A man is moved to action by a boon long denied, determined to avoid being cheated by Miss Elizabeth Bennet again.

In the Wilds of Derbyshire
Elizabeth Bennet goes to her uncle's estate in Derbyshire after Jane's marriage to Mr. Bingley, feeling there is nothing left for her in Meryton. She quickly becomes close to her young cousin and uncle, though her aunt seems to hold a grudge against her. She also meets the handsome Mr. Fitzwilliam Darcy, and she realizes that she can still have everything she has ever wished to have. But there are obstacles she must overcome . . . .

Netherfield's Secret
Elizabeth soon determines that her brother's friend, Fitzwilliam Darcy, suffers from an excess of pride, and it comes as a shock when the man reveals himself to be in love with her. But even that revelation is not as surprising as the secret Netherfield has borne witness to. Netherfield's secret shatters Elizabeth's perception of herself and the world around her, and Mr. Darcy is the only one capable of picking up the pieces.

The Companion
A sudden tragedy during Elizabeth's visit to Kent leaves her directly in Lady Catherine de Bourgh's sights. With Elizabeth's help, a woman long-oppressed has begun to spread her wings. What comes after is a whirlwind of events in which Elizabeth discovers that her carefully held opinions are not infallible. Furthermore, a certain gentleman of her acquaintance might be the key to Elizabeth's happiness.

What Comes Between Cousins
When Mr. Bingley leases Netherfield, a rivalry springs up between Mr. Darcy and Colonel Fitzwilliam, each determined to win the fair Elizabeth Bennet. As the situation between cousins deteriorates, clarity begins to come for Elizabeth, and she sees Mr. Darcy as the man who will fill all her desires in a husband. But the rivalry between cousins is not the only trouble brewing for Elizabeth. There are others who have an interest in keeping her apart from her gentleman.

For more details, visit
http://www.onegoodsonnet.com/genres/pride-and-prejudice-variations

ALSO BY ONE GOOD SONNET PUBLISHING

THE SMOTHERED ROSE TRILOGY

BOOK 1: THORNY

In this retelling of "Beauty and the Beast," a spoiled boy who is forced to watch over a flock of sheep finds himself more interested in catching the eye of a girl with lovely ground-trailing tresses than he is in protecting his charges. But when he cries "wolf" twice, a determined fairy decides to teach him a lesson once and for all.

BOOK 2: UNSOILED

When Elle finds herself practically enslaved by her stepmother, she scarcely has time to even clean the soot off her hands before she collapses in exhaustion. So when Thorny tries to convince her to go on a quest and leave her identity as Cinderbella behind her, she consents. Little does she know that she will face challenges such as a determined huntsman, hungry dwarves, and powerful curses . . . .

BOOK 3: ROSEBLOOD

Both Elle and Thorny are unhappy with the way their lives are going, and the revelations they have had about each other have only served to drive them apart. What is a mother to do? Reunite them, of course. Unfortunately, things are not quite so simple when a magical lettuce called "rapunzel" is involved.

If you're a fan of thieves with a heart of gold, then you don't want to Miss . . .

THE PRINCES AND THE PEAS
A TALE OF ROBIN HOOD

A NOVEL OF THIEVES, ROYALTY, AND IRREPRESSIBLE LEGUMES

BY LELIA EYE

An infamous thief faces his greatest challenge yet when he is pitted against forty-nine princes and the queen of a kingdom with an unnatural obsession with legumes. Sleeping on top of a pea hidden beneath a pile of mattresses? Easy. Faking a singing contest? He could do that in his sleep. But stealing something precious out from under "Old Maid" Marian's nose . . . now that is a challenge that even the great Robin Hood might not be able to surmount.

When Robin Hood comes up with a scheme that involves disguising himself as a prince and participating in a series of contests for a queen's hand, his Merry Men provide him their support. Unfortunately, however, Prince John attends the contests with the Sheriff of Nottingham in tow, and as all of the Merry Men know, Robin Hood's pride will never let him remain inconspicuous. From sneaking peas onto his neighbors' plates to tweaking the noses of prideful men like the queen's chamberlain, Robin Hood is certain to make an impression on everyone attending the contests. But whether he can escape from the kingdom of Clorinda with his prize in hand before his true identity comes to light is another matter entirely.

About the Author

Jann Rowland is a Canadian, born and bred. Other than a two-year span in which he lived in Japan, he has been a resident of the Great White North his entire life, though he professes to still hate the winters.

Though Jann did not start writing until his mid-twenties, writing has grown from a hobby to an all-consuming passion. His interests as a child were almost exclusively centered on the exotic fantasy worlds of Tolkien and Eddings, among a host of others. As an adult, his interests have grown to include historical fiction and romance, with a particular focus on the works of Jane Austen.

When Jann is not writing, he enjoys rooting for his favorite sports teams. He is also a master musician (in his own mind) who enjoys playing piano and singing as well as moonlighting as the choir director in his church's congregation.

Jann lives in Alberta with his wife of more than twenty years, two grown sons, and one young daughter. He is convinced that whatever hair he has left will be entirely gone by the time his little girl hits her teenage years. Sadly, though he has told his daughter repeatedly that she is not allowed to grow up, she continues to ignore him.

Website: http://onegoodsonnet.com/
Facebook: https://facebook.com/OneGoodSonnetPublishing/
Twitter: @OneGoodSonnet
Mailing List: http://eepurl.com/bol2p9

Made in the USA
Columbia, SC
31 October 2018